BOOKS BY TINA FOLSOM

Scanguards Vampires

Samson's Lovely Mortal (#1)

Amaury's Hellion (#2)

Gabriel's Mate (#3)

Yvette's Haven (#4)

Zane's Redemption (#5)

Quinn's Undying Rose (#6)

Oliver's Hunger (#7)

Thomas's Choice (#8)

Silent Bite (#8 1/2)

Cain's Identity (#9)

Luther's Return (#10)

Mortal Wish (# 1/2)

Blake's Pursuit (#11)

Fateful Reunion (#11 1/2)

John's Yearning (#12)

Ryder's Storm (#13)

Damian's Conquest (#14)

Grayson's Challenge (#15)

Isabelle's Forbidden Love (#16)

Cooper's Passion (#17)

Vanessa's Bravery (#18)

Patrick's Seduction (#19)

Stealth Guardians

Lover Uncloaked (#1)

Master Unchained (#2)

Warrior Unraveled (#3)

Guardian Undone (#4)

Immortal Unveiled (#5)

Protector Unmatched (#6)

Demon Unleashed (#7)

Out of Olympus

A Touch of Greek (#1)

A Scent of Greek (#2)

A Taste of Greek (#3)

A Hush of Greek (#4)

Venice Vampyr

Wicked Lover (#1)

Final Affair (#2)

Sinful Treasure (#3)

Sensual Danger (#4)

Thriller: Eyewitness

Code Name Stargate

Ace on the Run (#1)

Fox in plain Sight (#2)

Yankee in the Wind (#3)

Tiger on the Prowl (#4)

Hawk on the Hunt (#5)

A big thank you to you, my dear reader, for supporting my writing by purchasing my books. This is truly the best job in the world!

COOPER'S PASSION

SCANGUARDS VAMPIRES #17

TINA FOLSOM

1

"Chief wants to see you."

Anita Diaz hung her jacket over the chair and turned to the woman who'd spoken. Like Anita, Eloise wore a uniform identifying her as a member of the Elko County Sheriff's Department. She was ten years older than Anita and at least half a foot shorter. At five foot nine, Anita was tall for a woman and taller than some of the male officers she worked with. At the police academy, her male colleagues had seen her as competition, because her height and strength helped her outperform the male trainees in many physical disciplines. In hand-to-hand combat, she'd lifted plenty of men off their feet. They'd been embarrassed that a woman could best them. It had made her less than popular among her peers.

"Did he say what he wanted?" Anita asked tilting her head in the direction of the closed door to the sheriff's office.

"Didn't ask." Eloise lowered her voice. "But he didn't sound happy."

"Well, better get it over with then." Anita walked to the door and knocked briefly. When a sound akin to a bark came from inside the office, she opened the door and entered.

"You wanted to see me?"

He motioned behind her. "Close the door."

She followed his command and looked at him. He was still handsome despite his age. At sixty-one, he could still turn a woman's head. His tall, athletic frame, dark hair, and bronzed skin was unusual for a man his age, but he'd always looked after himself.

He rose from his chair, his jaw clenched tightly, his brown eyes piercing. "I'm disappointed in you."

Anita sucked in a breath, her spine straightening as she steeled herself for the dressing-down that was to come. Yet, she didn't say anything, knowing that he hated being interrupted when he was about to launch into a tirade.

"I've cut you a lot of slack, more than I should. Nobody else is taking the liberties you are."

He pointed to the window that would have allowed him to look into the open-plan office outside were the blinds not drawn.

"But to misuse department resources to chase some cockamamie theory? That goes too far! Enough is enough. I warned you before not to go down that rabbit hole. There's nothing to find there. There's no case here."

"But Janet Fillmore was abducted. I know it! She's in danger."

He narrowed his eyes. "Did I say you could speak?" He paused for a moment. "Didn't think so." He walked closer, his entire body looking tense. "Janet and Hank had marital issues. She left him. And why wouldn't she? He's a drunk and a lazy bastard. Without her business and hard work, Hank would have been out on the street a long time ago."

Defiantly, Anita braced her hands at her hips. "I'm not saying he's not. But I saw what I saw. She was taken."

"Just because you saw her get into a van with a stranger, doesn't mean she was abducted. It was probably the man she left Hank for. End of story."

Anita filled her chest with air, ready to defend what she'd seen five weeks earlier when she'd left a local bar. But she didn't get a chance.

"Not another word on that subject!"

"You can't stop me from looking into these disappearances. It's connected to Mom. I know it. She didn't leave me. She was abducted. She would have never—"

He blanched. "Your mother left us! And she didn't even have the guts to say good-bye." His voice became louder with every word. "Don't dig up the past. It's been twenty-one years—"

"Dad, please," she begged. "She didn't leave us. She loved us." Anita felt tears sting in her eyes.

José Diaz shook his head. "Stop making excuses for her. If I'd known that you would use sheriff's department resources to chase a ghost, I would have never supported you to become a deputy." He glared at her. "I can't change that now, but I'm not going to show any more leniency. You'll take two weeks of vacation, starting right now. And when you're back on duty, you'll follow orders. No more chasing wild theories."

"You can't do that! You can't force me to take a vacation."

"Would you rather be suspended without pay?"

Anita's heart stopped. The threat was clear. "You wouldn't—"

"Try me, and I'll have your badge and gun," he challenged, his voice a low grumble now.

Anita didn't doubt that he meant it. After all, she was his daughter, and she'd inherited his doggedness, even though physically, she resembled her fair-skinned, blonde mother. José Diaz wouldn't be swayed, not in the mood he was in right now. There was no talking sense into him. He'd made up his mind that Janet Fillmore had left her husband, just like Helen Diaz had left him. But somehow, Anita had to find proof to make him see the truth.

She thrust her chin up. "Fine. I'll take a vacation." Without waiting for his response, she turned on her heel and ripped the door open.

"Anita, it's for your own good, and deep down you know it."

She didn't acknowledge his words, and instead slammed the door shut behind her. In the open-plan station, she noticed that several of her colleagues turned their heads to her. She ignored them too, snatched her uniform jacket and her bag, and stormed out of the building.

When she reached her house in the outskirts of Elko, she was still seething. She got out of the car and looked at the house. Her father had bought it shortly after her mother's disappearance. Before that, they'd lived in Reno. José Diaz had insisted on moving away, claiming their old house held too many memories. As a nine-year-old, Anita hadn't had a say in the matter, even though she'd wanted to stay where she felt closest to her mother. The sale of the house and the move to Elko had driven a wedge between her and her father.

When he'd married a widow after being granted a divorce in absentia from Anita's mother, Anita had felt betrayed. But deep down, she couldn't blame him. He was still a young man, virile, and handsome. Why wouldn't he start a new family? When his new wife had given birth to two strapping boys within three years, the house had become too small for the growing family. They'd moved, and Anita, now a young adult, had agreed to her father's suggestion that she stay in the house, and he and his new family moved to a larger one in the city. It gave them the physical distance they needed. Slowly, their relationship had improved.

Until today.

Anita locked the car and went inside. She was glad she lived alone now and only saw her father at the station or at his house, because it meant she didn't have to explain why one entire wall in her living room was covered with maps, photos, printouts, and post-it notes. The map spanned five states: Nevada, California, Oregon, Washington, and Idaho. Blue and red dots were marked on the map. The blue ones indicated the disappearance of a woman, and the red ones stood for women who'd been found dead. Flanking the map on all sides were photos of women as well as information on where they were last seen and where they finally turned up dead.

Her father was right: she had indeed used department resources to look into the disappearances and murders of young women not just in Nevada, but also in the surrounding states. She'd realized very quickly that none of the women she'd identified were found in the same state from which they disappeared. When she'd made that connection, she'd realized she was onto something: the killer was travelling through these states, picking up women on his way, then killing and dumping them in another state. She guessed that this was by design to make it harder for local police and sheriff's departments to connect the dots.

A *Jane Doe* in Nevada wouldn't immediately be matched up with a missing person in Idaho. In addition, in the six years that Anita had found data for, the perpetrator had never abducted anyone from the same town twice. The same went for the dead bodies: each and every single one had been found in a different city. Yet, two things remained a constant, and therefore pointed to a serial killer. He only killed tall, blonde women aged between 30 and 45, and the cause of death was always the same: exsanguination.

Yet one thing gave her hope that Janet Fillmore from Elko was still alive. The serial killer kept his victims alive for six to eight weeks. The bodies that had been found in all five states had been dead for less than twenty-four hours. Janet Fillmore had disappeared five weeks earlier. She was still alive—somewhere.

Anita scrutinized the map again. If her theory was correct, the serial killer was traveling in a clockwise pattern, which meant that the missing woman from Elko would show up somewhere in Northern California. The previous year, a missing woman from Las Vegas had shown up in Oakland, California. Before that, it had been Sacramento, and before that Santa Rosa.

"Where did you go this time?" she murmured to herself and looked at the post-it notes she'd placed around Janet's photo.

White van, it said on one. *License plate: couldn't read it; dirty. Time: 12:25 am.*

She stepped closer to look at Janet's face again. She was thirty-seven, blonde and tall. Her driver's license had indicated that she was five foot eight, an inch shorter than Anita. Janet ran a successful business in Elko, a furniture store. She'd inherited the business from her parents, and she'd improved it to make it into a very profitable enterprise. Anita was certain that having put all this hard work into her business, she wouldn't just leave without a word. No, Janet had been abducted. Anita removed a post-it note that said *left voluntarily?* and discovered another note beneath it. She'd almost forgotten about it.

There'd been a sticker on the white van in which Janet had disappeared.

Sticker on van: two letters intertwined. S, F?

It had to be a logo. Maybe that of a company?

Janet sat down at her laptop and booted it up. Moments later, she did a search for logos with S and F. There were a multitude of hits. She clicked on *Images*. Various images all depicting the letters S and F in different fonts, colors, and configurations appeared on the screen. She started scrolling, when she stopped abruptly. The orange on the screen popped, drawing her eyes to it. This was it! This was the sticker she'd seen on the van. She clicked on it.

San Francisco Giants logo, was written below it.

Whoever had taken Janet had a connection to San Francisco. She glanced back at the map. So far, the killer had never dumped a body in San Francisco, nor had he kidnapped anybody from there either. At least not anybody who fit the profile she'd developed.

Anita knew it was a long shot, but by her estimate, Janet only had one to three weeks left, before she would show up too, dead by exsanguination. Sick bastard! This time, she had to stop him. She had to get there before he could kill her, and stop him once and for all.

And maybe then she could prove that he was the one who'd taken her mother twenty-one years earlier, and find out where he'd dumped her body. Then her father would finally have to acknowledge that her mother had loved them both and hadn't left them like a thief in the night. It hadn't been her choice. She'd been forced.

2

One week later

"Where's the body?" Cooper asked as he rushed into the small command center on the first level of Scanguards' headquarters in the Mission. Inside the room, monitors were mounted on one wall, and a large desk stood in the center, Nicholas, a twenty-nine-year-old vampire hybrid, the son of Zane, one of the meanest vampires Cooper had ever met, looked up. It was Nicholas's week to staff the command center, which handled all incoming emergencies dealing with vampires and vampire-related crimes.

"They already removed it from the crime scene and brought it here."

"Without doing forensics on scene? Who the fuck ordered that?"

"I figured you'd want the body removed as quickly as possible so nobody sees what state it's in." Nicholas thrust his chin up, now in defensive mode.

"Have I taught you nothing?" Frustrated, Cooper grunted. "Did you at least have them take photos of the crime scene?"

Nicholas shifted and clenched his jaw. "I'm not an idiot. Of course, I had them take photos. But it's not the crime scene anyway."

"What's that supposed to mean?"

"The body was dumped there. There was no blood anywhere. He must have sucked her dry somewhere else and then tossed her in that alley."

"Who knows about this?"

"The human who found her." Nicholas looked on a notepad on the desk. "Michael Lavine. He was on his way to a restaurant and cut through the alley. He called 9-1-1. They sent out two unis. By the time they cordoned off the scene and reported that the body was bloodless, Donnelly made sure to keep SFPD's forensics team away from the scene, and contacted us."

This news made him feel somewhat better. At least there were only a few people who knew about it, and with some luck they could keep this out of the newspapers. The discovery of an exsanguinated body would spark all kinds of speculations.

"Good. Is Maya already examining the body?"

Nicholas nodded. "Yes. Buffy is helping her."

"I'll go see them shortly. What do we know about the victim?"

Nicholas shrugged. "Not much. No ID, no jewelry, no clothes."

Surprised, Cooper snapped his gaze back to the younger hybrid. "She was found naked?"

"Yep."

Cooper ran a hand through his short hair. "That'll make it harder to identify her. As soon as Maya has DNA, let's run it through CODIS. Do you already have the fingerprints?"

"I was about to get those so I can run them through AFIS," Nicholas said hastily. "Ahm, let me find the scanner." He jumped up and walked to the opposite wall. He opened several drawers of the large cupboard, rummaging through them.

Cooper rolled his eyes. Nicholas still needed a lot of supervision, even though he was only three years his junior.

"I'll be in the med center with Maya," Cooper announced, not willing to wait until Nicholas got his act together.

"I'll be down there in a sec," he promised without looking over his shoulder.

Cooper left the room. He hadn't seen Nicholas that nervous before.

He knew what it meant to have to prove himself, and with a father like Zane it probably wasn't easy for a guy like Nicholas to distinguish himself and forge his own path. Having Zane's shadow loom over him would make anybody nervous. This was the first time Nicholas was running the command center by himself. Cooper and the older hybrids had done it many times before, but now it was time to train the younger ones so they were ready to lead when the time came.

Cooper thrived on pressure like this. Nicholas clearly didn't. At least not yet. He needed a few more years to grow into his role, whereas Cooper knew he was ready to lead, which was also the reason why anybody working in the command center reported to him. He'd fought long and hard for this position. Samson, the founder and owner of Scanguards, a three-hundred-something-year-old pure-blooded vampire had promoted him soon after he'd been instrumental in saving Isabelle, Samson's daughter, from an evil and demented vampire.

Instead of waiting for the elevator, Cooper took the stairs to get down to the underground level where the medical center was located. It was run by Dr. Maya Giles, the vampire female blood-bonded to Gabriel Giles, the second-in-command at Scanguards.

Cooper marched along the corridor that led to the medical center, but stopped before he reached the double doors leading into the reception area. Instead, he briefly knocked at the door to his right and swiped his access card. He heard a faint beep, then pushed the door open and entered.

Maya, the dark-haired beauty who'd been a human physician at UCSF before she'd been turned into a vampire against her will, stood bent over the body of a woman. She glanced up briefly.

"Hey, Coop."

"Hey, Maya. So that's her, huh?" He'd never seen a dead body so pale. Her blonde hair was long, but tangled, her cheeks hollow. Other than that, he couldn't tell much else.

Maya nodded grimly. "There isn't a single ounce of blood left in her."

"Puncture wounds?"

"Yes." She turned the woman's head, and Cooper was able to see two small round holes on the side of her neck.

"He didn't hide what he did," he murmured to himself. "Why not lick over the incisions so the flesh would mend without leaving any evidence that a vampire did this?"

"He probably tried," Maya suggested, "but if she was already dead by the time he withdrew his fangs, his saliva wouldn't have been able to heal her skin. Even vampire saliva can't heal what's already dead."

"He gorged himself on her." Disgust rose in Cooper, together with the need to hand out punishment for this crime. "What can you tell me about her?"

"Not much. She has blue eyes, good teeth; she's five foot eight, pretty tall for a woman. As to her weight, I can't really say, because she looks to me like she lost weight before her death. Her skin is sagging in places, but that can also be from the fact that he sucked her dry."

"Age?"

"In her late thirties I'd say. She had sex in the last forty-eight hours, but I can't tell if it was consensual or not. If the vampire who killed her had sex with her, he could have used mind-control to make her comply, which would explain the absence of wounds around her genitals."

"Still makes it rape."

"Agreed."

"Can you tell me when she died?"

Maya looked at the large clock on the wall. "Around 4 p.m. today."

Cooper contemplated her words. "That means Nicholas was right when he said that she wasn't killed in that alley but somewhere else, and then just dumped there."

"Makes sense," Maya said. "He would have had to wait until nightfall before he could move her."

"Nicholas said she had no ID on her. When do you think you'll have her DNA for us to run through CODIS?"

"Buffy is in the lab right now, working on it."

"Buffy? I didn't realize she was doing that kind of work yet."

Maya smiled for the first time since he'd entered the room. "She's been with me for over a year now, and she's a great student. She's very capable."

"I don't doubt that. You're a great teacher."

"Charmer," Maya said with a smile. "Now, go, and let me take an impression of her teeth in case we don't get a hit on her DNA or her fingerprints."

"That reminds me: Nicholas is on his way down here—just as soon as he can find the fingerprint scanner." Cooper rolled his eyes.

"Cut him some slack. Doing your first shift as the leader in the command center is nerve-racking. Ethan was a mess when he had to coordinate every emergency that landed at Scanguards."

From what Cooper remembered, Maya's youngest son, Ethan, had done fine in the command center and everything had gone like clockwork. "Ethan had everything under control."

"And Nicholas will too. Just be patient with him. Trust me: he's getting enough flak from Zane for not being one-hundred-percent perfect one-hundred-percent of the time."

Cooper sighed. "You're probably right. Zane is a slave driver." Then he pointed to the body. "Keep me posted."

"I'll call you as soon as I know more."

Cooper left the morgue and made his way to the elevator. When the elevator doors finally opened, he heard a sound from the end of the corridor and saw Sebastian coming toward him, transporting two heavy looking wooden boxes on a dolly.

"Hold the elevator," Sebastian called out. The half-Asian twenty-five-year-old was Oliver's son. Oliver, a pure-blooded vampire, had been with Scanguards for decades, and Sebastian, like so many other sons and daughters of vampires was following in his father's footsteps and working for Scanguards.

Cooper grinned and held the elevator door open. "Did somebody relegate you to delivery boy?"

Sebastian reached him and rolled the boxes into the elevator. "Far from it. This is the first batch of my latest invention."

Cooper stepped into the elevator and pressed the button to the parking garage, while he looked into the top box. "Bottled blood? Hardly the latest invention."

Scanguards had started bottling human blood several decades earlier to make it more convenient for their vampire and vampire hybrid staff to feed without having to use unsuspecting humans. Cooper, his sister, and friends had all grown up on bottled human blood, though of course, they'd all at one time or another bitten humans to drink blood straight from the source.

"Not just any bottled blood. It's carbonated. You know, fizzy." Sebastian beamed. "You should try it. I'm calling it *Blood Splatter*." He pulled a bottle from the case and handed it to Cooper. "Cool name, right?"

"Blood Splatter? You're killing me." But he had to hand it to Sebastian: he had interesting ideas and the technical knowledge to turn them into reality. Whether this type of bottled blood would catch on, however, was anybody's guess. The blood didn't come in the usual glass bottle with the Scanguards label indicating what blood type it was, but in a light-weight silver-colored aluminum bottle hiding its contents. "All right. I'll try it."

"Great!" Sebastian slapped him on the shoulder, clearly happy. "Let me know if you like it, okay? But be honest. If it doesn't taste right, just let me know, and I'll refine the recipe. I'm still in the testing phase."

The elevator doors opened.

"You bet." Cooper left and headed for his SUV.

He made his way through heavy evening traffic to North Beach, the San Francisco neighborhood known for its vibrant restaurant scene. It bordered on Telegraph Hill, where he, Lydia, and their parents lived—though in separate homes. Since his condo was being repaired due to water damage caused by his upstairs neighbor, Cooper currently stayed with his Uncle Wesley, an accomplished witch, and his wife, Virginia, a Stealth Guardian, a preternatural creature able to make herself invisible and walk through solid matter.

Cooper finally found a parking spot on a side street, in between Washington Square and the alley where the body of the naked woman had been found only a few hours earlier. His stomach growled. He'd rushed to Scanguards the moment he'd been notified about the exsanguinated body and had forgotten to eat. As a vampire hybrid he could supplement human blood with regular human food if he wanted to, but like many of his friends, he almost exclusively drank blood. Drinking human blood was as essential to a vampire hybrid as to a pure-blooded vampire. It made him strong and gave him endurance, keeping his senses sharp.

It was best if he fed right now, so he'd be sharp when he visited the crime scene. He opened the compartment between the two front seats of the SUV and pulled out the bottle Sebastian had given him a little while earlier. He read the label and chuckled. Sebastian had indeed named the brew *Blood Splatter*.

Cooper unscrewed the top of it. Like a geyser, the red liquid spewed from the narrow bottleneck, splashing his face and neck.

"Fuck!"

He held the bottle over to the passenger side of the car, away from him, to prevent more carbonated blood from soaking him. But the damage was already done. The collar and upper part of his white shirt was splattered with blood.

Cooper reached for the box of Kleenex behind his seat to wipe the blood off his face and neck. But there wasn't anything he could do about his shirt. He looked down his front. He looked like he'd just slaughtered a pig.

"Sebastian, I'm gonna throttle you!"

As soon as he was done checking out the alley where the dead woman had been dumped.

3

____

Anita got the call when she'd finished her dinner at a small Italian restaurant not far from the Airbnb she'd moved into upon her arrival in San Francisco. The one-bedroom apartment was located on the edge of North Beach, and she'd been surprised that she'd been able to get something so cute on short notice.

She'd spent the past week wandering around the city, showing Janet Fillmore's photo to shopkeepers and waiters in restaurants, while keeping her eyes out for a white van with a San Francisco Giants sticker. Unfortunately, there were too many white vans, and by now, the suspect had had plenty of time to disguise the plain white van she'd seen in Elko with decals on its sides to make it look different.

She'd also gone to the police department, shown her Elko Sheriff's Department credentials to an officer and asked to be notified if a woman matching Janet Fillmore's description was found in the city, dead or alive. She knew that the San Francisco Police Department had no obligation to work with her, since she wasn't going through official channels, but she knew that they would contact her as a courtesy should Janet show up in San Francisco.

"Deputy Diaz? It's Stan Drummond, SFPD."

Anita's heart pounded out of control. She'd both dreaded and hoped for this call. "Officer Drummond? Has she been found?"

"I'm not a hundred percent certain, but a couple of hours ago a woman matching your friend's description was found dead in an alley in North Beach."

"Oh my God." A cold shiver ran down her spine. If this was Janet, then she was too late. "You said you're not a hundred percent sure. Was there no ID?"

"That's what I've been told. And worse: apparently, she was naked when she was found. I'm sorry, Deputy. Wish I could give you better news."

Anita swallowed away the bile that rose inside her. "Can I come and identify her?"

"Ahm, yes, but you'll have to wait until tomorrow. Just go to the city morgue. I hope you have the stomach for it. I haven't seen the body, but from what I'm told, she's been drained of her blood."

"Exsanguinated?"

Anita closed her eyes to push down the rising tears. But she couldn't give in to her emotions right now. If the body was exsanguinated, the killer was almost certainly the same one who'd abducted and killed other women in Nevada, Idaho, Oregon, Washington, and California. She was on the right track. Just a little bit too late.

"Thanks, Officer Drummond. One more thing. Do you know where exactly she was found? I'd like to see the crime scene for myself."

He sighed. "Ahm, I shouldn't really tell you this, cause it's all hush-hush, because we don't want to create a panic in the city. So far, the press hasn't gotten wind of it yet, but you're law enforcement, so I don't see the harm in it. I'll text you the address."

"Thank you. I really appreciate your help."

"You take care now."

There was a click in the line. A moment later, her cellphone buzzed with a message from Stan Drummond: the address where the body had been found. She tapped on it and opened the map app. The address was only a few blocks away from the restaurant. According to the app, walking there would take ten minutes.

Anita settled her bill and got up. In the restroom, she dug into her handbag and pulled out her gun and shoulder holster. She was glad now that her father hadn't suspended her, or she would be without her gun. With it, she felt safer roaming the streets at night, particularly in a city she didn't know very well. She had to be prepared for everything. Anita slipped the shoulder holster over her sweater, then slid the gun into it and donned her casual windbreaker. She adjusted her clothing, so the gun wasn't visible, before she left the restaurant. Outside on the pavement, she oriented herself and memorized the route her cellphone app suggested. She put her cellphone into her jacket pocket, because she didn't want to look like somebody who didn't know her way around. It would make her look like easy prey. And the last thing she needed right now was a mugger distracting her from her mission.

It was damp and foggy, just like it had been during the day. *May Gray* the residents called this weather. Apparently, it was followed by *June Gloom*. Welcome to sunny California! She was glad that she'd packed jeans and T-shirts. On her first day in the city, she'd bought a couple of sweaters to keep the cold air at bay. The summer dress she'd packed was still in her suitcase and would remain there for her entire stay.

Now, in the darkness, the fog made the city look spooky. Instinctively, she shivered despite her sweater and jacket. Nevertheless, she was excited to be here, not just because she wanted to catch the serial killer she'd nicknamed *Midnight Bleeder*. There was something else here in San Francisco that made her want to explore the city more thoroughly. She loved the Victorian architecture, the narrow and steep streets, the old cable cars, the excellent restaurants, and the lively bars and clubs.

For a moment, she allowed herself to dream that she would leave small town life behind and live in the big city in relative anonymity. It would be an escape and maybe even the best solution. Perhaps leaving Nevada would give her closure and help her finally come to terms with her mother's death—and she had to be dead, because were she still alive, she would have contacted her only daughter by now. Maybe a new city would give her a new start, a new life. Not that she could even dream of living in San Francisco. The real estate prices were through the roof, and even renting a one-bedroom apartment was out of her reach.

As she continued walking, she noticed that it got quieter around her. She was several blocks away from the main drag of North Beach, Columbus Avenue, where most of the restaurants and bars were located. But here, in the narrow streets that stretched up onto one of the many hills in San Francisco, she encountered nobody. An occasional car drove slowly past her, most likely searching for an elusive parking spot. Anita had left her own car in the parking spot assigned to the Airbnb, because she'd realized on her first day that finding a parking spot in San Francisco bordered on a miracle.

She pulled out her cellphone to check her GPS location. The dot showed that she'd arrived at her destination. She would have missed the alley, had she not looked at the map. The reason for it became clear instantly: the streetlamp at the entrance had burned out, and the alley itself was so narrow that only one car would be able to pass through. A few trash containers lined the side. Standing at the entrance to the dark alley, Anita looked up and noticed that the left side was flanked by what appeared to be a large apartment building. On the right side stood a commercial building without windows facing the alley. It was the perfect place to kill somebody.

Anita peered into the darkness, ready to pull her flashlight out of her handbag, when she perceived a movement in the distance. She made one step into the alley so she was in complete darkness, and whoever was farther back in the alley couldn't see her. When she quickly glanced back to the street, she realized that there was no police tape anywhere to restrict access to the crime scene. Had forensics already processed the scene?

Anita remained as quiet as possible, while her eyes adjusted to the darkness. The sound of footfalls reached her ears. Who was walking around in the alley? Had the killer come back, and was looking for something he might have lost when he'd killed his victim? It was possible. Or maybe he'd come back to relive his kill. Serial killers in particular enjoyed reliving their deeds over and over again. Had he maybe even watched the police as they arrived to process the scene and take away the body? A sick bastard like the Midnight Bleeder had most likely stuck around to watch.

Knowing she had to be careful, Anita pulled her gun from her shoulder holster and quietly edged along the wall deeper into the alley. She was glad that she'd opted for sneakers rather than her heavier boots, which would have alerted the person in the alley to her presence. When a light suddenly illuminated a part of the alley, she realized that somebody on the second or third floor of the apartment building to the left had switched on a light in a room facing the alley. The dim light source shone directly onto a tall man, who now looked up too.

She heard him murmur something to himself as he turned just a few degrees in her direction. It was enough for her to see his face and torso clearly.

Anita suppressed a curse, instinctively clasping her gun more tightly. The face was that of a man in his twenties or thirties—she'd never been very good at guessing a person's age—and he was rather handsome. His face was clean-shaven, his chin chiseled, his cheekbones high, his dark hair ultra-short. There was a red rim around his irises, making them look blood-shot, but that could be an optical illusion. What was definitely not an optical illusion was the blood on his white shirt. She could clearly see red dots of various sizes on his collar and down to the third button of his shirt. She'd seen plenty of blood splatter patterns during her training at the police academy and while assisting at crime scenes to know what she was looking at. The pattern gracing this man's shirt looked like it had been caused by somebody slashing a person's artery. Slashing an artery to exsanguinate a woman. The woman who'd been found here only hours earlier.

This could mean only one thing: he was the killer, and he'd returned to the scene of the crime. It didn't matter why. All that mattered was that he couldn't be allowed to escape. She had to act before he disappeared again, and abducted and killed another woman. He had to be stopped at all costs. There was no time to wait for backup.

Anita lifted her gun and aimed it in the direction of the suspect.

"Police! Hands behind your head! Now!"

4

Cooper spun on his heel and faced the person who'd barked the brusque command, expecting to be confronted by an over-eager uniformed officer of the SFPD. Instead, he saw a young woman in plain clothes pointing a gun at him. Although she stood in the darkness, his superior vampire vision allowed him to see her well enough to give her a quick assessment.

The woman was about his age, maybe a few years younger. Her long blonde hair was tied back in a ponytail, revealing her perfect facial structure and her olive skin. She was beautiful. Her blue eyes pinned him, and despite the aggressive stance she'd taken with her weapon—pointing it straight at him, finger on the trigger—he recognized a glimmer of fear in her expression. She was brave but also scared. She perceived him as a threat. Had he accidentally shown his vampire side? Cooper quickly ran his tongue over his canines to confirm that his fangs weren't extended. They weren't. He also knew that his eyes weren't glaring red, otherwise his vision would be tinted red, which it wasn't.

"I said hands behind your head! I'm not gonna say it a third time."

It would be easy to use mind control on her to make her drop her weapon, but he hated having to explain to the chief of police that he'd had to wipe a police officer's memory of the incident. While Police Chief Mike Donnelly had kept Scanguards' secrets for decades, he preferred that vampires not expose themselves to his staff if it could be avoided. And in this case, it could be avoided.

Cooper slowly raised his arms and put his hands on the back of his head. "Excuse me, Officer, but I think you're making a mistake. I haven't done anything wrong."

She scoffed, tipping her chin toward him. "Your shirt says otherwise."

He glanced down at himself. He was surprised that she'd seen the bloodstains in the dark. Apparently, the woman had excellent eyesight. And the way Sebastian's *Blood Splatter* had stained his shirt looked indeed like he'd brutally killed somebody. He couldn't argue with that. But he had to clear up the misunderstanding.

"I can explain that."

"Sure you can. At the police station." She stepped closer, the gun still pointed at him. "Now get down on the ground, face down."

"You're making a mistake."

She gestured with the gun. "You said that already. Now lie down."

He shrugged. "Fine." She would owe him an apology shortly. And he was looking forward to those words rolling over her kissable lips. Cooper lowered himself onto the ground, keeping his hands on the back of his head. He knew the drill.

He turned his head to look at her as she approached. "You're really gonna handcuff me, aren't you? It's not that I'm not into handcuffs, but this isn't really the place for it." When he noticed her huff indignantly, he couldn't help himself and chuckled. "You should at least buy me dinner first."

A moment later, she gripped his left hand, clicked one cuff around it and pulled it down to his back, then did the same with his right arm. With his hands cuffed behind his back, she ordered, "Get up."

Cooper rose and turned to her. "So now that you've had your fun, how about you call dispatch and ask for the chief. He'll clear this up. No need wasting police time with a false arrest."

"You think I'm stupid? This is the exact spot where only hours ago somebody was found dead, and I find you here, blood all over you, clearly looking for something. Tell me, did you lose something that might lead back to you? Is that why you came back?"

Fuck! How many people knew about the dead body already? Hadn't Donnelly made sure that this was kept quiet?

"You weren't one of the unis who found her," he said, scrutinizing her. "What's your name?"

"None of your business."

"Fine. You wanna play hard-ass? Let's play hard-ass. I want you to call the chief of police, Mike Donnelly. Now. Here. I'm not making another step until you do." And if she gave him any more trouble, he'd simply break the handcuffs—since they weren't made of silver, a metal no vampire could break—and wipe her memory of the incident.

She glared at him, but then finally, after a few seconds that seemed like minutes, she pulled out her cellphone and punched in a number.

Cooper heard the faint sound of the phone ringing even though he was standing several feet from the woman who'd arrested him.

"San Francisco Police Department, how may I direct your call?"

"The chief of police please."

"Your name please?"

"Deputy Anita Diaz, Elko County Sheriff's Department."

Cooper raised an eyebrow. "This isn't even your jurisdiction."

Anita cast him a reprimanding look.

"I'm afraid the chief has left for the night. Can anybody else help you?"

She hesitated.

"Tell them it's regarding Scanguards," Cooper said quickly.

"What's that supposed to—"

"Just tell them," he insisted. "He'll take my call. I'm Cooper Montgomery from Scanguards."

"Deputy?" the operator prompted.

"Ahm, could you let the chief know that it's in regard to Cooper Montgomery from Scanguards."

"Oh, of course, one moment, I'll patch you through to his cellphone."

Stunned, Anita looked at him. She'd clearly not expected that the chief of police was suddenly available. Cooper stood there, smirking. Oh yeah, he'd definitely get an apology, and now he was looking forward to it even more. And if he played his cards right, he could probably get even more than that.

"This is Donnelly. Coop? What's going on?" Donnelly's voice was loud enough so even a human without his superior auditory senses would have heard him.

"Sir? Chief Donnelly? This is Anita Diaz. I'm a deputy with the Elko County Sheriff's Department."

"Elko County? Where's that?"

"Nevada, sir. I've arrested a Cooper Montgomery."

"What the fuck is he doing in Nevada?"

"He's not in Nevada. He's in San Francisco."

"But you said you're from Nevada. Is this a prank?"

"No, sir. No prank. I'm here in San Francisco, and I've arrested Mr. Montgomery on suspicion of murder."

"Murder? What the fuck?"

Cooper couldn't keep his smirk to himself. He knew how annoyed Donnelly could get when people didn't get to the point right away.

"Yes, ahm, it's about the woman who was found dead tonight. I found him in the alley where it happened. He's got blood splatter all over his shirt." Anita was talking fast, the words fairly tumbling over her lips.

"First of all, that's where Cooper is supposed to be. He's investigating the murder. Second, how do you even know about the dead woman? We've kept this under wraps. And thirdly, you're way out of your jurisdiction! You can't just arrest one of my men. Let me talk to him! Now!"

"Yes, sir. I'm sorry, sir."

Her face red like a ripe tomato, Anita bridged the distance between them with two steps and tried to hand him the cellphone, but Cooper shrugged, indicating his hands, which were still cuffed behind his back.

"Just hold it for me," he quickly ordered Anita, and she held the cellphone to his ear. "Hey, Mike."

"Coop? Wanna tell me what's going on?"

Donnelly's voice was just as loud as before, and even without putting the call on speaker, Cooper knew that Anita could hear every single word of their conversation.

"Just a little misunderstanding. I'm at the dump site looking for clues. I guess I looked a little suspicious." He winked at Anita, who blushed even more. He hadn't meant to embarrass her, but when she'd insisted on cuffing him, he'd had no other option but to have Donnelly vouch for him. "Don't worry. My team is on it. I'll keep you posted."

"Thanks, Coop. Call me anytime in case another country bumpkin deputy wants to arrest you."

"You know she heard that, right?"

"Tell her to keep her hands off my men. Night, Coop."

There was a click in the line. Donnelly had hung up.

"Don't worry, he's not really mad," Cooper said with a look at Anita's flushed face. He turned halfway, showing her his cuffed hands. "Do you mind uncuffing me?"

Anita reached into her handbag and pulled out the key. He turned his back to her, and she unlocked the cuffs. "Why didn't you identify yourself as a police officer?"

Now free, Cooper turned around to face her. "Because I'm not. I'm a private investigator."

"And you're on a first name basis with the chief of police?"

He shrugged. "I've known Mike all my life." Then he took a breath. "So, about your apology for falsely arresting me..."

"What apology?"

"The one you haven't given me yet." He smirked.

She pointed to his blood-stained shirt. "I merely followed the evidence. So, how did that happen? Looks like blood splatter to me."

"It is." And he'd just come up with an excuse of how to explain it away without exposing his secret. "I stopped a bloody fistfight between a couple of drunks. Who knew that a nose can bleed that profusely?" He grinned, turning on his charm. "No good deed goes unpunished, right?"

She gave him a doubtful look. "I guess."

"So, how about that drink?"

"What drink?"

"The one you're going to buy me to make up for handcuffing me." He winked at her. "Not that I'm totally against cuffs. Under the right circumstances."

5

—————

Anita had to hand it to him. Cooper was disarming, although, given the circumstances, he had every right to be angry, yet he wasn't. Being arrested and handcuffed hadn't phased him at all. Rather, he was asking her out for a drink. She studied his face. His grin made him look even younger and more handsome than when she'd thought he was a brutal killer. The fact that the chief of police had vouched for him made her pounding heart settle back into an even rhythm.

Maybe it wasn't such a bad thing to have a drink with him. After all, she'd accused him of being a murderer, and she owed him an apology.

"All right," she finally said. "I'll buy you a drink."

He smiled broadly. "Perfect. Do you mind if we swing by my flat so I can slip into a clean shirt? I live only a few blocks from here."

Anita hesitated. "I can wait in a bar for you."

"And ditch me?" Cooper shook his head, laughing. "Besides, my flat's on the way to the bar. We're practically passing by it anyway."

She reminded herself that Chief Donnelly had confirmed that Cooper was working for him, and that had to mean that he was one of the good guys. Why did she always have to see the worst in people? Was that why she rarely dated? Because she expected every guy to turn out to be a criminal, or at the very least a total jerk?

Anita took a deep breath. "Sure. Otherwise, other people might wonder too why you look like you slaughtered somebody, and call the cops on you."

He grinned. "Don't want that to happen twice in a night." He pointed past her. "This way."

They started walking next to each other.

"So how come you knew about the dead body?" Cooper asked.

She wasn't surprised that this was his first question. She didn't know what to say. If she told him that she was on the trail of a serial killer, he would probably think that she was crazy. Hell, her own father thought her theory was crazy. It was best to keep things simple.

"A woman from Elko County went missing six weeks ago. I spoke to somebody at SFPD to find out if she's turned up here. I got word tonight that a woman matching her general description was found dead in North Beach."

"So you think it's her?"

"I don't know yet. I'm planning to look at the body tomorrow."

Cooper nodded. "Good, you should definitely do that. We found no ID on her, and if you can identify her, it'll help us in our investigation. Tell me why you thought she'd show up here."

Anita shrugged, not wanting to divulge too much. "A hunch. It's hard to explain. There were a few clues that she might have come to San Francisco. I guess we'll find out tomorrow if it's her."

"I guess." Then Cooper gestured to a small older building that looked like it was divided up into six units. "This is where I live." He pulled his keys out and unlocked the entrance door. He held it open for her, so she could enter ahead of him. "Second floor. Sorry, no elevator."

"Don't worry, I'm fit," she said, looking over her shoulder as Cooper followed her. "I've walked up a lot of hills this past week."

"Is that how long you've been here? A week?"

Arriving on the second floor, Cooper went to one of the two doors and unlocked it. He pushed it open and ushered her inside.

"Yes, I got here a week ago."

"Excuse the mess, but the place is undergoing some major repairs." He pointed to the ceiling. "A pipe burst in my upstairs neighbor's flat, and it flooded my bathroom and kitchen."

Anita glanced around. The condo had a large living/dining area with big windows overlooking the city. There was one bedroom as well as the kitchen and bathroom. The entire place looked like a construction site. Furniture was piled up in the living area, and floorboards had been removed to expose pipes. She peered into the bathroom, where the sink, tub, and toilet had been ripped out, and the tiles had been removed as well.

"Don't tell me you're living here right now."

"God, no." He walked into the bedroom, leaving the door open. "I'm staying at my uncle's house in Buena Vista until this mess is repaired."

Through the open door, she saw him take off his shirt and toss it into a hamper. His naked torso was a beautiful sight to behold. Cooper was muscular, his arms flexing as he reached into the closet to pull out a fresh shirt. He slipped into the shirt, before walking to his bed where he pulled something small from the drawer of his nightstand. He slipped it into his pants pocket and turned around. Had he just put a condom in his pocket? Their gazes met, and Anita felt heat shoot into her cheeks. Slowly, as if this was a striptease in reverse, Cooper buttoned the casual shirt without breaking eye contact.

Anita cleared her throat and ripped her gaze from him, not wanting to drool at such male perfection. Her mind was doing cartwheels. Was Cooper preparing for the eventuality of having sex? No, she'd probably seen wrong. Maybe he'd put a handkerchief into his pocket.

"So, Buena Vista. Where's that?" Was her voice shaking? Was it obvious that she was nervous?

"It's clear across town. Nice area, and some great views of the city," he said casually and walked toward her, fully dressed now. He reached for his jacket and put it on. "So, let's go for that drink, and you can tell me all about yourself."

She turned to the door, but he was faster and opened it for her, his hand suddenly on her lower back to guide her outside. When he removed it seconds later, she was disappointed. Damn, this man conjured up all kinds of desires in her, even though she didn't know anything about him. But seeing his naked torso and the way he'd looked at her with such intensity in his brown eyes while he'd dressed without inhibition, had awakened everything female in her. This man exuded pure sex from every pore of his skin. She had no doubt that whenever he set his sights on a woman, he got exactly what he wanted. What woman in her right mind could resist a man like Cooper?

The place Cooper took her to was an intimate wine bar with small, half-moon-shaped booths lined with red velvet and candles on the tables. The lighting was muted, and soft jazz music came from the hidden speakers.

"I should have asked if you like wine," Cooper said as a staff member led them to a table in the back of the establishment.

"I do, but only red. And I'm not a connoisseur. You might have to help me choose," she admitted, slightly intimidated by the many bottles of wine that were lined up behind the bar and others that were hidden behind a glass front to keep their contents at a steady temperature.

Sitting down at the table, Cooper handed the menus back to the waiter. "We'll have the Wilson Zin, the Tori if you have it."

"An excellent choice, sir," the man said and disappeared.

"I guess you know your wine," Anita said, feeling even more flushed now that they were inside. It was rather warm in the bar, and she was still wearing her jacket. She adjusted her collar to allow more air to reach her skin.

"You must be warm. Why don't you take off your jacket?" he suggested.

She leaned closer, lowering her voice. "I can't. I'm wearing a shoulder holster."

Cooper chuckled. "I almost forgot about the gun." He pointed to a door. "Why don't you take it off in the restroom and put it in your handbag?"

"Good idea." She rose.

"As a matter of fact, I'd better wash my hands. After all, I was lying on the ground in a dirty alley not too long ago."

"You'll never let me forget about that, will you?"

He grinned, and the dimples in his cheeks made her heart jump with excitement. "Maybe if I could replace that memory with a better one..."

She decided not to reply to his comment. It was a minefield, and there was no good answer to it.

6

Cooper entered the men's room and locked the door behind him. He pulled his cellphone from his pocket and tapped on the number for the Scanguards command center.

Nicholas answered on the first ring. "Scanguards. State your emergency."

"It's me, Cooper."

"Hey, I already fed the fingerprints into AFIS," Nicholas said quickly.

"I'm not calling about that. I need you to do a background check for me as soon as possible."

"Sure."

"Okay, the name is Anita Diaz. She's a deputy with the Elko County Sheriff's Department. That's in Nevada. I need to know whether she is who she says she is. And see if you can find out what she's doing in San Francisco. She claims she's working a missing person's case."

"Okay, got it."

"Thanks. If I don't answer my phone, leave me a detailed voicemail with whatever you've found." He was about to disconnect, when he remembered something else. "And one other thing: send somebody to clean the interior of my car—there's blood all over the seats and the dashboard."

"What happened? Are you okay?"

"Yeah, yeah, I'm fine. Let's just say that drinking one of Sebastian's *Blood Splatter* concoctions after the bottle has been in a moving car, isn't a good idea."

A suppressed chuckle came from Nicholas. "Where's the car?"

"In North Beach. Use my GPS location. And when it's clean, have somebody park it at Wesley's house." After all, he couldn't very well allow Anita inside his SUV in the current state it was in. "Thanks. Talk later."

"Later," Nicholas replied, and Cooper disconnected the call.

He washed his hands and double-checked his appearance in the mirror. There wasn't much he could do on the case of the exsanguinated woman right now, and there was no harm in having a few drinks with a beautiful woman. The way Anita had looked at his naked torso had pleased him. She wasn't immune to his charms. Besides, it was best to keep her close until he could establish if she knew anything about the dead woman. Sure, he could take her to Scanguards right now to identify the body, but this move wasn't wise until he'd checked her out and was sure that she wasn't a danger to him or Scanguards. She wouldn't be the first person who'd infiltrated their community and turned out to be a bad guy. Better safe than sorry.

Back at the table, the waiter set two glasses of wine down, when Anita reappeared. Cooper barely recognized her. The determined sheriff's deputy who'd arrested and handcuffed him was gone and had made way for a blue-eyed seductress who was well aware of her sex appeal. She'd not only taken off her jacket, but also her thick sweater, and hung both over her arm. She now wore a simple pink T-shirt, accentuating her well-formed breasts. Her hair hung loosely over her shoulders, making her face look even more feminine. Only now he realized how tall she was, five foot eight or nine, if he had to guess. Tall for a woman, tall and athletic. Her long legs seemed to be endless, and he could already imagine what it would be like to feel those strong thighs wrap around his hips once he got her into bed.

Damn, just thinking about that made his cock harder than a crowbar. He was glad that he was sitting on the bench with the table hiding his lower body, or she would have instantly seen what he had planned for tonight.

Anita sat down on the half-moon bench and placed her handbag, jacket, and sweater next to her, preventing him from scooting closer to her. Maybe it was better this way, so he wouldn't be tempted to slide his hand onto her thigh while they were engaging in conversation.

"Feeling better?" he asked and lifted his glass.

"Much better now." She reached for her glass and clinked it to his. "I'm sorry for falsely arresting you." Her blue eyes sparkled, and a smile formed on her lips.

Cooper smirked. "You don't look very sorry."

He took a sip of his wine, and watched her do the same, while she lowered her eyelids as if timid.

"You didn't seem to mind the cuffs that much."

"Are they in your purse now?"

"Yes, why?"

He leaned closer. "So I know where they are when I need them later."

"Don't you have your own? I mean, you work for the police."

He recognized a fishing expedition when he saw one. And Anita was definitely fishing for information. "Actually, the company I work for has a contract with the police to help out with investigations that require our expertise. But let's not talk about me. Tell me about yourself. Is this your first trip to San Francisco?"

"It is." She took another sip from her wine. "It's an impressive city. Did you grow up here?"

"Yes. I've lived here all my life. My father's family is from here too. My mother is from the East Coast. And you? Diaz is a Latino name, but you're a natural blonde. That's unusual for a Latina."

"My dad is from Mexico, but my mother's family is from Sweden. How do you know that my hair isn't dyed blonde?"

He shrugged. "I just do." He could smell it. Dyed hair had a different smell, even once it had been washed fifty times. "Did you grow up in Elko County, or did you move there just for the job?"

"I spent my entire life in Nevada. But we lived in Reno until I was nine. After that, my father and I moved to Elko, and we've been there ever since."

He noticed that Anita hadn't mentioned her mother. "Just you and your dad? You don't have any siblings?"

She shook her head. "Do you? Have siblings, I mean."

"An older sister, Lydia."

He stretched out his hand and put it on Anita's forearm, enjoying the feel of her soft skin, the warmth of her body. He noticed her breath hitch. Her eyes snapped to his.

"How about we stop with the twenty-questions-game we've got going here? What I really want is to get to know you. You're a beautiful woman, and I think we both know that I'm attracted to you." He winked at her. "Despite you arresting me." He stroked over her forearm down to her hand, allowing his fingers to brush over hers. "Please tell me a little about yourself, about what drives you, about your life, your dreams."

She inhaled deeply, and her chest rose, drawing his gaze to it instinctively, before he lifted his eyes back to her face.

"I'm not used to talking about myself. I've spent a lot of my childhood on my own, without family other than my father, and now, working in law enforcement, it's even harder to let anybody come close, when you have to behave a certain way. It's difficult to let go of that. You must know how that is. I mean, you're in law enforcement too."

Cooper took her hand and simply held it. "I think it's different for me. I work with my family. And everybody at Scanguards—that's the company I work for—is part of my extended family. We might not all be related by blood or marriage, but we're all one big happy family. I couldn't imagine doing anything else, and not being part of Scanguards."

"Your entire family works there? They're all private investigators?"

"No. Scanguards' main purpose isn't investigations. It's security. I'm actually trained as a bodyguard, and virtually everybody working there is also a bodyguard."

Anita's eyes widened in surprise. "Your parents too?"

"Yes. That's how my parents met. Mom was protecting a young actress, and Dad got tangled up in it. It's complicated. But it worked out in the end."

Yes, it had worked out, but only because his father, Haven, had sacrificed his human life in the end, and his mother, Yvette, had saved him by turning him into a vampire. But those were details he couldn't divulge to a human who knew nothing about the existence of vampires and other preternatural creatures.

"It sounds like you're very close to your family, and to the people you work with."

Cooper nodded.

"My father and I have always had a complicated relationship. It didn't get any easier after Mom was gone." Anita hesitated, searching his eyes before she continued, and he didn't interrupt, didn't prompt her, and instead gave her the time she needed to open up. "We lived in Reno, when Mom disappeared one night. Dad still believes that she left us because she didn't love him anymore, but I think she was abducted."

Cooper squeezed her hand. "I'm sorry."

"We never heard from her again. That was twenty-one years ago. Dad thinks she's living somewhere else, maybe under an assumed name, but I think she's dead."

"Why do you think that?" he asked with interest.

"She would have contacted me if she was still alive. She would have never put me through the pain of losing her if she was still alive. She loved me. And I loved her."

"Have you tried to find her?"

"Yes. Her leaving was the main reason why I went into law enforcement. It gave me the resources I needed."

"So that's what drives you." He felt her heartbreak, felt the pain she carried with her. "Thank you for telling me about it. Now I can see who you are." And he liked what he saw: a woman with a hard shell to protect the soft heart inside. A woman who loved deeply and was trying to protect herself from further hurt.

Anita smiled softly, then sighed. "You don't think I'm crazy thinking that my mother didn't leave us voluntarily?"

"Why would I think that? I've dealt with plenty of tragedies like yours to know that these things happen more frequently than people think. Unfortunately, many of these cases are never solved. But at Scanguards we try our best to help victims and their families get closure. It's very rewarding when we close a case. The cases the police hand us are some of the more egregious ones, because we have people with the right expertise." Or rather, the police handed them cases that involved vampires, but he couldn't very well tell her that, even though he wanted to open up to her just like she'd opened up to him.

He took the last sip of his glass of wine. "How about another glass?"

Anita smiled at him. "I'd like that."

7

Anita was surprised at how easy it was to talk to Cooper. He was witty, charming, and above all else, caring. She'd never met a man like him, a man who played no games and was straightforward. His confession that he was attracted to her had sent her heartbeat into the stratosphere. He exuded confidence, both as an investigator and as a man. He was so different from the men she worked with in Elko. Many of them were overly macho and thought that their uniform made them superior to others, a fact that often translated into arrogance and egotism.

She saw none of these traits in Cooper. It attracted her to him. Not that she didn't find the rest of him equally attractive: his handsome good looks, his broad grin, the sparkle in his eyes when he laughed, and his deep voice that made her want to melt like an ice cream cone in 100-degree weather. He was still holding her hand across the table long after the waiter had brought their second glasses of wine. It felt natural to allow him to touch her, though it felt in no way innocent. His touch was electrifying, and the way he rubbed his thumb over the back of her hand, caressing her gently, made her imagine what his touch would feel like on other parts of her body.

"You still find it too warm in here?" Cooper suddenly asked.

The question made her feel even more flushed. Was it written on her face what she was thinking? "Just a little."

A mischievous glint in his eyes, he leaned in and brought his mouth close to her ear. "Then I'll have to wait until we're outside in the cold before I can kiss you, or we might both get burned."

His hot breath scorched her skin, and she let out a shuddering breath of air. "You sound very sure of yourself. What if your kiss doesn't have that kind of effect on me?" She'd never been so bold, teasing a guy like she teased Cooper now. But she liked it. For the first time in her life, she felt that she had power that didn't come from the uniform she wore. The power a woman had over a man.

"Are you challenging me?" A soft chuckle accompanied his question.

"What if I am?"

"Then I'll have to meet your challenge. Just so we know who's right," he suggested.

Her breath hitched. "I think that's a good idea."

Cooper shifted a little, and his face was now only inches from hers. There was a golden shimmer around his irises, and it reminded her of the reflection she'd seen when he'd stood in the alley. Just like then, the light was playing tricks on her, making his eyes look like molten lava. He was a man so full of passion that it stoked a fire inside her belly that made her crave something she had no words for: a connection beyond sex. Beyond the here and now, even though this could only be a one-night stand, at most a brief holiday fling. Nevertheless, she wanted this, wanted him.

His lips were gentle when he touched hers, while he took her hand and pressed it to his cheek. She felt the warmth of his skin, and tilted her head to the side, asking him to deepen the kiss. Cooper placed his hand on her nape and licked over her lips, making them part. His intoxicating taste filled her mouth as he slipped his tongue between her lips and explored her. She greeted him with eagerness, meeting his invasion by dueling with him. The kiss instantly intensified, and she felt heat flare up in her core. A bolt akin to an electrical charge traveled south and ignited the tender flesh between her thighs, wringing a moan from her lips.

Cooper pulled back, severing the kiss, and exhaled on a long hum. "Yeah, I definitely think we should do this outside where it's colder."

Anita stroked her thumb along his jaw, leaning in again. "Or inside with fewer clothes."

"That sounds even better." He turned his head to the side and lifted his hand toward the bar. "Check, please." He looked back to her. "You've seen the state of my flat. It's not exactly inviting. We should go to your hotel."

"I'm not staying at a hotel."

He raised his eyebrows. "Where then?"

"I rented an Airbnb in North Beach."

"Even better." He smirked. "No housekeeping staff that can disturb us."

"But housekeeping only comes in the mornings."

He rolled his eyes, then leaned in to whisper into her ear. "Do you really think I'd sleep with you once and then sneak out in the middle of the night?"

"Oh." Was he really planning to stay the night? "But I thought guys—"

Cooper put a finger to her lips. "Yeah, other guys maybe. But I prefer to spend the whole night with a woman. And I'm not a once-a-night kind of guy either." He winked at her. "I'm pretty insatiable when it comes to sex."

Excitement charged through her body. Men like Cooper didn't exist. At least, she'd never met a man who was not only straightforward about what he wanted, but also wanted more than just a quick tumble in the sheets. He wanted the whole night.

"How insatiable?" Anita teased, unable to stop smiling.

"Extremely." He kissed her again but was interrupted by the waiter presenting him with the bill.

"I'll take care of that," Anita said quickly and reached for it.

Cooper was faster. "Not a chance."

"But that was my apology drink. We agreed I'd pay."

Cooper handed his credit card to the waiter, who quickly walked away. "If you'd been an ugly guy who'd falsely arrested me, I would have allowed him to buy me a drink. But you?" He shook his head. "From you I'd rather receive a different kind of apology."

He smirked, and the dimples in his cheeks became more pronounced, making him look even more handsome. Damn, this man could work as a model or an actor. With his looks, he'd get plenty of work. But he hadn't chosen the easy way. Being a bodyguard and an investigator was a difficult and dangerous profession.

"Then I'd better make sure you get that apology." She looked into his brown eyes, more confident than she'd ever been around a man.

"I'm looking forward to it," he murmured against her lips and kissed her again, until somebody cleared their throat.

Anita pulled back and saw the waiter place the credit card receipt and Cooper's credit card on the table. "Have an enjoyable night," he said with a smile and retreated.

A few minutes later, they were sitting in the back of a taxi. Anita gave the driver the address of the Airbnb, and leaned back in the seat. Cooper pulled her to him, and kissed her passionately, while his hands weren't idle. He slipped one underneath her jacket. She hadn't bothered to put on her sweater or the shoulder holster with her gun. She was too hot for that despite the cool evening temperature and the fog that blanketed the city. And considering what Cooper's caresses did to her, she shouldn't have bothered with the jacket either. But at least the jacket concealed what he was doing.

Cooper slid one hand underneath her jacket and moved it up until he reached her breasts. He cupped one and kneaded it through her T-shirt. She wore no bra beneath it, a freedom she allowed herself only when she was off duty. Now she welcomed this fact, because it made her experience his touch more intensely. He was skillful, alternating between gentle strokes and firm kneading motions, interrupting every so often by rubbing her nipple and capturing it between thumb and index finger.

Anita moaned into his mouth and pulled him closer to her, one hand on his chest, one on his nape, caressing him there. She felt him shiver, and he ripped his lips from hers. Cold air blew against her heated lips.

"Baby," he whispered, his voice hoarse. "You keep doing that, and we're not gonna make it to a bed."

"You started it."

His eyes shimmered almost golden now. "Can't argue with the truth." He sank his lips back onto hers, and continued his sensual onslaught.

This time, he pulled the seam of her T-shirt from the waistband of her pants, and tunneled underneath it until he palmed one breast. The contact of skin on skin made her entire body tingle with anticipation.

"We're here."

The words drifted to her ears, and for a split second, she didn't know what they meant and who'd spoken. Cooper released her and leaned forward, handing the cab driver a few banknotes, while she adjusted her clothing, still hot and dazed from their passionate encounter.

Cooper helped her out of the cab, and they walked up to the building that housed several flats. The front door was unlocked like it had been the day she'd arrived. The Airbnb she rented was on the second floor. When they arrived at the door to it, Anita punched the six-digit code into the keypad. She was glad that many vacation rentals had this kind of entry system. It meant that no keys needed to be exchanged.

Cooper pushed the door open and ushered her inside the one-bedroom flat.

"Where's the bedroom?"

"This way."

Cooper pulled her with him and opened the door to the bedroom wider. Only the light from a streetlamp illuminated the dark interior. Anita reached for the light switch, but Cooper stopped her.

"Curtains first," he said and quickly pulled the curtains shut.

Anita flipped the light switch, and the two bedside lamps bathed the room in a warm light. She dropped her handbag on the floor, and slipped out of her jacket. Cooper did the same and tossed it on a nearby chair.

Before she could reach for him and begin to unbutton his shirt, he was already pulling her T-shirt over her head. She welcomed the cool air that blew against her naked skin. Cooper gazed at her, and his eyes shone with desire and admiration.

"You're beautiful," he murmured and made a motion to embrace her, but she stopped him.

"Now you."

He smirked. "Haven't you already seen what's beneath my shirt?"

"And I bet you did that on purpose so I'd get a preview of what I'd get to touch if I took you home with me."

Cooper flipped one button after the other open. "I'm glad it worked." He shrugged the shirt off his shoulders, revealing his hairless chest that was sculpted as if Michelangelo himself had created him. She'd never seen so much male perfection close-up.

Anita licked her lips, then tipped her head toward his lower body. "How about the rest?"

With two fingers hooked into the waistband of her pants, Cooper pulled her to him. "Let me help you with yours first."

With expert hands he undressed her, until she stood in front of him in only her bikini panties. With relief she noticed that she wore her sexiest pair. Cooper cast an appreciative glance at her, before he proceeded to rid himself of his shoes, socks, and pants. When he stood in front of her only wearing his boxer briefs, she dropped her gaze to them and noticed the heavy bulge that stretched the fabric.

"Oh." She reached for it, but Cooper gripped her wrists.

"Not yet, or I'm not gonna last. I'd much rather take care of you first." He motioned to the bed. "Lie down."

She followed his command without hesitation. When she lay on her back and looked up at him, he stepped closer to the bed. He suddenly held something in one hand. It shimmered silver. Her eyes zeroed in on it. Her handcuffs. Air rushed out of her lungs. When had he taken them out of her handbag?

"What are you gonna—"

He sat down on the edge of the bed, facing her. "I thought I'd handcuff you like you did with me. And then—" He caressed her breasts with his free hand. "—I'll make you come."

Her heart thundered, the thought of being helpless scaring her, yet exciting her nevertheless. "And you need the handcuffs for that?"

"Yes. Because I can't have you touch me while I pleasure you, or I'm gonna give into the temptation too quickly."

"What temptation?"

"To sink my cock into your sweet pussy."

It wasn't just his words that convinced her that being at his mercy would be a good thing, it was also the way he looked at her with passion and desire.

"All right. Just one thing, before you handcuff me."

"Anything."

"I want you fully naked."

Cooper smiled and rose. He freed himself of his boxer briefs. His cock was hard and heavy. It curved upwards toward his navel despite its weight. He was beautiful, just as perfect as the rest of his body. She couldn't wait to feel him inside her. Anita licked her lower lip, before she stretched her arms over her head to grip the wooden slats of the headboard.

Cooper bent over her with a grin, looped the handcuffs around one sturdy slat, and fastened the cuffs around her wrists. She tested the cuffs. They held. Cooper dipped his face to hers and looked into her eyes.

"Now relax and enjoy."

He kissed her just as deeply as he had in the taxi, before he lifted himself off her and scooted down. His eyes shimmered again, this time with a red glint. He reminded her of a hungry animal and the sight made her heart thunder. Had she made a mistake by allowing him to handcuff her?

8

The picture before him was perfect. Anita was handcuffed to the headboard of the bed, her arms stretched out above her head, her blonde hair fanned out around her flushed face. Her blue eyes sparkled, and he noticed two conflicting expressions in them: desire and fear. He would rob her of the latter, because he had no intention of hurting her. All he wanted was to find pleasure with her and give her the same in return.

Her breasts lay in front of him like a sumptuous buffet, the ample swells topped with hard little buds that confirmed that she was aroused. But it wasn't the only sign that she wanted him to make love to her. Her pussy was weeping for him already, he could smell it, and he hadn't even touched her yet. But he would rectify that oversight quickly.

Cooper hooked his thumbs into Anita's panties and pulled them down her legs until he could free her from them completely. Then he brushed his hands up her calves, over her knees to her thighs, applying just a small amount of pressure, until Anita let her legs fall open, giving him an unobstructed view of her pussy. The blonde curls guarding her center of pleasure were damp from her juices, and the scent of it now wafted to him more freely.

Inside him, he felt the vampire awaken, eager to taste the delectable woman who lay on the sheets like an offering. But the vampire would have to wait. Cooper slipped into the space between her legs and dipped his head to the apex of her thighs.

"You're beautiful," he murmured, connecting with her gaze for a brief moment, before he pressed his face to her pussy and inhaled the aroma of her arousal. He pushed her thighs farther apart, making her set her feet flat on the bed, thus exposing more of her pink flesh. Unable to wait another second, he licked over her drenched folds and began to explore her.

Beneath him, he felt Anita relax. Her body began to move in synch with his, and soft sighs and moans rolled over her lips. He licked along her slit, then stroked upwards to give the same attention to her clit, bathing it in the juices he'd collected with his tongue. Anita undulated her hips, silently asking for more pressure, and he complied and caressed the small organ with more fervor, applying a faster tempo.

"Oh, yes, please," she begged, twisting beneath him.

He lifted his head for a brief second to look at her face, and saw perspiration collect on her chest. Anita looked at him, her eyelids at half-mast. It was the picture of a woman in the throes of passion. The sight made his cock even harder, and all he could do was rub it against the sheets in an attempt to alleviate his need.

"Tell me what you need," he demanded, knowing that every woman's body was different.

She lifted her head off the pillow. "Are you for real?"

"I wanna make you come. Tell me what you like."

"You're already doing it." She dropped her head back in the pillow.

Cooper licked over her clit again and again, then used his fingers to spread her folds farther apart, exposing her center of pleasure fully. With quick flicks of his tongue, he caressed her flesh, wringing more and more moans from her lips.

"Cooper, yes, yes, please, almost... almost."

He sucked her clit into his mouth and pressed his lips together. Suddenly, her body spasmed. He drove his middle finger into her tight channel. Her interior muscles squeezed him, spasming around his digit as the waves of her orgasm charged through her body.

He gave her the time she needed until the waves subsided, before he withdrew his finger and lifted his head from her pussy. Anita lay there, eyes closed, breathing hard. He scooted up sufficiently to reach her breasts and captured one hard nipple in his mouth. He sucked on it and heard Anita moan softly. He did the same with the other breast, before he lifted himself off her and got off the bed. He found the spot where he'd dropped his pants and reached into the front pocket.

"Are you leaving?"

Cooper turned back to her and showed her what he'd retrieved. "Just getting a condom."

"Oh. That's not gonna work."

Surprised, he froze in place. Had she changed her mind about wanting to sleep with him? Before he even knew how to react, she added, "I have a latex allergy."

He looked at the condom. It was a latex condom, like most of them were. "Sorry. I can run down to the drug store. There's a 24-hour-pharmacy not too far from here. I'm sure they have latex-free condoms."

She shook her head. "Don't. I'm on the pill."

Cooper tossed the condom on the nightstand and bent over Anita. "Are you sure? I don't mind getting some if that's what you need."

"All I need right now is your cock inside me."

He smirked. "That can be arranged." Then he looked at the handcuffs. "But without the cuffs. As much as I love to have you at my mercy, I want to feel your hands on me."

"I'd like that."

Moments later, Cooper retrieved the key from Anita's handbag and uncuffed her. Anita sat up and pulled him down until he lay with his back on the mattress.

"Now I'll be in charge," she announced and swung herself over him like a rider would mount a horse.

Cooper put his hands on her hips and grinned up at her. "I love a woman who likes to take the reins. I'm game." Then he gave her a gentle slap on her backside.

Anita gasped.

"Ride me already." He cast a meaningful look at his cock, which stood fully erect. "Or are you planning to torture me longer?"

She smirked. "Well, you *did* handcuff me."

"Which, if I'm not mistaken, you enjoyed."

The rose blush was back on her cheeks, and with her blonde hair hanging over her breasts, she looked like an innocent. Damn, she made him hot.

"I did. So, I hope you'll enjoy this." Anita lifted herself onto her knees and guided his cock to her center, before she bore down on him.

All air rushed from his lungs, and he closed his eyes and pressed his head into the pillow, the pleasure so intense he had to fight against the urge to extend his fangs.

He opened his eyes and stared at Anita. "Fuck, you feel good!"

She bent over him. Her hair caressed his skin and her breasts bounced up and down, side to side while she moved up and down on his cock. Her plentiful juices turned every descent and every withdrawal into a sensual caress. Her pussy was tight and her interior muscles gripped him like a glove one size too small. The absence of a condom made him even more sensitive, and every sensation was more intense, more pleasurable.

Releasing one of her hips, Cooper pulled Anita's head to his. "Go slowly so I'll last longer, 'cause I love being inside you."

"I love having you inside me."

He took Anita's lips and kissed her, while he placed both hands back on her hips to adjust her tempo. When she complied with his wishes, he removed his hands again and began to caress her breasts. They were full and firm and in perfect proportion to her tall stature. He was glad that she'd decided to ride him, because it tamped down his urge to go all caveman on her. At least like this, he could keep a modicum of control over himself, though he knew that soon that self-control would snap no matter what he did. And then the beast in him would take over and fuck her until neither of them could move another limb.

Anita moaned with every move, and he realized that she was close to another climax. He ripped his lips off hers, barely holding on to his control now, the sensation of her pussy squeezing him too intense.

"Sorry, baby, gotta take over now," he pressed out.

COOPER HAD BARELY FINISHED his sentence, when Anita found herself with her back on the bed. She gasped in surprise just as he pushed her legs apart and plunged his rock-hard cock deep into her. She'd never been with a man who'd taken her with such determination, never been with anybody who'd made her feel so desired. As he pumped his hard-on deep into her, filling her, stretching her farther than she thought was possible, she allowed herself to submit to him again. When he'd gone down on her while she'd been handcuffed, she'd marveled at his selflessness and considerable skills in pleasuring a woman. Her initial fear of giving him free rein had subsided instantly, and she'd let herself go in his arms. Just like she did now.

"Oh God, that's... oh... that's..."

"Good?" he asked and thrust again.

"Amazing."

He continued to ride her hard and fast, their bodies slamming together more forcefully than before. Her body was on fire. Every nerve ending was vibrating, and her arousal spiked. Her breathing accelerated, and her heart thundered.

"Come with me," Cooper murmured.

She met his gaze, seeing his eyes shimmer almost golden now, and lost herself in their beauty. Cooper slipped his hand between them and rubbed his finger with unerring precision over her clit. In the matter of a few minutes, he'd learned what her body needed.

Cooper caressed her while he thrust deep and hard. Finally, Anita felt the approach of her orgasm, and all tension left her body while her interior muscles spasmed. In the same instance she felt Cooper's cock spasm inside her. The hot spray of his semen filled her, making his thrusts even smoother.

A few more thrusts, a few more breaths, and he collapsed. He rolled off her instantly, before he pulled her to him and kissed her with so much tenderness that it felt as if he was a different man. When he let go of her lips, he gently brushed his fingers over her face. She'd never felt such satisfaction, such contentment with anybody. Was it because they were strangers and there were no expectations, no inhibitions, because they might never see each other after tonight?

"You were amazing," she confessed.

"Because you turn me on," he admitted. "You're a very sexy woman, Anita, and I'm even more attracted to you now that I've felt you come in my arms."

"Twice." And she'd enjoyed every single second of it.

He chuckled. "Yes, only twice. But the night is young. Give me a few minutes, and we'll double that number." Cooper put his fingers under her chin and drew her face closer to his. "Now kiss me, Baby, or I'll have to handcuff you again so you'll do what I want."

His words and actions made her bold. "Is that what you do with all the women you sleep with? Handcuff them?"

He hesitated, before he finally answered, "Only when the woman needs to be restrained."

Her forehead furrowed. "You thought I needed to be restrained?"

Cooper put his hand on her lower back and pulled her closer. "Don't get me wrong, I would have never forced the cuffs on you, if you'd said no..." He sighed. "But I had the feeling that you don't find it easy to let somebody get close to you, and that you don't often let yourself go. So I figured that giving the reins over to me for a little while would make it easier for you to enjoy yourself."

Stunned, she gaped at him. How had he seen through her so easily? She'd spent years perfecting her iron-clad façade as a sheriff's deputy so nothing could faze her. As a consequence, she'd found it difficult to open up to men who wanted to date her, and many had thought her emotionally cold.

"Did I say something wrong?" Cooper's eyes bored into her.

"No, no, you didn't," she said quickly. "It's just that you're the first man who's figured out who I am. Most guys I go out with barely get past the first date. They think I'm too reserved, too cold."

"You're not. You're full of passion. Making love to you, feeling how you responded to me, was breathtaking. Just thinking of it…"

He took her hand and pulled it down his torso until she felt his cock beneath her palm. Instinctively, she wrapped her hand around his erection. "You're hard again." Her pulse kicked up.

"Of course, I'm hard again. You're in my arms, naked, and utterly sexy. Why wouldn't I be hard? Are you not even aware of how hot you are?"

"I've never seen myself like that."

"Anita, Anita," he said softly, a chuckle rolling off his lips as he put two fingers beneath her chin to tip it up so her mouth was only an inch from his. "Do I have to make love to you all night so you'll believe me when I tell you what a desirable woman you are?"

She smiled mischievously. "If it's not too much trouble."

"No trouble at all," he murmured and kissed her, while he rolled over her.

9

I t was almost midday, when Cooper woke. He was famished and lusted for blood. Anita had wrung the last bit of energy out of his body, yet he didn't regret a single second of their night together. Making love to her was the most natural thing he'd ever done. And the most satisfying. It was also evident to him that he wasn't just attracted to her. It was more than that. He was drawn to her like a moth to the light. And even now, in the harsh morning light, he wanted to be close to her rather than leave her place. That had never happened with other women. Certainly, he'd always enjoyed spending the entire night with a woman, but in the morning, he'd always had the urge to leave. Not so this morning. But before he could welcome this feeling, he had to do one thing.

Cooper got out of bed, careful to be quiet, pulled his cellphone from his jacket pocket and walked into the bathroom. He shut the door behind him, before navigating to his messages.

The first message was from Sebastian. *"Hey, bro, sorry about the blood splatter accident. Your car is clean again, and I've parked it in Wesley's garage. Next time maybe don't have the bottle rattle around in your car before you open it. Just saying. I mean you wouldn't do that with a bottle of champagne either. Anyway, see ya."*

Cooper rolled his eyes, but he wasn't mad at him anymore. After all, had he not had blood splatter on his shirt, he might have never made Anita's acquaintance.

The next message was from Nicholas. *"Coop, I've got the background on that woman you asked for: Anita Diaz. She's 30 years old, never been married. Lives alone. She's a deputy in the Elko County Sheriff's Department. And get this: her father, José Diaz, is the Sheriff in Elko County. There's no record of what happened to her mother. Apparently, she's not been seen in the last twenty-one years. And here it gets interesting. Her father divorced her mother in absentia about fourteen years ago and remarried. He has two sons with his second wife. It doesn't appear that Anita is close to them. Rumor has it that she's been using sheriff's department resources to look for her mother. And another thing: according to one of her colleagues I could reach on the phone, she's looking for a local woman who left Elko about five or six weeks ago. The woman's husband didn't file a missing person's report, but Anita thinks she was abducted. The sheriff was apparently so pissed off about her looking into this that he made her take a vacation. So, that's all. Hope it helps. Let me know if you need anything else."*

Pleased about Nicholas's thorough report, Cooper typed a quick text message to thank him, before he placed his cellphone next to the sink and stepped into the shower. As he began to soap up, he thought about the information he'd received from Nicholas. Everything Anita had told him was true, even down to the detail of when her mother had disappeared. The fact that her father had divorced his wife in absentia rather than having her declared dead fit with Anita's assertion that her father believed that she'd left them and lived somewhere else under an assumed name.

However, Anita had left out that her father was the sheriff of Elko County and therefore her superior, and that he'd forced her to take a vacation, most likely to stop her from investigating the disappearance of a woman whose husband hadn't even filed a missing persons' report. So what had convinced Anita that this woman was truly missing and had ended up in San Francisco? There was something Anita hadn't told him yet. She'd called it a hunch the night before, but he suspected there was more to it. Why would Anita drive all the way to California to spend her forced vacation looking for this woman?

By the time Cooper left the bathroom, a towel wrapped around his lower half, Anita came out of the bedroom, dressed in a short Kimono-style robe. Her long blonde hair was ruffled, her cheeks rosy, and she looked even more enticing than the night before. But he knew he couldn't have sex with her right now, because if he did, he would bite her and drink her blood. He desperately needed to replenish, and right now, a good amount of regular food would help stave off the hunger for blood, until he could get his hands on bottled blood.

"Good morning," she murmured, a smile curving her lips upwards.

He pulled her against his naked chest. "It's almost midday. How about you get ready, and I'll take you out for lunch? I'm famished."

"That's a great idea."

Cooper released her from his embrace and gave her a gentle slap on her bottom as she turned to walk to the bathroom. "Don't take too long, or I'm coming in there." And God help him what would happen then.

While Anita got ready in the bathroom, Cooper collected his clothes and got dressed. In the kitchen, he gulped down a glass of water, and munched on a few crackers. He sat down at the dining table to check his emails on his phone, when he realized that the table was covered with file folders, maps, and photos. He didn't want to snoop, but it was hard not to notice that some of the documents looked like they were police reports and autopsies. He took a closer look and realized that he was right. These were cases, but not from the Elko County Sheriff's Department, rather they were from police departments all over the western United States. He saw files from Washington State, Oregon, Idaho, and even California.

The bathroom door opened, and he looked over his shoulder to see Anita come out of it, her hair damp from the shower.

She approached, and he pointed to the table, deciding it was best to grab the bull by the horns. "Do you always take work with you on vacation?"

There was hesitation on her face, and he could fairly see the wheels in her head spinning like a caged hamster, trying to figure out how to answer. He didn't push her, simply waited for her to make a decision.

Finally, she sighed. "Let me get dressed, and then I'll tell you all about it. Maybe it'll even help with your current case."

"Okay." Now he was positively curious.

He was glad that Anita didn't take a lot of time to get dressed. She joined him at the dining table only a short while later and sat down next to him. He met her gaze and noticed that she was still hesitating.

"Can you promise me to keep an open mind?" she asked.

He nodded. "Of course. So, what's this about?"

"I believe there's a serial killer roaming the western U.S. abducting and killing women."

Stunned about her confession, Cooper's chin dropped. "You're chasing a serial killer?"

Her shoulders stiffened visibly. "Don't say I'm crazy. I get that enough from my dad."

Cooper lifted his hands in a show of capitulation. "I'm not. Is that why you're in San Francisco? Because you think the serial killer is here?"

"Yes, and if I'm right, then the dead body that was found last night is his latest victim."

Instinctively, Cooper tensed. He hoped that Anita was wrong, because if she was right, it would mean that the serial killer she was chasing was a vampire. "Okay. Show me your evidence. Let's see if it checks out."

"Thank you for not dismissing it outright," she said and kissed him on the lips.

Cooper put one arm around her and pulled her close to deepen the kiss, before he released her, knowing if he kissed her any longer, he'd drag her right back to bed.

Anita unfolded a map and pointed to the blue and red dots on it. "Over the last six years, there have been at least thirty-five abductions and murders that I believe were committed by the same person. He never abducts more than one person from the same jurisdiction. And he always kills them in a different state. For example, if he abducts a person from Washington State, that person will show up dead in Idaho about six to eight weeks later. He travels in a clockwise direction from Washington to Idaho, then to Nevada; from there to California; then back up north to Oregon, and then back to Washington."

Cooper studied the map and noticed that the red and blue dots never coincided. He nodded to himself. "It makes it harder for law enforcement to connect the crimes if they're being committed in different jurisdictions, I get that. How did you connect them?"

"I started seeing a pattern. He only abducts women between the age of thirty and forty-five. All victims so far were blonde and blue-eyed. And all women were tall. He definitely has a type. And it looks like he keeps the women alive for several weeks before he kills them, because according to the autopsies that I was able to obtain, when the bodies were found six to eight weeks after the abductions, they'd been dead for less than twenty-four hours."

Cooper remembered what Maya had told him about the time of death of the exsanguinated woman. She'd been dead for only a few hours, and she fit the type: blonde, blue-eyed, tall, and in her thirties or forties.

"You don't believe me." Anita looked at him, looking disappointed.

"That's not it. Show me more. How did these women die? Stabbed? Strangled? Shot?"

"That's just it. They died of massive blood loss, but they weren't stabbed or shot. But I wasn't able to get all the autopsies. Some jurisdictions aren't quite as accommodating when it comes to sending copies of autopsies to out-of-state law enforcement. Particularly since I couldn't really go through official channels."

Massive blood loss translated to exsanguination by a vampire. Shit! This wasn't good.

Anita opened a file and pulled out several photos. "This is Sandra Thacker, a store manager from Olympia, Washington. She was found dead in Ketchum, Idaho." She pointed to another one. "Here. Clare Grundy, a professor at a community college in Boise, Idaho. She was found in Reno, Nevada."

She reached for another one, but Cooper put his hand over hers. "I believe you. I can see the pattern too." He was impressed with her work. Anita knew how to analyze data. "You need to identify the dead woman from last night. If she's indeed the missing woman you mentioned, we've got a huge problem on our hands."

And he couldn't even let her know how terrible a prospect this was. To reveal to her that vampires existed, and that one might be a serial killer wouldn't exactly start them off on the right foot. It was hard enough to reveal to a human that vampires existed, but how could he convince Anita that most vampires were peaceful people living normal lives and meant her no harm, when he had to admit in the same breath that the serial killer she'd been hunting was a vampire?

Anita nodded. "Let's do that. Let's look at the body."

She already got up from her chair, when there was a sound at the door. Cooper whirled his head in the direction. Somebody was inserting a key in the lock. He jumped up and rushed toward the door, ready to fight the intruder, while he issued a command.

"Anita, stay back!"

10

Startled, Anita stared at Cooper as he rushed to the door of the Airbnb. At first, she hadn't heard anything strange, but now she could hear what Cooper was reacting to: somebody was trying to unlock the door. She charged toward the bedroom where she'd left her handbag and pulled her gun from it.

When she re-entered the living room, the entrance door was already open, and a young Asian couple entered, before freezing. The woman shrieked, and the man quickly pushed her behind his body to shield her.

"What the fuck!" the guy cursed. His gaze fell on her gun, and he lifted his hands. "Don't shoot. Just take what you want and leave us alone."

The woman behind him started to cry. "Please, don't hurt us. Please."

Cooper suddenly turned to Anita. "Lower your gun."

Anita let her gaze sweep over the couple, but they weren't armed. Reluctantly, she lowered her gun.

"What are you doing here?" Cooper asked. "Where did you get the key from?"

The couple exchanged confused looks.

"And you can lower your hands," Cooper added. "Just don't make any sudden movements."

Slowly, they lowered their arms, and Anita noticed the set of keys in the man's hand.

"Now talk! Where did you get the key?" Cooper repeated.

"From the real estate agent. My wife and I closed escrow today," the man explained. "We were assured that the tenants would be gone by close of escrow."

Anita took a step closer. "You bought this place?" She shook her head. "I rented it on Airbnb. I've paid for two weeks."

"But this is our place as of today," the woman added, now stepping next to her husband, her tears drying up.

"Can you prove it?" Cooper asked.

"Can you prove you rented this place as an Airbnb?" the man shot back.

Anita put the gun in the back of her waistband and pulled her cellphone from her pocket. "I can." She scrolled through her emails, then tapped on the one that confirmed her reservation. "Here. That's the confirmation that I paid for two weeks. I arrived a week ago." She turned her cellphone around, and the man reached for it.

He perused it for a few seconds, then handed her back the phone. "Looks real, but it's impossible. We didn't put this place up for rent. We're moving in."

"But... but..." Anita didn't know what to say.

Cooper put a hand on her forearm, then looked at the young couple. "Do you have the papers showing that you bought this place?"

The man nodded and pulled his cellphone out. Moments later, he handed his phone to Cooper. Anita looked at the document that the man had scrolled to, while Cooper paged through it. It was an escrow statement, signed and notarized.

"It's legit," Cooper said, before he handed the phone back to the man. "This is their place, and whoever rented it to you had no right to do so."

"Fuck!" she cursed. "I'm gonna give that asshole a piece of my mind!" She tapped on her phone, and scrolled to the confirmation. She clicked on the link to contact the Airbnb host and let it ring. It rang only once, before a recording sounded. *"The number you are trying to reach has been disconnected."*

Anita let out another curse. "Goddamn it!"

"Ahm," the young woman said. "I'm sorry that you got scammed. But you can't stay here. This is our place."

"Of course," Anita said quickly.

Inside, she was fuming. She'd been cheated. The person who'd posted the apartment as available on Airbnb—most likely the previous owner or the owner's agent—had taken advantage of her. What would she do now? She wasn't ready to go home to Elko, and from looking at accommodations prior to her trip, she knew that most hotels were out of her price range. She'd paid in advance for this stay, and it would take weeks, if not months to get a refund once she complained about this dishonest host to Airbnb. What would she do in the meantime? Max out her credit card?

"I'll help you pack."

She looked at Cooper, who'd spoken, and let out a sigh. Tears threatened to overpower her, but she pushed them back. She couldn't be weak, not in front of Cooper, nor in front of the young couple.

The woman looked at her with pity. "Why don't we give you a half hour? My husband and I will wait outside."

Anita forced a smile. "Thank you. You're very kind. And I'm sorry I pointed my gun at you."

The couple left the apartment and pulled the door shut behind them.

Alone with Cooper, she inhaled a shaky breath. "Where am I gonna stay now? Can you recommend any hotels that aren't too expensive? I can't just go home now. I need to see this through. It's gonna take forever to get my money back. Damn crook! No wonder the place was available on short notice. I should have seen it. I should have realized that if it's too good to be true, it's not true. I don't—"

"Shhh." Cooper pulled her into his arms and pressed a kiss to her forehead. "Don't worry about that right now. Just pack, and I'll take care of the rest."

"How? And don't say you're gonna lend me the money for a hotel room, because I can't accept that. You don't owe me anything."

"I'm not gonna give you any money, but what I would like to offer you is to stay with me."

She stared at him. "But your condo is uninhabitable right now."

"I'm not talking about my condo. You can stay with me at my uncle's house in Buena Vista."

She was floored by his generosity, but she couldn't accept this either. "But what about your uncle? You can't just bring another guest with you. I can't impose on him like that. And you don't know me."

He put a finger over her lips. "I know enough about you to know that my uncle and his wife will have no problems with you staying at their house with me. It's a huge place. And I would love to spend more time with you." Cooper brushed his finger over her lips.

"I don't know what to say."

"Say yes."

"Yes."

Anita tilted her face up, and Cooper followed her invitation for a kiss. His lips were warm and inviting, the kiss just as passionate as the night before. What should have been a simple thank you for his kind offer turned into a smoldering fire in seconds. She found herself crushed against his chest, while Cooper delved deep into her mouth, his tongue demanding and experienced, his hands possessive as he yanked her pelvis to his. She could already feel the hard outline of his cock underneath his pants and wished she could undress him now and take his hard-on into her mouth to suck him until he came. But there was no time for that now. They both knew it.

When she peeled herself out of his embrace, she met his heated gaze.

"We have twenty-five minutes to get out of here. If we had more time, I'd toss you on that table..." He didn't complete his sentence, but he didn't have to. She knew exactly what he wanted.

"And I would get on my knees and suck you until—"

"Fuck, Baby, not another word, or we'll never get out of here."

11

———

Cooper directed Anita to park her car in front of Wesley's house. Offering Anita to stay with him at his uncle's house had been a spur-of-the-moment decision, but he didn't regret it. Indeed, it was fortuitous. It would make it easier to introduce Anita to his family, and for her to see that they were just as normal as humans, even though they were all preternatural creatures: vampires, vampire hybrids, witches, and even a Stealth Guardian. Of course, he'd have to wait until he could tell her the truth about himself, his family, and Scanguards, but he knew he would eventually come clean.

When the young Asian couple had surprised them, and he'd thought that somebody was trying to break in and harm Anita, his protector instinct had immediately emerged, and he'd been prepared to defend her no matter the cost to himself. It had revealed the depth of his feelings for her. Anita wasn't just a one-night stand or a fling for him. He wanted more, so much more, even though they'd only just met. And soon, he would no longer be able to suppress the need to bite her and drink her blood. And while he could do this without her knowledge and consent by simply using mind control, he wouldn't do it. He wanted Anita to know what he wanted, and he wanted her to experience the pleasure of his bite. He wanted her to want it.

"This is your uncle's house?" Anita asked, pointing at the Victorian home, admiration in her voice.

"Yes. That's his. It's gorgeous inside too. Come, I'll show you." Cooper got out of the car, and opened the trunk to lift out Anita's suitcase and her computer bag with her files on the serial killer.

Anita joined him and took the computer bag from him, then locked her car. Together they walked up to the front entrance, and Cooper unlocked the front door, then ushered her inside. He shut the door behind them.

Inside the home it was quiet.

"Wes? Virginia?" Cooper called out but didn't receive a reply. "They're probably at work." He walked up the stairs with the suitcase, and Anita followed him closely.

"What do they do? Are they bodyguards too?"

"No, ahm, Wes works in a lab." Which was mostly true. He was a talented witch, and did indeed spend a lot of time in a lab at Scanguards that he shared with another witch: Charles. "And Virginia sits on a board." That wasn't a lie either, only that the board was the ruling body of the Stealth Guardians, an ancient race whose preternatural skills included making themselves and others invisible, and being able to walk through solid objects like walls.

"Do they have kids?"

"No. Guess they're not quite ready for that." Cooper opened the door to a guestroom on the second floor and set the suitcase down.

Anita followed him into the room and dropped her computer bag and handbag on a chair. "Wow, this is so cute."

The room was large and furnished with a queen-size bed, an antique dresser, matching nightstands, and an armchair. Two sash windows let lots of light into the room.

Cooper pointed to a door. "This door leads into the bathroom. I can access it from my room on the other side. We're sharing the bathroom."

Her forehead furrowed. "We're not sharing a room? I thought..."

"Here's the thing..." he started.

"Don't tell me your uncle and aunt are religious and won't allow us to share a bed."

Cooper threw his head back and laughed. "God no! Those two would be the last ones to do that." He shook his head and put his hands on her shoulders, drawing her closer. "No. I'm giving you your own room so that you can have a place to withdraw to if you want some time to yourself. Because the moment you're in my bed, I'm going to make love to you. And if that gets too much for you, all you need to do is sleep here in this room, and I won't intrude."

Anita slid her hands around him, putting them on his ass. "And where are you going to withdraw to when it gets too much for you?"

Pleased about Anita's reply, he smiled and pressed a tender kiss to her lips. "Trust me, it'll never get too much for me. You've whetted my appetite for a lot more than what went down last night. Now, why don't you unpack, and I'll quickly check on a couple of things downstairs? Just come down when you're ready."

Cooper left the guestroom and shut the door behind him, before he rushed downstairs. He went straight into the pantry, where bottles of blood were stocked in a separate refrigerator. When he'd moved in with Wes and Virginia, he'd brought a supply of blood for himself, since his uncle normally only kept a few bottles for emergencies or for when Cooper's parents came to visit.

Cooper unscrewed a bottle and gulped down the cold liquid. He felt better instantly. The blood strengthened his body and replenished his energy stores. Normally he only needed a bottle a day, and occasionally supplemented with human food, but today he needed more. He opened a second bottle and drank it down just as quickly. Finally, he was his normal self again. On the drive from Anita's Airbnb to Wes's house, when he'd been confined in the car, Anita's scent had driven him almost insane with hunger. Another ten minutes, and he wouldn't have been able to resist the urge to taste her blood. But now, his immediate hunger was gone.

He still wanted Anita's blood, but he knew he could wait until it was the right time to tell her what he was, and hope that she could accept him as a vampire. In the meantime, he had to double his intake of bottled blood so he wouldn't give into the temptation to bite her while they made love. And they would make love. Anita had practically assured him of that, when she'd shown her surprise when he'd offered her her own room.

Cooper wiped his mouth, making sure there were no remnants of the blood he'd consumed, and left the pantry, just as Anita came down the stairs.

"Are you hungry? We can go out, or I can make us something here," Cooper suggested.

"I'm hungry, but I think I'd rather eat after I go to the morgue to look at the body." She placed her hand on her stomach. "I still get a little queasy when I see a dead body."

"I get it. It's not pretty. Let's eat later then."

"Good. Did you want to come with me to the city morgue?"

"Actually," Cooper explained, "the body isn't at the city morgue. It's at Scanguards."

Surprise registered on her face. "But why?"

"Like I said last night, when the police have a complicated case, they call us in. And we have a very capable physician and the facilities to examine dead bodies at Scanguards." He motioned for her to follow him to the door that led down into the garage. "We'll take my car."

He took Anita's hand, and together they went into the garage and got in his SUV. Moments later they were on their way to Scanguards' headquarters building in the Mission neighborhood of San Francisco.

On the short drive, Cooper called the medical center at Scanguards. He knew that Maya wouldn't be there during daylight hours, when the clinic was staffed by trusted humans as well as vampire hybrids.

Buffy answered the phone. "Med center."

"Hey, Buffy, it's Cooper."

"Hey, Coop. What do you need?"

"I'm coming in with a civilian who might be able to identify our Jane Doe." Civilian was Scanguards' code for a human who wasn't aware of the existence of vampires. "Can you please make sure we can have access to the body right away?"

"Not a problem. I'll get it ready for you. How far out are you?"

"About ten minutes."

"See you shortly."

"Thanks, Buffy." He disconnected the call and looked at Anita. "You ready for this?"

She nodded.

"Did you know the missing woman personally?"

"I've seen Janet Fillmore at her store and spoken to her a few times. She owns a huge furniture store. And I know her husband. I've arrested him a couple of times for drunken disorderly conduct."

"Given his brushes with the law, don't you suspect him of having something to do with her disappearance?"

"No, he might be scrounging off his wife and living high on her money, but he also knows that if anything happens to her, his meal ticket is gone."

Surprised, Cooper furrowed his forehead. "But wouldn't he inherit her store?"

Anita shook her head. "No. The store's in a family trust, and the way it was set up by Janet's parents, is so only a blood relative will inherit. Guess her parents didn't trust her to use good judgement when choosing a husband."

"Yeah, when it comes to love, people throw all caution to the wind." He gazed at her from the side. "There's always the risk that you fall for somebody who's not right for you. But without taking that risk, you might miss out on the person that's perfect for you, even if there are obstacles to overcome." And the obstacles he had to overcome to win Anita were monumental.

She turned her face to him. "We're not talking about Janet anymore, are we?"

"No, we're not." He smiled at her before he concentrated on traffic again. "How come you're still single? Or are all the men in Elko County blind?" When she didn't immediately answer, he added, "I mean at least I hope you're still single."

***

"I wouldn't have slept with you if I wasn't," Anita said, glancing back at him.

Cooper surprised her. He was so different from other men. More sincere. More approachable. She still couldn't believe that he'd offered her to stay with him in his uncle's house. Who did such a thing? What man invited a woman he'd had sex with for the first time, a woman he barely knew, to stay with him? Was he too good to be true? There had to be a catch somewhere. But so far, she hadn't found one.

"I'm glad."

"And you, are you still single?"

"Yes. I would never cheat on a woman once I've committed to her. I live by my parents' example. They're devoted to each other."

How she would have loved to have parents like that. But even before her mother's disappearance, she'd sensed that her parents' marriage hadn't always been a happy one. And as a deputy, she'd been called to plenty of domestic disturbances and seen the state of people's relationships.

"How long have they been together?"

"Thirty-six years. And when you see them together, you'd think they're still on their honeymoon. So, Lydia and I moved out quite a while ago to give those lovebirds some privacy."

Anita smiled. Was that why Cooper was such a considerate man? Because he was raised in a home with loving parents as an example? So where was the catch?

"I'm curious," she started. "Ahm…"

"Curious about what?"

She sighed, not really sure how to ask what she wanted to know. "Why did you offer me to stay with you? I mean you didn't have to do that. And if it's just for the sex…"

Cooper put his hand on hers and squeezed it. "I wanted to do it. I enjoy spending time with you." He cast her a sideways look. "I've dated a lot, but I've never been with a woman like you."

She wasn't sure what he meant by that. "How like me?"

"Brave, smart, strong," he said with a smile. "Passionate, beautiful, and direct. Most women play games with men. You don't. When I look at you, I can see exactly what I get. And I like that. Work is stressful enough. It feels good to be with somebody I can relax with."

No man had ever spoken with such openness, and she was unprepared as to how to answer. All she could do was to show him that she appreciated his confession. She put her hand on his thigh, and felt his muscles flex under her touch.

"I like being with you too," she said quietly.

Cooper took her hand, and she thought that he wanted to remove it from his thigh, but to her surprise, he pressed her palm over his crotch. When she felt a hard ridge there, she gasped. Cooper had a full-blown erection.

"That's how much I like being with you," he murmured and looked at her, his gaze heated.

Around them, it was dark all of a sudden. They'd entered a parking garage, and Cooper was pulling into a parking spot. When he switched off the engine, all she could hear inside the car was Cooper's breathing and her own heartbeat. Their gazes connected, and Anita inhaled sharply. She could think of all kinds of things she wanted to do right now. All of them involved unzipping Cooper's pants and taking out his cock. It would be so easy.

She reached for his waistband, about to pop the button open, when he snatched her wrist and stopped her.

"Trust me, I want nothing more than for you to suck me." He leaned over to her and kissed her on the lips. "But I'd rather enjoy that when we're somewhere we won't be interrupted by my colleagues."

Cooper opened the car door and got out. Anita did the same, and together they walked to the elevator. Inside the elevator, Cooper swiped his access card, before he pressed the button to one of the lower levels.

"How many people work for Scanguards?"

"A few hundred," Cooper replied.

His answer appeared vague, but she didn't dig deeper. "How long have you worked for them?"

"I started with their bodyguard training when I was eighteen."

"So about five years then," she said with a grin.

He chuckled. "I'm not that young!"

"You look it though. You could easily pass for a college kid."

"If that's a roundabout way of you asking how old I am, I'd better put you at ease. You're not robbing the cradle. I'm thirty-two."

"That's a relief. I wouldn't want to have to arrest myself for sleeping with a minor."

The elevator doors opened, and Cooper ushered her along a well-lit corridor. The walls were pastel-green, and the floor reminded her of a hospital. At a door, Cooper swiped his access card again, and held the door open for her. She entered the sterile looking room. A young black woman was already waiting for them. She stood in front of a steel gurney. The body on it was fully covered with a large white sheet.

"Hey, Buffy," Cooper said as he entered behind her. "This is Anita Diaz. She's with the Elko County Sheriff's Department."

Buffy nodded. "Nice to meet you."

"Nice to meet you too," Anita replied.

Buffy turned to the gurney. "Are you ready to look at her?"

Anita dreaded the moment. If this was Janet Fillmore, then she'd failed. She'd come too late. "As ready as I'll ever be."

Buffy lifted the sheet and drew it down to the dead woman's cleavage, where she let it rest. Anita took another step closer and looked at the dead woman's face. She looked ashen, completely drained of blood. Her hair was still blonde, but it had lost its brilliant sheen. She didn't have to open the woman's eyes to know that they were blue, because she recognized her. She had no doubts.

"It's Janet Fillmore. She disappeared from Elko County six weeks ago."

"I'm sorry," Cooper said from behind her and put his hand on her shoulder, squeezing it gently.

Anita nodded, acknowledging his condolences. "How did she die?"

Buffy cleared her throat and cast a glance past her to Cooper. "Ahm, massive blood loss."

"Gunshot wound? Stab wounds?"

"None." The answer came from Cooper.

Anita looked back at Janet's dead body and saw something on her neck. She brushed the dead woman's hair away from her neck and revealed two small puncture wounds. She looked up at Buffy. "What is this?"

"We believe that this is how the killer drained her," Buffy said.

"Hmm." Anita inspected the tiny holes more closely. They were approximately two inches apart. What weapon or tool could create such puncture wounds? Why not take a large intravenous catheter? Two puncture wounds didn't make sense. Had the other dead women had the same kind of puncture wounds, and she'd overlooked them in the autopsy reports? She had to go back and read them again. Something wasn't right.

She looked up and noticed that Cooper and Buffy were watching her intently.

"Do you have any idea what could have made these puncture wounds?" she asked Buffy.

"I'm afraid I don't know. Even Maya is baffled," Buffy said.

"Maya?"

"Our physician," Cooper said quickly. "She did the autopsy."

"Can I speak to her?"

"I'm afraid she's on the nightshift." Cooper nodded to Buffy. "Thanks, Buffy. You can put her back in the refrigeration unit."

"Sure thing."

Anita allowed him to lead her outside into the hallway. There they stood, and Cooper put his arms around her.

"You were right when you guessed that she would show up here," he said. "I'm sorry. For your sake, I wish it wasn't her, but now we know who she is, and it will help us find her killer."

Anita lifted her head from his chest. "I know that. But I was so close. And still, I couldn't save her."

"That's not on you. You went out of your way to find her."

"I have to make some calls."

"To her husband?"

"Yes, and to the sheriff."

"Let's go to my office. It's quiet there. You can make your phone calls. Ask the sheriff's department to email us photos of Janet so we can use them when we canvass the city for any sightings prior to her death."

"I have a photo of her."

While she dreaded both phone calls she had to make—the one to Janet's husband, and the one to her father—Anita was glad to have something productive to do rather than beat herself up about her failure to find Janet alive.

At the same time, the odd puncture wounds on Janet's neck puzzled her.

The only time she'd ever seen anything of the sort was in a movie.

A movie about vampires.

12

———————

Carrying a serving tray laden with yogurt, fruit, pastries, and a selection of water and sodas, Cooper entered his office. He'd picked up the food from the H lounge, the Scanguards lounge meant for human employees and visitors, while Anita was making phone calls. She was still on the phone.

"I could have prevented this," Anita said into the phone, sounding agitated and louder than what he was used to from her. There was a short pause, then she added, "No, Dad. You just never wanted to believe me. You have no confidence in me. I'm not a little girl anymore. I'm a cop. A good one. But you can't handle that, can you?"

Cooper placed the tray in front of her, and she looked at him.

"Let me talk to him," Cooper murmured and reached for the receiver of his landline.

With a huff, Anita handed it to him. "He's infuriating."

Cooper kissed her on the forehead, before he pressed the speaker button and put the phone back on the cradle. "Sheriff Diaz? I'm Cooper Montgomery. I work with the SFPD."

"Officer Montgomery," Sheriff Diaz replied.

Cooper didn't correct him. He'd mentioned the SFPD on purpose, and he hadn't lied. He indeed worked *with* the SFPD, just not *for* them.

"Is it true what my daughter is saying? Janet Fillmore was found murdered in San Francisco?"

Anita looked annoyed, gesturing toward the speaker, whispering. "See what I have to deal with?"

"Yes, sir, every single word. We found Mrs. Fillmore dead last night. And if it hadn't been for your daughter, she would still be a Jane Doe. We're immensely grateful to her for her diligent police work."

"Hmm. Well, we trained her well here in Elko County."

Anita's mouth gaped open, and Cooper could see that she was about to hurl an insult at her father for taking credit for her work. But Cooper put a finger to her lips and shook his head. A shouting match would help nobody and only damage Anita's relationship with her father even further.

"Yes, Ms. Diaz is an exceptional law enforcement officer." He put his arm around Anita and pulled her to his side. He felt her relax in his arms.

"But this talk about a serial killer," the sheriff said, "that can't possibly be true. That must be an exaggeration."

"I'm afraid it's not," Cooper said firmly and held Anita's gaze. She looked at him with gratitude. "I've looked at the evidence your daughter has collected, and I have to agree with her. There's a serial killer on the loose. And I have reason to believe that he's in San Francisco."

"Oh." The sheriff appeared to be taken aback by his statement. "Well, that's, uhm... I guess she was right after all."

It sounded like it was hard for him to make that admission.

"Sheriff, I know your daughter is currently on vacation, but I'd like her to work with us on this case until we've apprehended the suspect."

"Is that what she wants?"

"Yes, Dad!" Anita said firmly. "I have more knowledge about this serial killer than anybody else. And I saw Janet disappear."

Cooper snapped his gaze to her. "You saw her with the killer?"

"Yeah, sorry, forgot to mention it. I'll give you the details after this." She motioned to the phone.

"Honey, I'm sorry I didn't believe you," Sheriff Diaz said, his voice softer now.

Anita sighed, looking much calmer than at the beginning of this conversation. "It's all right, Dad. I probably wouldn't have believed myself either."

"What can I do from here? I should call Janet's husband."

"I've already spoken to him," Anita said. "I told him we'll be in touch regarding the transport of the body once it's been released."

"I should have known you already thought of that."

Cooper exchanged a look with Anita, who now rolled her eyes. Her father was switching from disbelief to praise so quickly that they were both getting whiplash.

"Sheriff," Cooper interjected. "There is something that you could do for us. We need everything you have on Janet Fillmore. We're trying to establish what made her vulnerable to him; what made him choose her."

"Of course, I'll send it to you."

Cooper glanced at Anita. "Go ahead and email it to Anita. We'll take it from there."

"If there's anything else, please let me know. And Anita, honey, you can call me anytime you want to talk."

"Thanks, Dad."

"Thank you, sir." Cooper disconnected the call. "That didn't go too badly."

"Thanks to you."

He winked. "Didn't want you guys to start a screaming match."

Anita hugged him tightly.

"So, tell me, you saw Janet Fillmore disappear with the killer?"

She nodded. "I was out for a drink at one of the dive bars in Elko. It was a busy night, and I had a few drinks. Maybe one too many. Anyway, I left the bar just after midnight. I went into the parking lot to get my car, but then I thought better of it and called an Uber. So I waited. That's when I saw her. She was getting into a white van. I saw the guy only from behind. But I recognized Janet. She looked like she was drunk or under the influence of something. I called out to her to see if she was all right, but she didn't even turn her head as if she hadn't heard me."

Cooper knew what that indicated. Janet had been under the influence of a vampire's mind control. "She got into the van without him forcing her physically?"

"Yes. It was so odd. At first, I thought maybe he was an acquaintance, and she'd been drinking, and he was offering to drive her home, but she never got home. That's the last time anybody saw or heard of her. I wish I'd gone over there to check on her. I could have stopped him."

The thought sent a chill down his spine. Anita wouldn't have been able to fight him. No human could best a vampire. "Don't go there. You couldn't have known. Janet's husband, he didn't file a missing persons' report?"

"No. He's a loser, and they probably had a fight, and he figured she'd finally left him."

"Hmm. Tell me about the van."

"It was a plain white van like thousands of others. I couldn't see the license plates. Too dirty. But he had a sticker on the back of it. SF. I later found that exact symbol on the internet. It was a San Francisco Giants sicker."

"And that led you to San Francisco?"

"Yes. He'd already abducted and left bodies in Sacramento, Santa Rosa, Oakland, and a few other towns in northern California, so the sticker was as good a lead as any I'd ever get. I figured he has a connection to San Francisco."

"Hmm. Did you try to trace the van? I mean you must have had access to traffic cams."

"I tried that. But there was nothing. He must have stayed off the main roads and somehow gotten to the freeway via an on-ramp where we had no cameras nearby."

Cooper nodded. He'd half expected this. Anita was a good cop. She knew how to track a suspect. But this suspect was smart, smarter than the average criminal. And more dangerous. As a vampire, he would know how to stay out of sight, and he would only travel at night. Few people would notice him. Or his van.

"Okay," Cooper said with a deep breath. "Let's put a plan together of how to catch this guy."

"Do you think he's still in the city?"

"I think so. If he has a connection to San Francisco, and being a San Francisco Giants fan suggests so, it's likely that he has a place here that he uses regularly, a place where he can keep his victim locked up until he's ready to kill her, a place where he can park his van out of sight." And a place where he could hide from the sun, but Cooper couldn't tell her that.

"Okay, then let's start with the van. Can we get SFPD to give us access to the traffic cams?" Anita asked.

"Already done," Cooper confirmed. Scanguards had continuous access, courtesy of the chief of police himself. "Text me Janet's photo. I'll distribute it to everybody to see if there have been sightings in the days before her death. It might lead us to him. I'll have our IT team run it through facial recognition."

Anita looked energized, ready to go into battle. "That's great. Let's do that. And I need to go over my files again. There has to be something else besides the physical attributes that define his victims."

"That's what I think too. I have to read your files anyway to see what else you've dug up. In the meantime, my team can comb through the traffic cams and run Janet's photo through facial recognition."

13

The sun was about to set over the Pacific Ocean, when Cooper drove into his uncle's garage. Two other cars were parked there. Anita looked at the dark BMW and the smaller sportscar.

"Looks like your uncle and aunt are home," Anita said as she exited the car. When they'd left to drive to Scanguards earlier, only the smaller sportscar had been parked in the garage.

"Looks like it," Cooper replied and waited for her until she came around the car. "Let me introduce you to them."

He put his hand on her lower back, and she took a deep breath, a little uncomfortable that Cooper had invited her to stay here without clearing it with his aunt and uncle first.

"Are you sure they'll be all right with me staying here?"

"You worry too much."

Cooper took her hand and opened a door leading into a corridor. They were still in the basement of the house. From here, a staircase led up to the first floor, while the two other doors in the corridor looked like they led to storage areas. One of them was open.

When Cooper opened the door leading into the foyer of his uncle's house, Anita heard a baby crying. She cast him a sideways glance. "I thought you said they didn't have kids."

Cooper winked at her and headed for the back of the house. "Looks like we have a little visitor."

Together they entered the large eat-in kitchen, where a man with dark hair cradled a crying toddler in his arms, while he tried to cook.

"Need a hand, Wes?"

The man turned around to them, a look of relief on his face. "Thank God you're here. Can you take your cousin for a moment, while I puree his food?"

"Hey, Jacob." Cooper wrestled the toddler from his uncle's arms, swung him back and forth while making sounds as if the boy was an airplane.

Anita had a chance to cast Wesley a closer look. The man had handsome and charming written all over him. His blue eyes were penetrating, and his dark hair was longer than Cooper's. But there was no way that this was Cooper's uncle. He looked barely a day over thirty-five.

"Coop, don't you wanna introduce us?" Wes asked as he spooned vegetables and cooked meat into the blender.

"Sorry, Jacob distracted me," Cooper said with a grin, while he blew a raspberry at the little boy. Jacob chortled and clapped his hands, the tears forgotten. "Wes, that's Anita, she's working on a case with me. And she's staying here, because something went wrong with her Airbnb. Anita, this is my uncle, Wesley."

"Hey, Anita."

"Hi, nice to meet you, Wesley," Anita said quickly. "I hope it's all right that I stay here. I didn't want to impose, but Cooper said you wouldn't mind, but I know he didn't ask you ahead of time, so, if it's a problem for you and your wife—"

"Anita, breathe," Cooper interrupted.

Wesley smiled. "It's totally fine with us. In fact, you're the first woman he's brought back here since he moved in with us over a month ago. I was getting worried that something was wrong with his sex drive."

"Wes!"

The reprimand came from behind Anita. She whirled around, her heart pounding. She hadn't heard the door open. A woman with red hair dressed in black leather pants, a tank top, and a leather jacket stood right behind her. She was about the same age as Wesley.

"Babe, you were wondering the same thing last week," Wes said casually.

"Yeah, but I didn't do it in front of Cooper and his, uhm..."

"He called her a colleague," Wes helped, completely ignoring the fact that she and Cooper were in the room, "but honestly, I think she's his girlfriend."

"Really, guys?" Cooper said, shaking his head. "You can be more embarrassing than my parents, and that's not easy."

The redhead ignored Cooper's comment and extended her hand to Anita. "I'm Virginia, Wesley's wife."

Anita shook her hand. "Nice to meet you, Virginia. I'm Anita. I hope it's all right that—"

"We love having guests," Virginia said. Then she turned to Wesley. "I've gotta go. There's a last-minute council meeting."

"That's convenient," Wes said with a look at the toddler. "Strange how you always have last-minute meetings when we're babysitting Jacob."

Virginia smirked and put her arms around her husband, before she kissed him for more than just a few seconds. "I'll make it up to you."

"Well, if you put it that way..."

Virginia turned toward the door. "Nice to meet you, Anita. I'll see you all later." Then she left the kitchen.

"She's got you totally wrapped around her little finger," Cooper commented.

"Well, there's something we Montgomery men aren't immune to: beautiful, hot-blooded women. Get used to it, 'cause we're all sitting in the same boat, you, your father, and I." Then he motioned to the toddler. "And when Jacob is old enough, he'll be joining us."

Anita suppressed a laugh. She liked Wesley and his wife. They were easy-going and witty. And they didn't behave like uncles and aunts were meant to behave. They seemed much younger too.

"So who are this cute boy's parents?" Anita asked.

She noticed how Cooper was rocking Jacob gently in his arms, the action so natural that she realized that this wasn't the first time he'd done this.

"Jacob is Katie's son. I'm just on babysitting duty today," Wesley said.

"She's Wes and my father's younger sister," Cooper added, before he addressed his uncle. "Where are Katie and Luther today?"

"Fundraiser for the theater." He grimaced. "They promised me to be back before ten to pick up this rascal."

"He doesn't seem like a rascal," Anita said and smiled at the boy. She approached, and he smiled back at her.

"Wanna hold him?" Cooper asked and already transferred him into her arms, before she could protest.

"Hey, Jacob," Anita cooed, and the boy looked at her with curiosity.

"Is that his dinner?" Cooper asked, just as Wesley pressed the button for the blender, and the sound drowned out everything else.

Jacob jolted in her arms, and stared at her, his eyes suddenly blood-shot, his mouth wide with only two tiny teeth protruding. The loud sound was clearly scaring the child, and she instinctively pressed him closer to her, when he finally leaned his face against her biceps.

"Ouch!" Her involuntary yelp coincided with the blender stopping.

"Anita? Jacob?"

Cooper was at her side in a flash, while she looked at Jacob who was just now pulling back his head. She noticed something red on his tongue, and with horror, Anita looked at her biceps, where two tiny pinpricks marked her skin.

"Jacob bit me."

"Uh, oh," Wes said from behind Cooper. "I'd better feed him."

While Wes reached for the toddler, Cooper rubbed his fingers over the tiny wounds.

"That's the age," Cooper said. "Don't worry, I'll kiss it and make it better." He winked at her and dropped his face to her bicep, then kissed her softly. "See, it's all gone. He just nicked you a little."

When she looked back at her biceps, she realized that Cooper was right. No more blood seeped from her skin, and she couldn't even see the pinpricks anymore.

She gave Cooper a grateful smile, hoping he didn't think that she was hysterical or didn't like kids, when it was so obvious to her that he loved his little cousin and knew how to handle him.

"Sorry, I didn't mean to overreact," she said, before she looked past Cooper to Wes who was now placing Jacob into a high chair and fastened a bib around his neck. "I hope I didn't scare him."

"He's made of sturdier stuff, right, Jacob?" Wes said and fed him a spoon of the pureed food he'd prepared.

The boy instantly spit it out.

Wes rolled his eyes. "I have the feeling this'll take a while."

Cooper chuckled, glancing at her. "Guess he's had better."

"Yeah, and I can't give him that." He gave Jacob a stern look. "You're gonna have to eat what I've cooked for you, little man."

Cooper turned to her. "How about I make us something to eat? You must be starving by now."

"Actually I am."

"We've got everything for a stir-fry in the fridge," Wes added. "If you make enough, I'll have a bite too."

"Stir-fry okay for you, Anita?" Cooper asked.

"Sounds perfect. Can I help you prepare it?"

He shook his head. "No, I've got it. Why don't you bring your files down, and set them up in the living room, and we'll go over them once we've eaten something?"

"You sure you don't want my help?"

"I'm sure."

She pivoted and left the kitchen. As she walked upstairs, she reflected on the incident with Jacob, but another glance at her biceps confirmed that his teeth hadn't broken through her skin, or the puncture wounds would still be visible. They weren't. She shook her head. She was probably just tired and famished. Too much had happened in the past twenty-four hours.

In the guestroom, she grabbed her computer bag, when she realized that her handbag wasn't in the room. Had she left it in the foyer? She walked downstairs, but didn't see her bag in the entrance hall either, and now remembered that she'd put it behind her seat in Cooper's SUV.

Anita put the computer bag on the little bench next to the coatrack and opened the door that led downstairs into the basement and the garage. She searched for the light switch, but couldn't find it. As she walked downstairs, she noticed that with every step she made, lights along the steps began to illuminate her path, triggered by motion sensors. She hadn't even noticed them earlier, maybe because Cooper had flipped a light switch at the bottom of the stairs to switch on the overhead lights. In the basement, she turned to her left and headed into the garage. Cooper's SUV was unlocked, and her handbag was indeed where she'd left it. She grabbed it, and closed the car door, when her gaze fell onto the other cars in the garage. Both the BMW and the smaller sportscar were still parked here. It appeared that Virginia hadn't left by car.

She opened the door to the hallway again, when she saw a dark figure at the other end of the corridor. There was no light back there, and the person moved as if leaving in a hurry. But there was no exit at the back of the property. After all, the house stood on a hill, and only the garage part of the basement was above ground.

Before she could even finish her thoughts, she saw long red hair swaying, then the person simply disappeared. Anita blinked, but the person was gone. Had this been Virginia? She'd only seen a glimpse, but who else could it have been? Her heart pounding like a sledgehammer, Anita made a few tentative steps into the corridor, glancing around. She passed the stairs, and peered through an open door into the room to her left. It was a small storage room, but nobody was inside it. Slowly, she walked toward the second door. It was closed. Hesitantly, she turned the knob and eased the door open very slowly.

"Virginia?" she called out hesitantly.

There was no reply. She opened the door wider, but the room was entirely empty. There were no windows and no other doors or any place to hide. The person had disappeared as if swallowed up by the ground.

"Fuck!"

Was she losing her mind? She took a few deep breaths, feeling dizzy all of a sudden. She leaned against the doorframe for support. Maybe her blood sugar was low. After all, she hadn't eaten anything in almost twenty-four hours. She'd skipped not only breakfast, but also lunch, and it was almost time for dinner.

"Don't go crazy now," she chastised herself.

The stress was getting to her. If she was honest with herself, she'd admit that she'd been running on empty for a while now, not just since she'd arrived in San Francisco. She'd been immersed in the serial killer case for months, and hadn't taken a break to recharge, and now it was showing. She was starting to hallucinate, to see mysterious things that weren't there, to suspect everyone and everything. She needed to get a grip.

Anita forced herself to take a few calming breaths, before she headed for the stairs.

14

———

"She did what?" Wesley asked, while he wiped little Jacob's mouth with a clean cloth.

Cooper tossed sliced vegetables into the wok. "She handcuffed me."

"And you let her?"

Cooper winked at his uncle. "Don't worry. She made it up to me later."

"I bet she did. She's quite the looker. Pretty hot body if you ask me."

Cooper rolled his eyes. "You shouldn't even be noticing that."

"I'm married, not blind. Besides, even if I wanted to make a play for your girl—which I don't— I wouldn't have the energy for it. Virginia is a demanding woman." Wes smirked, and the sparkle in his eyes confirmed that he wouldn't have it any other way.

"Yeah, so I hear—every night."

"Maybe you should have chosen a guestroom that's further away from our bedroom."

"With my sensitive hearing, I doubt it would make a difference. Or why do you think Lydia and I moved out from home the moment we could?"

Wes laughed and lifted Jacob out of his high chair. "My big brother was quite the stud when he was human. I shudder to think what he's capable of now."

"Thanks for that visual." Cooper added spices into the wok and tossed the mixture several times.

"Let's see if I can get this little man to take a nap," Wesley said.

The door opened, and Anita entered. "Hmm, it smells good in here."

"Dinner is almost ready," Cooper replied with a smile at Anita.

"I can set the table if you tell me where everything is," she offered.

"I've got it." Wesley handed Jacob off to Anita. "Here, hold him for a sec."

When Anita held the boy a foot away from her, clearly surprised, Cooper shook his head. "Nice handoff, Wes. You could have asked her first."

Wes shrugged and went to pull plates from the cupboard.

"It's okay," Anita claimed, rocking Jacob in her arms now. "I think I remember how it's done. I was a teenager, when my half-brothers were born."

A phone suddenly rang, and Wes dug into his pocket and pulled it out.

"Hey, what's up?" he answered. For a few moments, he listened intently, and Cooper would have probably been able to hear the other side of the conversation had the vent over the stove not been switched on.

"Oh, crap! Wow. No way! I'll be there shortly." Wes disconnected the call and looked at him. "You're not gonna believe this. Charles blew up the lab."

"Is he all right?" Cooper asked.

Anita gasped. "Is somebody hurt?"

"No, no, he's fine. But I've gotta get over there now."

"What for?" Cooper asked, his forehead furrowing.

"To gloat. Why else? This is the first time that Charles has blown up the lab. It wasn't me! Finally, I can prove to him that I'm not the only one who has the occasional little accident." Wesley already turned toward the door.

"What about Jacob?" Cooper asked.

"You're here now. You and Anita can watch him for a little while. I'll be back soon. Besides, it's time for his nap anyway. And Luther and Katie won't be out late." He pushed the door open. "See you."

A moment later, Wesley was gone.

Cooper made a grimace. "I guess we're on babysitting duty until either he or Luther and Katie are back."

Anita met his gaze with a smirk. "How much trouble can a little boy like this be?"

"You have no idea!"

For starters, the little vampire hybrid had already developed a taste for blood. It was only a matter of time, until Anita noticed that Jacob's sharp teeth were actually fangs that he could extend at will. It was best to make sure the little boy was sleeping so he couldn't cause any more trouble. Luckily, Cooper had been able to quickly close the tiny wounds caused by Jacob biting into Anita's biceps by kissing the spot and depositing a small amount of saliva on it to close the puncture wounds instantly. Anita hadn't been the wiser, and he hoped he could keep it that way until he'd gained her trust and secured her affection, before he had to come clean about what he was.

Cooper took the wok off the stove. "You hungry?"

"I could eat a horse."

"How about a cow?" He took two plates and spooned a good amount of the beef stir-fry on both.

"What are we gonna do with this guy?" She brought her face to Jacob, and her voice changed when she addressed the toddler. "Are you gonna let the grownups eat?"

Jacob snatched strands of her blonde hair. "Na. Na."

"I think he means no." Cooper took some cutlery and walked toward the arch that connected the kitchen with the dining and living area. "There's a playpen in the living room. Let's put him in there."

Anita followed him as he walked into the dining room and placed the plates on the table.

"I'll get us something to drink."

He walked back into the kitchen, and by the time he'd brought a serving tray with glasses, water, and wine, Anita had placed Jacob in the playpen, where the boy was crawling around, babbling happily.

Cooper joined her at the table, and they began to eat. He wasn't very hungry anymore. The two bottles of blood he'd guzzled when they'd dropped off Anita's luggage were still keeping him satiated. But he didn't want Anita to wonder why he wasn't eating, so he forced himself to eat the stir-fry.

"This is delicious," Anita praised as she put another forkful of food into her mouth and chewed.

"Thanks."

"Did you learn cooking from your mother?"

"No, she doesn't really cook." And why should she? She didn't eat either. "I taught myself. And I got a few tips from my aunt, Katie, and of course from Wes. He's an excellent cook."

"He seems really nice. But he looks so young. I can't believe he's your uncle."

Of course, Anita had noticed that. Time to use his usual excuse. "Oh, he's older than he looks. And we all have good genes." He pointed to his own face. "I mean, look at me. You said yourself that I look like I'm a college kid."

"Yeah, you do. I feel like Mrs. Robinson."

Cooper laughed at her reference of the movie *The Graduate*. He winked at her. "I think I have a little more experience than Dustin Hoffman in that movie."

Anita promptly blushed, and the sight delighted him. He reached for her hand and squeezed it. If they didn't have work to do right now, he would toss her on the couch and make love to her. But there would be time for that later.

He pointed to her empty plate. "Want some more?"

"No. I'm full, thanks. We should go through my files."

"Let's do that. I'll clear the dishes, and then we can start."

"I'll help you."

He put his hand on her shoulder. "Just relax. I've got it."

It took him only a few minutes to take care of the dishes and tidy up the kitchen. When he returned to the dining room, he saw that Anita had spread out her files on the coffee table in the living room and was sitting on the couch. Jacob was still in his playpen, but he was lying on the soft cushions, his eyes closed.

Cooper approached quietly and took a seat next to Anita on the sofa. He put his arm around her back and leaned in. "How about a kiss for the chef?"

Anita brushed her lips over his, and he accepted her invitation and kissed her, while he pulled her closer to his body. He angled his head for a deeper exploration and dueled with her tongue. She was just as receptive as she'd been the previous night, and his hunger for her was growing again. But they had important things to do. Making love to her would have to wait.

Cooper severed the kiss and pressed his forehead to hers. "Damn, Anita, you get me so hot."

She chuckled. "Maybe you shouldn't kiss me if you can't handle the consequences."

"Hmm. You little vixen. Trust me, I can handle you. I'll prove it to you later. But right now, we've got work to do."

"Okay, let's get to it then." She turned toward the coffee table and picked up a file. "Here's an overview of what I've found."

15

─────────

Anita went over all the details she'd been able to piece together about the serial killer's victims, where they were from, where they were abducted, and where they were eventually found dead. Cooper turned out to be a good listener, only interrupting her when he needed anything clarified. Telling him about every case she'd unearthed helped her to refresh her own memory about the various different victims and why she'd concluded that they'd all been killed by the same man.

"Let me go over these again," Cooper said after over two hours and reached for a stack of printouts.

"Go ahead. I want to look over some of the autopsies again," she said and picked up the file which contained all the autopsies she'd been able to obtain.

Anita leaned back in the sofa cushions, and closed her eyes for a moment, when she felt Cooper's hand on her thigh.

"Tired?"

"Just a little." She opened her eyes.

"Come, put your feet up while you're reading."

Cooper helped her lean back against one corner of the sectional sofa, while he freed her of her shoes, and took her legs and laid them over his thighs.

"Hmm. That feels much better. Thanks."

He smiled at her, then turned his gaze back to the stack of papers in his hands. Anita began reading the autopsies, this time specifically searching for any mention of puncture wounds. When she'd read them previously, she hadn't really looked at smaller wounds, scratches, and tiny cuts, because she'd assumed that most of them were defensive wounds the women had sustained while fighting for their lives. But now, she knew what to look for. She went through report after report. Some were more detailed than others, but only a few of them noted two unexplained puncture wounds. Some medical examiners wondered if an animal could have left the puncture wounds, one theorized that the victim could have been bitten by a snake. However, since there was no swelling around the bite wound, and no venom was found in the victim, a snake bite seemed unrealistic. Besides, the space between the two puncture wounds was too wide to belong to a snake. Their fangs were closer together.

What all autopsies had in common was the fact that the female victims had been exsanguinated, though the method was unknown.

Jacob's crying pulled her from her thoughts. Cooper jumped up from the couch and lifted the boy out of the playpen. She noticed him sniff.

"Looks like this little boy needs a diaper change." He walked toward the hallway. "I'll be back."

She heard him soothe the toddler by talking to him in a calming voice. Anita had to smile at that. Despite looking so young, Cooper was a real adult, a man who pitched in wherever help was needed, a man who was good with kids and seemed to have a great relationship with his family. And he even cooked. Was there anything this man couldn't do?

Anita put the autopsies aside and reached for the stack of notes about the thirty-five victims. Well, it should be thirty-six now, if she included Janet Fillmore, but she hadn't had a chance yet to write out a profile sheet for her. She grabbed another file, fished an empty profile sheet out of it, and began noting everything she knew about Janet in the various boxes.

She booted up her computer and checked her emails. Her father had already sent her more information about Janet. There wasn't much that looked important. Janet had a business degree from a university in Arizona. She'd never had any brushes with the law apart from a speeding ticket when she was barely nineteen. She was a member of a Wednesday night book club that met at the local library. All in all, she'd had an unremarkable life. Nothing tied her to the other women the serial killer had targeted, nothing apart from her blonde hair, blue eyes, and tall stature. By that measure, Anita herself fit the profile too. What was she overlooking?

She paged through the stack. The women had nothing in common. They worked in different industries. There was a lawyer, a doctor, a schoolteacher, a branch manager of a bank, a business owner of a furniture store, a manager of a restaurant, a supervisor at a meat packing plant. None of these women had the same skills, the same education, the same kind of job.

When it came to their family situation, they had just as little in common. Some of them were married, some single, some divorced, some widowed, some with children, some without, some looking after their elderly parents, some without any family at all. Again, they didn't fit a pattern.

"Hey."

Anita looked over her shoulder, and saw Cooper returning with a happy and calm looking Jacob in his arms. Instead of putting him back into his playpen, he sat down next to her and rocked the boy on his knees.

"I'm frustrated," she confessed. "I've looked at these files for so long that I can't see anything anymore. Nothing apart from their physical appearance ties these women together. But that can't be all there is. Serial killers get drawn to their victims by something more than just looks. There has to be something."

"It's in there, I'm sure. We just can't see it yet," Cooper said, his voice calm. "Don't beat yourself up." He motioned to the documents on the coffee table. "You put all this together by yourself. Nobody else saw the patterns you detected."

"I know, but it doesn't seem to be enough. And no matter what I look at, there's nothing that makes these women similar in anything else but their looks. One was a schoolteacher, another one a branch manager of a bank, Janet was a business owner, another woman a lawyer, another one a doctor. They didn't work in the same industries, or the same positions. Their family situations were different too. They—"

"Did you say positions?" he interrupted.

"Yes, why?"

"Show me the victim profiles again," he demanded and switched Jacob onto his other knee.

Anita held the pages out for him so he could read them.

"Managers, supervisors, business owners, schoolteachers..." Cooper murmured. "That's it. The positions all these women held were positions of power, of authority." He pointed to one sheet. "Even the doctor is in a position of power, telling her patients what to do. And the teacher, she tells children what to do."

"Oh my God, how did I not see that?" She could barely contain her excitement.

"You were too close to it. But when you step back, you can see it. He's selecting women in positions of power who are blonde, blue-eyed, and tall. That can only mean one thing."

Anita nodded excitedly. "He's been rejected or humiliated by a woman in power, and he's taking it out on women who remind him of the woman who hurt him. He's taking revenge on them for something another woman has done. He's not gonna stop, not after that many kills. And these are only the ones I could find. I bet if we go farther back, we'll find more."

She tried not to think it, but she couldn't stop herself. It was always in the back of her mind. If they went far enough back, they would find that Helen Diaz was one of his victims. She'd held a position of power as the principal of a small elementary school, and physically, she fit the profile too. But Anita couldn't give voice to her suspicion, not yet.

"We'll have to find him fast." Cooper pulled his cellphone from his pocket and scrolled through it. "I have an idea."

16

"Wes got held up at the office," Cooper reported to Anita, while he shoved his cellphone back into his pocket. "But Luther and Katie are on their way back. Once they're here, we can leave."

He glanced at Jacob, glad to see that he was asleep in the playpen.

"Good." She suddenly wrapped her arms around him. "Have I thanked you already for figuring out what these women have in common?"

He slipped one arm around her and drew her closer. "I don't think so, and I do have a very good memory." Then he looked at the large clock in the living room. "We have about fifteen minutes, Jacob is sleeping." He grinned. "That's just enough time for you to thank me."

Anita smirked and rolled her eyes. "You're incorrigible, Cooper. I was thinking of a kiss, not of having sex."

He held her tightly and brought his face to hers. "You should know by now that one kiss with you is not enough for me. Just the thought of it does things to me." He pressed his groin against hers.

A breath of air rushed from her lips. "Oh. I forgot about that."

"Liar," he teased and pressed a soft kiss on her lips, before pulling back a little. "You know exactly what you're doing to me, and you're enjoying it. Wait until the shoe is on the other foot, and I'll turn you into a woman who can think of only one thing, and that's my cock inside her."

She blushed. "I thought you already did that last night."

"Babe, I haven't even started yet. Last night was just a test drive to see if we're compatible."

"And are we? Compatible?"

"Oh yeah, very compatible. In fact, we fit so perfectly together that it's a wonder we got through this day without me pinning you to the nearest flat surface and fucking you senseless. I've been thinking of all kinds of things we could do."

It was something he would take care of later tonight, once they'd dealt with a few things about the serial killer case.

"Do those things include me on my knees in front of you, sucking you?"

Cooper palmed her ass with both hands and yanked her toward him, his cock rapidly filling with blood. "Most definitely."

She batted her eyelashes at him, looking at him like the seductress she was, and leaned in, offering her lips.

"If you kiss me now, I have to warn you: I will toss you over the back of the sofa and sink my cock into you and fuck you. And I won't care if my aunt and uncle walk in on us."

Anita gasped and shrank back but didn't free herself from his embrace. "You do have a wild streak, don't you?"

"You have no idea." It was the vampire in him who was untamed.

She looked deep into his eyes, and the blue color of her irises seemed to smolder like an icy fire. "I like a little wildness in a man."

"That's what I thought." It gave him hope that she would welcome his vampire side too, once he was ready to reveal that untamed side of himself. "Maybe I'll let you tame me."

"You think I can manage that?"

"If anybody can, it's you."

"Do you say that to every woman you sleep with?"

He chuckled, enjoying their lighthearted banter. "As a matter of fact, I don't." He heard a faint sound from the entrance door. Somebody was putting a key into the lock. He released Anita from his arms. "I think they're here."

"I don't hear anything."

The sound of the heavy entrance door opening drifted into the living room. Anita gave him a surprised look.

"You must have better hearing than I."

Cooper shrugged it off. Anita would find out soon enough just how sensitive all his senses were. "Come, I'll introduce you to them."

Luther and Katie were already entering the living room through the open archway from the foyer. Both were dressed elegantly. Luther wore a smoking jacket, and Katie was dressed in a long red dress, looking stunning as ever.

"Hey, Coop," Luther greeted him. "Did Jacob behave?"

"He was an angel." Cooper smiled at Katie. "Hey, Katie. Did you guys have fun at the fundraiser?"

"Yes, but let's not talk about that," Katie said and made a step closer to Anita. "Why don't you introduce me to your... uhm, friend?"

"Katie, Luther, this is Anita Diaz. She's with the Elko County Sheriff's Department, and she's helping me with a case." He smiled at Anita, who already extended her hand to Katie. "This is my father's sister, Katie, and her m— uh, husband."

Mate, he'd almost said, because couples in their vampire society were more than just husband and wife. They were blood-bonded, mated for life.

As they exchanged polite greetings, Katie cast him a sideways look. "Wes said she's your girlfriend."

Cooper shot a look at Anita and noticed that her cheeks were flushed. "So, Wes had time to update you on my life, but didn't have time to come home to babysit. Why does that not surprise me?"

Luther chuckled. "Must run in the family."

Katie elbowed her husband in the side, but the big vampire wasn't deterred. He put his arm around Katie's waist and pulled her closer.

Katie looked up at him, smiling. "Are you complaining?"

"You know that I have absolutely nothing to complain about." Then he motioned toward the playpen. "Let's get Jacob so you guys can get out of here. Thanks so much for taking care of him."

"It was really no trouble," Anita said. "He's such a sweet boy."

Luther furrowed his forehead. "Are we talking about the same child?"

Cooper laughed and winked at Luther. "Well, Jacob has inherited many of your traits." Then he took Anita's hand. "We'd better go. Have a good night."

Moments later, they were in Cooper's car heading for the Tenderloin, an unsavory neighborhood in downtown San Francisco.

"Your aunt and uncle look really young. Katie can't be older than you."

"Oh, she's definitely older than me, but she's the youngest of the three siblings. My dad is the oldest. And like I said, we've got good genes. We all look younger than we are." In fact, as a vampire hybrid he would never look a day older than he looked now.

He glanced at her from the side. What else had she noticed? He'd smoothed over Jacob's bite, and was certain that she'd accepted his explanation. He'd been careful so far, and as long as he kept himself on a tight leash, he'd make it through another few days, before he had to think about how to approach telling her about the existence of preternatural creatures.

"So why are we meeting your colleague Vanessa so late at night? Is she always working that late?"

"Comes with the job. She does outreach to some of the more vulnerable populations in San Francisco."

"The homeless?"

He nodded. "And the prostitutes. They all know her, and she'll be able to get them to talk to us."

"But how would that help us? We've just established that the serial killer picks women in positions of power. I've yet to find a case where he abducted a prostitute."

"You're right, he's not after prostitutes. But they can help us. You'll see."

17

Anita had seen enough homeless people, drug addicts, and prostitutes in her time as a sheriff's deputy to know that the Tenderloin in San Francisco was a breeding ground for all kinds of crimes. She got out of the car, her handbag slung across her body, her gun inside it. Despite carrying a gun, she felt safer when Cooper came around the car and walked next to her. It was odd, really, because as a law enforcement officer she was used to being in shady areas at night, but this wasn't her city, and she wasn't wearing a uniform. Her uniform always felt like a shield, an additional defense, because even criminals thought twice about attacking a cop. A woman in plain clothes was an easier target.

Therefore, she was surprised when Cooper approached a beautiful young woman in plain clothes waiting at a corner. The woman didn't show any signs of feeling uncomfortable or worried despite her surroundings.

"Vanessa, thanks for meeting us."

The woman was in her twenties, and her wavy long brown hair caressed her elegant face like silk. She was slim too, which was emphasized by the skinny jeans she wore. Her turtleneck sweater hugged her curves, confirming that she wasn't armed, unless she was hiding a weapon in the handbag that was slung diagonally across her torso.

"Hey, Cooper," she replied with a smile and stretched out her hand to Anita. "I'm Vanessa."

Anita shook her hand. "Anita. Nice to meet you."

"So, you're looking for a serial killer, huh?" Vanessa asked.

"Yeah." Cooper glanced at Anita. "I filled in Vanessa earlier while you were getting ready." Then he looked back at Vanessa. "You're all right with us tagging along on your route tonight?"

"The more the merrier." Vanessa motioned in a direction, and they began walking next to each other.

"Cooper said you do outreach," Anita started, trying to get a better idea of what Vanessa did. "What does that actually mean? Are you like a social worker?"

Vanessa cast her a sideways look. "Kinda. I'm employed by Scanguards, and we have a contract with the city to take care of the prostitutes, and anybody living on the streets. I check in with the homeless and the sex workers to see if they need help."

"You mean if they become victims of crimes?"

"Yes, on occasion, but most of the time I make sure they get to see a doctor if they're sick, and they take their meds. I get them to a free clinic, and contact the shelters if they need to sleep indoors. Though there's a lot of people who prefer sleeping outside." Vanessa shrugged. "You can't force them, so I try to get them to accept help when they need it."

"And the prostitutes?"

"I make sure that they're not mistreated by a pimp or a john. I've been doing this for a while now, and they know me and trust me. I hear a lot of what's going on out here on the streets."

Impressed, Anita continued asking, "What do you do when you find out that a pimp or a customer is mistreating them?"

Vanessa exchanged a look with Cooper and grinned. "That's the part of my job I like most."

Before Anita could wonder what she meant by that, Vanessa

continued, "I have a word with those guys and tell them what'll happen if they do it again."

"And they listen to you?" Anita shook her head.

"I'm very persuasive. And they know I don't bluff."

Anita couldn't quite believe that. What could a woman like Vanessa threaten a violent man with to make him comply? "Do you threaten them with jail time?"

"Something like that." Then she suddenly pointed to a corner. "There we are. Let's start with them. Cooper, do you have a picture of the dead woman?"

Cooper pulled out his cellphone. "Sending it to your cell now."

There was a soft ping, and Vanessa pulled her own cellphone from her bag. "Got it."

Two women stood at the corner, both dressed provocatively, wearing short skirts despite the cool temperature, and make-up that barely glossed over the fact that neither would win a beauty contest. They were very much like the women she'd seen ply the same trade in Elko County. Certain things were universal no matter the location, and the sex trade was one of them.

Anita watched with interest how Vanessa talked to the women, who were friendly to her, and addressed her by name. Vanessa seemed to have genuine compassion for these women, asking them about their well-being, and if anybody was giving them any trouble.

"I brought my friends tonight," Vanessa finally said and pointed to her and Cooper. "Anita and Cooper. They're investigating the murder of a woman, and we'd like you to look at her picture to see if you might have seen her around."

"Sure," one woman answered.

Cooper stepped closer and held up his cellphone with Janet's picture. "Did you see her in the last six weeks? Maybe in the company of a man?"

Both women looked at the picture, but shook their heads.

"Sorry, she doesn't look familiar."

"Never seen her," the second woman confirmed.

"Thanks," Cooper said. "Have you noticed any weird guys in the area lately? Maybe somebody who's interested in a tall, blonde woman?"

One of the women glanced at Anita. "You mean like her?"

Anita nodded in Cooper's stead. "Yes, like me."

"No, sorry. Wish I could help," the prostitute said.

"All right," Cooper said. "Thanks for talking to us."

"Take care of yourselves," Vanessa said.

Cooper took Anita's hand, and together they walked next to Vanessa, who was leading them onto another side street.

"Don't worry," Vanessa said. "This is just the beginning. There are a lot more sex workers we'll talk to tonight. Somebody is bound to have seen something."

They moved from corner to corner, talking to prostitutes as well as homeless people, showing them Janet's picture, and asking if they'd come upon a man who'd been interested in tall, blonde, blue-eyed women. Anita understood now why Cooper had suggested to go on a tour with Vanessa. Prostitutes noticed things other people didn't, and they often were good judges of character. Their lives depended on it. They also looked out for each other, watching each other's backs. But with every hour that passed as they walked through all the areas where sex workers hung out to pick up customers, she became more disillusioned about finding a lead. However, in the absence of a better idea, she continued trotting along.

"I know it's frustrating," Cooper said, squeezing her hand. "But until we find the white van, we have no other leads."

Vanessa glanced at them. "And now that we've alerted a whole bunch of people what to look out for, I'm sure we'll get some information. The girls all have my phone number. If I get a tip, I'll pass it on."

"Thank you, Vanessa," Anita said with a grateful smile. "I can't tell you how much I appreciate you taking the time to do this with us."

"It's all part of my job to keep people safe on the streets. The sooner we find that bastard, the better for everybody," she said, then nodded at Cooper.

The look the two exchanged was laden with something Anita

couldn't interpret. Was there something between them? No, that couldn't be. Vanessa had clearly noticed that Cooper was holding Anita's hand during their walk, indicating that they were intimate. Vanessa had looked entirely unconcerned about that fact, which had to mean that she didn't care about Cooper in a romantic way. But she could also sense that the two had lots in common and seemed to know each other very well.

"How long have you done this job for Scanguards, Vanessa?" Anita asked.

"About ten years?" she replied. "I kind of fell into it after I finished my bodyguard training at Scanguards."

Surprised, Anita stared at her. "You did the bodyguard training like Cooper? So that's how you met? During your training?"

Cooper chuckled. "Actually, I was already finished with my training, when Vanessa started. We've known each other since we were kids."

Vanessa nodded. "My parents work at Scanguards too. My mother runs the medical clinic there, and my dad is the second-in-command."

"Oh, wow. I didn't realize that. That's quite a coincidence that your parents and Cooper's parents work at the same place as you both. I always thought it was unusual that I followed into my father's footsteps and became a cop."

"It's not that unusual. It happens a lot among our friends," Vanessa said. "My brothers are bodyguards for Scanguards too. It's a great company to work for."

"It must be."

Vanessa pointed to the next intersection. "This way. I think I see Candy and Ginger."

"Where are we right now? I think I'm lost," Anita said.

Cooper motioned to his left. "Down there is the Financial District, and a few blocks this way is Lower Nob Hill and the Theater District, and Chinatown is just around the corner."

Anita smiled at him. "It looks so different at night. During the day, I can almost find my way around without a map. Almost."

"The longer you're here, the easier it'll get to navigate the city."

"And what areas to avoid," Vanessa added with a sideways glance.

She winked. "And I'm sure Cooper is happy to show you the city in his spare time."

"I don't want to take up all his time."

Cooper put his arm around her waist and pulled her closer, while they continued walking. "I'm happy to show you anything you want," he murmured into her ear. "As for my spare time: I'm sure we can find a way for you to compensate me for it."

She felt her cheeks heat despite the cool night air, at a loss of how to respond. "Not here," she whispered back.

Cooper chuckled, and they caught up with Vanessa and the two prostitutes a moment later. Vanessa was already showing them Janet's photo, and got the same answer as before. They hadn't seen Janet.

"Any strange guys lurking around looking for women like Janet?" Vanessa asked.

"No, sorry," one of them said.

The other one furrowed her forehead.

"Ginger? Did you see somebody?" Vanessa asked again.

"Hmm." Ginger seemed to contemplate something. "A couple of days ago, I saw something."

"Tell us, please. I'm Anita, and I think the man who killed Janet, killed lots of other women looking similar to her."

Ginger looked straight at her. "I saw some guy follow a woman who came out of a bank."

"Was it dark yet?" Cooper asked.

"Yes, it was late, and it was already dark. I think the blonde woman I saw worked late at the bank. She was dressed in a suit, you know. And she was walking along the sidewalk. I was just getting out of a client's car, and I wanted to walk back to my corner, but then I saw a guy follow that woman." She motioned to her friend Candy. "You know, that was the night you weren't feeling well."

Candy nodded.

"I was a little worried about that woman from the bank, because the guy was creepy. You know, I couldn't even hear his footsteps. I don't think she knew she was being followed. So I waited where I was, because they were both walking in my general direction. Then a car suddenly stopped next to the woman, and the driver opened the window and waved at her. She looked surprised, but happy. She got into the car with the guy, and they drove off."

"What happened to the man who was following her?"

"He was pissed off. I think he wanted to snatch her, but that woman's friend got there just in time."

"Did you see his face?" Anita asked.

Ginger nodded. "Yes, just for a moment when he stepped into the light of a streetlamp. He scared the hell out of me. I hightailed it out of there."

"Do you think you can describe him well enough for a sketch?" Cooper asked.

"Yeah, I think so. He was as tall as you, short dark hair like yours."

"I'll get a sketch artist to sit down with you." He looked at his watch. "I don't think I can get anybody until tomorrow morning."

"I can coordinate it with Ginger," Vanessa offered. "Is that okay with you, Ginger?"

"Sure."

"The sooner the better, while your memory is still fresh," Cooper said.

"Trust me, that's not a guy I'd forget very quickly. The sooner he's caught, the better for everybody."

Anita could only agree.

Finally, they had a tangible lead: a man who was following a woman matching the victim profile. And the fact that he was looking for a new victim after having disposed of Janet, meant that they were in a unique position to catch him.

18

———————

Cooper glanced at Anita as he put the car in drive and headed for home. "You must be tired."

She gave him a warm smile. "What time is it?"

"Past 3 a.m."

"At least we have a lead now." She took a breath. "And that's giving me an idea of how to catch him."

"Let me hear it."

"We know now that he's already looking for his next victim. And the woman that Ginger saw fits the profile: blonde, tall, and most likely with a job that gives her some sort of power."

"That's very likely. A bank teller leaves when the bank closes. A woman working late at a bank is probably in management."

"Exactly," Anita agreed and added, "I've seen several cases, where he actually abducted a woman *before* he killed the previous one, almost as if he *needs* a victim at all times."

Cooper knew that she was right with her assumption. This vampire most likely fed only from his female victims, and few vampires went without blood for more than a couple of days. The fact that some of his victims overlapped indicated that he wasn't a vampire who showed restraint.

"Good point. The incident Ginger reported happened before Janet was killed, so he was already looking for a replacement before he killed her, and we have to assume that after the woman from the bank slipped through his fingers, he's desperate for a replacement."

It had been over thirty-six hours since Janet's death, and the amount of blood the vampire had consumed would ordinarily tide him over for a few days. However, a killer like this one who gorged himself regularly had a lot less control over his hunger. He might already be on the edge of bloodlust, a state where he needed another fix just like a junkie.

"That's what I think too." Anita nodded, becoming more animated again, almost as if she could brush the need for sleep off like a dust particle on her sleeve. "Let's make it easier for him to find his next victim."

An odd sense of foreboding crawled up his spine, and he gave Anita a sideways glance. He didn't want to ask the next question, but he couldn't stop himself. "What are you suggesting?"

"I'm tall, I'm blonde, and blue-eyed, and I'm a woman in a position of power... well, of course I won't wear a sheriff's deputy uniform, but I can dress up like a businesswoman... and he won't know what hit him."

Cooper slammed on the brakes, bringing the car to a stop on a deserted side street, and spun his head to her. Had he heard correctly? "Are you fucking serious? You wanna play bait?"

"Hear me out. I'm trained for this."

He shook his head, his jaw tight from the strength it cost him not to let his vampire side emerge. "Not for this. You're not doing this! You're not putting yourself in the path of a psychotic serial killer."

She narrowed her eyes at him, showing her annoyance. "You don't have a say in this. I'm a sheriff's deputy. I can do this."

"Over my dead body!"

"You can't tell me what to do! I'll talk to the chief of police. He'll accept my offer—"

"No, he won't. He's gonna do what I tell him to do. And that is to keep you as far away from this killer as I can."

"You have no right—"

He leaned over to the passenger side and snatched her by the shoulders. "You don't have a chance against this perp."

Anita tried to shake off his hands, but he held her like she was in a vise.

"Let go of me!" she ground out.

"Try and fight me off! If you manage that, then, and only then, I'll let you play bait."

Cooper knew she would never have a chance against him in a fight. As a vampire hybrid he was so much stronger than her. So much more powerful. And the vampire who was abducting and killing these women would be just as strong if not stronger. He would snap her like a twig. And Cooper couldn't allow that. He had to protect her.

Anita lifted her hands up and pushed from her chest outwards in an effort to force his hands to lose their grip. But she hadn't counted on his vampire strength. Surprised, she glared at him, then tried again.

"Damn it!" she cursed and punched her fists into the inside of his elbows, but not even that maneuver made him lose his grip on her shoulders.

He leaned in. "You're not strong enough. If you can't beat me, you can't beat him."

"Oh, I can beat you."

The challenge in her eyes was clear. He braced himself for the next countermeasure. Instead of pulling away from him, she leaned in closer. A moment later, her hands were on his pants, and she was opening the button and lowering the zipper.

"Fuck!" This time he was the one who cursed. "That's playing dirty."

When she shoved his pants down and pulled his boxer briefs away from his body, he knew he'd lost. His cock was already readying itself for her touch, and there was nothing he could do to prevent it, except for letting go of her shoulders and pushing her away from him. By now his cock was out of its confines and hard as a crowbar.

Anita smirked. "Looks like I won."

"That's not a win!" He ran a hand over his head. "Damn it, Anita! Don't you get it? I don't want you to be in danger. I want to protect you."

"No, you want to control me! You want to tell me what to do! And I'm not gonna let you do that!"

He let out a sigh, dropping his shoulders. He wished he could tell her the truth of what kind of creature she was up against, that the killer was a vampire, but he couldn't.

"Anita, I know you probably won't believe me, because I barely believe it myself, but I have feelings for you." He raised his eyes to meet hers. "I'm falling hard and fast. For you. Or why do you think I offered you to stay with me? I've never done that before. I've never had a woman live with me, or even just stay with me temporarily. But you... damn it, when we met, I realized immediately that I have no defenses against you. You just get under my skin. You might think I'm crazy, because we don't really know each other, but when I'm with you, I just want to have more of you." He shook his head, looking away to the deserted street beyond the windshield. "I'm not trying to control you. I'm trying to protect you, because I couldn't live with myself if I let anybody hurt you."

Suddenly there wasn't a sound inside the car other than the sound of two people breathing.

When she didn't move and didn't say anything for a few very long seconds, he said, "Now you'll probably want to move into a hotel, because I sound like an obsessed stalker."

What had come over him to make this kind of confession? He'd made everything worse now. Independent women like Anita didn't like possessive men. But vampires and vampire hybrids were inherently possessive when they found their mates. And he knew he'd found his. But he'd screwed it up.

All of a sudden, he felt a warm hand on his thigh. He turned his head and looked into Anita's flushed face. Her anger was gone. Her lips were soft and inviting, her jaw relaxed. She leaned closer, their faces only inches from one another.

"You have feelings for me?"

He nodded. "I thought it was obvious. It's not like I can hide that."

Her hand on his thigh was moving until it made contact with his cock. The contact made him jolt. Slowly, she wrapped her hand around his erection. He closed his eyes, the sensation so intense that his fangs itched to descend. When he opened his eyes again, Anita dropped her head into his lap.

"Fuck!" he hissed, just as her breath blew against his sensitive skin and her lips wrapped around the tip of his shaft, imprisoning him in her warm mouth.

"Baby, you don't have to—"

But she'd already taken him as deep as she could. He let out an uncontrolled moan and pressed his head back against the headrest. He hadn't expected this, not after their fight, and certainly not in the car. After all, they weren't teenagers who had no other place to go. But fuck, if he didn't find it electrifying that Anita was blowing him in the car. And this was no mechanical blow job. The way she licked her tongue along his cock, and sucked him with such skill, was more than just a little arousing. He wished he could move a little to shove his pants farther down, but there was no space. He was wedged in and at Anita's mercy.

Her soft moans bounced against his hard flesh, sending shudders down his spine. Cooper put his hands around her head, gently pulling her back and making her slow down, knowing he would come in a few seconds if she continued with this pace.

"Baby, ease off a little, or I'll spill."

She raised her head until only the tip of his erection was still captured between her red lips, and looked up at him from under her lashes. He'd never seen a more tantalizing sight.

"Fuck, you're beautiful," he murmured and caressed her face. "If you were wearing a skirt, I'd lift you onto my lap right now and fuck you until we're both delirious."

She locked eyes with him, and slid back down on his erection as if to thank him for his words. Her sucking motion felt more intense now, and with every descent and every withdrawal he edged closer to his climax. But he still possessed a few thin threads of his self-control. He didn't want to presume that she would let him come in her mouth, and he didn't want to be selfish, so he pulled her up.

"Didn't you like it?" she whispered, her lips looking swollen and even more kissable than before.

"I loved it, every single second. I've never felt anything better than your lips around my cock." He pressed his lips to hers and kissed her passionately, dancing with her tongue, exploring the wet cave that had been home to his cock only a few seconds earlier. He brushed one hand over her torso, caressing her breasts through her top, pleased to be greeted by hard nipples. How he loved an aroused woman in his arms. He released her lips and pressed his forehead to hers, breathing hard.

"While I still have a few working brain cells, I think we should go home, so I can rip your clothes off you and sink my cock into you."

Anita sounded just as breathless. "I'm not done sucking you."

"We're only a couple of minutes from the house."

She looked outside, then back at him. "There's not a lot of traffic." She glanced down at his cock, which still stood upright as firmly as a flagpole.

"No, there isn't." His heartbeat accelerated again, guessing what she was implying. "And I know the route in my sleep."

Cooper put the car back in drive and pressed down the gas pedal, merging onto the empty street. Anita lowered her head back to his lap and took him back into her mouth, sucking him, while she gripped him tightly around the root.

<h1 style="text-align:center">19</h1>

———

Anita felt like she wasn't herself. She'd completely overreacted when Cooper had told her he wouldn't let her be the bait for the serial killer. She'd seen red and assumed the worst: that he was a man trying to control her. She hadn't expected him to confess that he was falling in love with her. At first, she'd thought he was lying so she would relent and give up her—admittedly—dangerous idea. But then she'd looked at him and had seen that he was crushed by the thought that she wanted nothing further to do with him. All he'd wanted to do was keep her safe, and she'd pushed him away. She knew now why: she too was developing feelings, and it scared her, because it was happening so fast.

Yet the rush of realizing that Cooper wanted her just like she wanted him, was too much to resist. So, for the first time in her life, she'd thrown caution to the wind.

More than that: she was doing something completely reckless. She was giving Cooper a blow job while he was driving. And the action sent a thrill through her body that she'd never felt before. She felt desirable and powerful in that moment, because she knew she could drive Cooper crazy with lust.

Anita felt the car slow down, and heard a garage door open, while she continued to suck Cooper's cock, unable to get enough of him. He was big and beautiful, so perfect that she couldn't believe her luck. He tasted even better, and his stamina was undeniable.

She heard his voice in the distance, almost as if she was in a trance, and had no idea how they made it out of the car and into the house. But somehow, they were finally in Cooper's room, tearing each other's clothes off, kissing and touching each other with an urgency she'd never before experienced.

When they were both naked, Anita fell to her knees before him and looked up at him. Cooper's eyes were shimmering in a golden hue caused by the bedside lamps, and he put one hand on her face, while he guided his cock to her lips with the other.

She met his gaze and held it while she swallowed inch after inch of his rock-hard shaft. She took him as deep as she could, before he put both hands on her face and began to withdraw gently, then thrust back into her mouth.

Cooper exhaled a shaky breath but didn't break eye contact. "Babe, you're amazing."

With his thumbs he caressed her cheeks, still cupping them lightly, giving her the freedom to pull back if she needed to.

Anita increased the tempo, moving faster up and down his erection, sliding her tongue along the underside of his hard flesh and swirling it around his crown before descending again.

Her hands weren't idle either. With one, she braced herself on his thigh, with the other she cradled his balls, alternately squeezing and releasing him.

Cooper's moans filled the room, and he seemed entirely unconcerned that his uncle and aunt might hear him.

"Oh, Baby, fuck! Fuck!"

All of a sudden, he withdrew from her mouth and pushed her back. Before she could protest, he'd pulled her up to stand and she found herself pressed with her back against the wall. A second later, she was suspended in the air, held up by Cooper's strong arms, her legs spread, her back pressed against the wall.

Cooper plunged into her pussy with one powerful thrust, seating himself deep inside her. All air rushed from her lungs, robbing her of the ability to speak.

"I'm sorry for being so rough," he said on a harsh breath, "but you've gotten me so hot—"

"I love it like this," she confessed. "I love your cock thrusting hard and deep and fast... please... please fuck me hard." She'd never begged a man before. But the way Cooper made her feel by taking her with such vigor was new to her, new and exciting, and intoxicating. As if she was getting drunk on the passion he shared with her.

Every nerve ending in her body seemed to vibrate, arousal and pleasure intersected, lust and desire collided until all she could feel were waves shooting through her body igniting little explosions of true bliss. Another wave followed, this one not created by her own body, but originating from Cooper as he climaxed and shot his semen into her.

At the same time, Cooper took her lips, kissing her hard, robbing her of the remaining air in her lungs, sending more waves of pleasure through her body. He suddenly ripped his mouth from hers, and she felt something sting her lower lip, as if a bee had stung her.

"Ouch!"

Cooper's head reared back, and for a brief second, she saw his lips peel back from his teeth. There was blood on his lips, and he licked it off. She blinked, her heart thundering in her ears. His teeth were hidden behind his lips again, and the blood was gone.

"I'm so sorry," he apologized quickly. "I was too rough."

She touched her lip with one finger and looked at the drop of blood she'd wiped away. "It's okay. It didn't hurt." It had only stung for a very brief split second.

"Let me kiss it better." He leaned in again, and this time his lips were gentle when he licked over her mouth, soothing it.

His tender touch made her relax. She caressed his shoulders, feeling the strong muscles beneath his skin flex, making her aware of how strong he was to be able to keep her suspended, supporting her entire weight as if she weighed nothing more than a feather.

Anita felt weightless and sated. Slowly, he took his lips from hers and withdrew from her sheath, before he set her back down on her feet.

She instantly swayed, her knees feeling like jelly. Cooper caught her, holding her in his arms, and she pressed her head to his chest, inhaling his male scent.

"That was..." She didn't even know how to describe it. "You're an amazing lover."

"It's easy to make love to you."

"Are you calling me easy?" she teased even though she understood what he meant.

Cooper chuckled. "No, I'm not. What I'm trying to say is that everything clicks when I'm with you."

He lifted her off her feet and carried her to the bed, where she slipped underneath the covers, and he joined her, pulling her back into his arms, spooning her. She pulled his arm around her front and held it to her chest.

"Hmm." She still felt weightless, her body still on a high. She'd never felt so relaxed and so satisfied after sex.

Cooper nuzzled his face in the crook of her neck, pressing gentle kisses to her skin. "I love the feel of a satisfied woman in my arms."

He pressed his groin to her backside, and she could feel his cock, still hard, still big. She wiggled against him, teasing him. To her surprise, he adjusted himself, and a moment later, he thrust back into her pussy.

She gasped at the welcome invasion. "Ohh!"

"Uh-huh," he murmured. "That's what you get for trying to seduce me again."

"I wasn't trying to seduce you."

"Yes, you were. You started it in the car." He began to move slowly back and forth, their combined juices making every movement smooth.

"You gave me no choice." Because he had been too strong, stronger than any of the cadets she'd practiced hand-to-hand combat with.

"Yeah, about that," he started, his voice serious now.

"I won," she said quickly to remind him of his promise. "You'll have to use me as bait to catch the killer."

He hesitated, before he finally replied, "All right, but I'll decide when and where." Then he plunged his erection faster into her. "But right now, you'll need to learn that sucking a man while he's driving has consequences."

"What kind of consequences?" She looked over her shoulder, trying her best innocent look, her lips in a pout.

"The kind that are best enjoyed naked."

20

———

Hunger awakened him, and Cooper realized with horror that his fangs were fully extended, his face nuzzled against Anita's neck.

Fuck!

It was bad enough that the previous night he'd accidentally bitten her lip because his fangs had extended automatically when he'd climaxed so hard he'd been afraid to black out. Now his need for Anita's blood was even more urgent. He'd expended a lot of energy making love to her, and his self-control was at an all-time low. His cock was already hard again, and all he would need to do was to thrust into Anita's pussy, waking her so they could both find pleasure again. He knew that Anita would welcome him just like she'd done before, but how would she react to his fangs? No, he couldn't spring it on her like this.

As quietly as possible, Cooper got out of bed, slipped into a pair of jogging pants, and left the room. He hurried downstairs. From the kitchen he heard voices and the clattering of dishes. He glanced at the large antique clock in the hallway. It was already past three o'clock in the afternoon. No wonder he was hungry.

In the pantry, Cooper went straight for the fridge. While he gulped down two bottles of blood, he relived his lovemaking with Anita. He'd never been so crazy about any woman before. And he had no qualms about telling her that she meant something to him. It was best that she got used to this fact as quickly as possible, because the way he felt about her, he knew that he wouldn't be able to restrain the vampire inside him for much longer. Because the vampire had found his mate and was ready to make her his, even though his human side was able to show more restraint.

When he stepped out of the pantry, he nearly collided with Wesley.

Wesley grinned unashamedly. "So, you're finally giving your girl a little break, huh?"

"Look who's talking," Cooper countered. "Like you ever let a night go by without making love to Virginia."

"Life's short. Gotta live every day like it's your last."

Cooper rolled his eyes. "Says the immortal."

Wesley chuckled, then he gestured to the upper floor. "So, Anita's the one, huh? I must say, you've got excellent taste."

"How do you—"

"May I introduce myself? I'm your uncle. I've known you since you were a baby, and trust me, I can see the change in you. You've never looked at anybody the way you look at Anita."

Cooper couldn't help but smile.

"Besides, you wouldn't risk exposing us and yourself and all our secrets by bringing her here if you only wanted to fuck her."

"You're quite perceptive as always. But don't worry, so far, she's not suspecting anything. I've been careful." Accidentally drawing blood by kissing Anita could have happened to anybody—well, any horny vampire. "Now, go, and mind your own business. I've got an insatiable woman to satisfy."

Laughing, Wes entered the pantry, while Cooper headed for the stairs.

ANITA SLAPPED both hands over her mouth in order not to cry out and give away that she was standing at the top of the stairs, hidden from Cooper's and Wesley's view, but able to hear their conversation. When she'd woken without Cooper by her side, she'd first assumed that he was in the bathroom, but the door had been open and Cooper was nowhere in sight. She'd slipped into her bathrobe, her feet bare, and had walked toward the stairs when she'd caught Wesley mentioning her name.

"So, Anita's the one, huh? I must say, you've got excellent taste."

"How do you—"

"May I introduce myself? I'm your uncle. I've known you since you were a baby, and trust me, I can see the change in you. You've never looked at anybody the way you look at Anita."

Her heart had made a somersault. If his uncle noticed how Cooper looked at her, everything Cooper had told her the night before had to be true. He was falling in love with her. She'd been ecstatic, but a second later Wesley had added something she couldn't make head nor tail of.

"Besides, you wouldn't risk exposing us and yourself and all our secrets by bringing her here if you only wanted to fuck her."

Exposing what? What secrets?

Cooper's cool voice interrupted her thoughts. *"You're quite perceptive as always. But don't worry, so far, she's not suspecting anything. I've been careful. Now, go, and mind your own business. I've got an insatiable woman to satisfy."*

Panic surged inside her. He'd been careful? Careful about what? What was he hiding from her? Her heart pounded out of control. Cooper was on his way upstairs, clearly to make love to her again. She couldn't let that happen, not now, not after what he and Wesley had said.

Barefoot she hurried back to the room, pulled the door shut soundlessly, and went into the bathroom. To her horror, she noticed that there was no lock on the bathroom door, maybe so a child couldn't lock itself in accidentally. Damn! What now? If she went back to bed and pretended to sleep, Cooper would most certainly want to have sex with her again. And if she turned him down, he might suspect that something was off. Maybe he had even heard her footsteps or the opening and closing of the door. She had to stall until she figured out what to do next.

The shower! She reached into the shower enclosure and turned on the water, then quickly took off her robe, tossed in on the vanity, and stepped underneath the lukewarm water. For a moment, she felt chilly, but then the water started to heat up. She forced herself to breathe evenly to calm down. Had she misinterpreted Cooper's conversation with his uncle?

The door opened, but she didn't turn around. She knew it was Cooper.

"Hey, Baby," he said, his voice dripping with tenderness. "Good morning."

Was it all fake? Every touch? Every sweet word? Every kiss? What did he want from her?

"Good morning," she forced herself to say, still not turning.

"How about I join you?"

It wasn't a question, she knew that immediately, because he was already stepping into the shower, and pulled her against his broad chest, his arms reaching around her, gliding up her torso, until he cupped both breasts possessively.

She gasped, apprehensive now. Was it just sex he wanted? Or something else too? Something nefarious?

Cooper dropped his head to the crook of her neck and kissed her there, while he continued kneading her breasts. Her nipples beaded automatically, not listening to her brain that warned her that something wasn't right about Cooper. He wasn't the honest man he pretended to be. He had secrets. Secrets even his uncle seemed to be concerned about.

"Hmm, you're getting me so hot, Anita," he murmured into her ear while he slid one hand down her body to caress her pussy. To her shock, she realized that she welcomed his touch and that her clit was already pulsing with need, with desire for his touch.

Before she knew what was happening, Cooper thrust into her from behind, plunging deep, his erection stretching her tight channel, while she moaned involuntarily as intense pleasure charged through her. Despite Cooper's lies, she couldn't resist him. Was this how women who were in a relationship with bad men felt? Did they feel just as helpless as she did now, unable and unwilling to push him away even though she suspected that she was getting into something that was bad for her?

Cooper moaned softly as he fucked her from behind, one hand still on her breast, while he caressed her clit with the other. How could a man be such a considerate lover while at the same time keeping secrets from her and lying to her? How was that possible?

She couldn't think straight anymore. Cooper's pistoning cock robbed her of her ability to keep a clear head, and his skill at caressing her clit just how she liked it, was sending her toward another earth-shattering climax, killing millions of brain cells in the process. When she came, she couldn't help but cry out in pleasure, then felt his cock spasm inside her, filling her with his semen once more.

"Anita, fuck, you're amazing," he murmured into her ear, his voice shaky as if he had trouble speaking.

"I didn't do anything," she deflected.

He chuckled. "Are you kidding? The way you grip me when I'm inside you... it's out of this world. I don't know if I'll ever again get any work done when you're around."

His words gave her an excuse to free herself from him. "I forgot about work. We need to find the killer. We can't stay here all day." It was probably afternoon already.

"Unfortunately, not," he whispered and pulled out of her. He reached for the liquid soap. "But that doesn't mean I'm going to forego the pleasure of washing you."

"You don't have to do—"

"But I want to," he interrupted and began lathering her skin, starting with her boobs. When her nipples pebbled under his gentle ministrations, he whispered, "Damn, Anita, are you always so horny when you wake up?"

He kneaded her breasts with firmer strokes, and she let it happen. It felt good, even though she knew something about Cooper wasn't what it seemed. And she had to find out what it was, and hope that he didn't turn out to be a bad guy, because despite all the warning signs she was falling for him.

21

———————

After they'd gotten dressed, Cooper had asked her if she wanted to eat something, but Anita was too nervous to eat, and had therefore claimed that she wasn't really hungry. Cooper had accepted her claim without questioning it, and hadn't eaten anything either. Had he noticed the change in her behavior? She hoped not, because she had no idea what he was capable of doing if he found out that she'd been listening in on his and Wesley's conversation.

In the car, she took some of the notes she'd made on Janet's case out of her handbag, leafed through them and pretended to read them again, just so Cooper wouldn't hold her hand.

"Is there anything else about Janet's file that looks like a lead?" Cooper asked as they headed into heavy late afternoon traffic.

Anita shrugged, but she knew she had to say something, or Cooper would wonder what was wrong with her. "I still think we're overlooking something."

"You mean apart from the victims' physical characteristics and their jobs?"

"I wish I knew."

When she saw him take one hand off the steering wheel, she

quickly snatched another paper with her free hand, and continued, "What about the abductions themselves?"

"What about them?"

"Janet was taken after midnight," she replied and searched for more things to say. "And if I remember correctly, all women were taken at night."

"That's not unusual." Cooper turned at the intersection and hit more traffic.

"I know. But for all thirty-five or thirty-six women to be taken at night, and not a single one during the day, is a pattern. Almost as if he doesn't want to be out during the day."

Cooper seemed to hesitate a bit and cast her a sideways glance. "You think he's worried that he might be recognized? That he's somebody well-known, a celebrity of sorts?"

"Hmm." Anita contemplated his words. "That might be the case if he limited the abductions to one state or one city, but it's not very probable that he thinks he can be recognized in five different states. That would mean he's nationally well-known. And I somehow doubt that."

"Then I'm not sure the time of the abductions gives us much of a lead." Cooper pulled into the Scanguards underground parking garage. "Besides, the prostitute, Ginger, didn't mention that she recognized him from somewhere."

"You're right. Well, let's see if we recognize him."

Cooper pulled into an empty parking spot and switched off the engine. Anita opened the passenger door and exited the vehicle. At the elevators, Cooper caught up with her and put his arm around her waist. She tensed involuntarily.

"Something wrong?" he asked, his voice laden with concern.

Anita forced herself to smile up at him. "No, it's just a little anxiety." She searched for another excuse. "I wasn't able to help Janet. What if we don't find him before he abducts his next victim?"

"I know the feeling."

He pressed a kiss to her forehead, his tenderness surprising her—and simultaneously confusing the hell out of her. How could he act like the most caring man and lover when he was keeping secrets from her? And how could he look so innocent doing it?

When the elevator door opened, the elevator wasn't empty. A young man with raven-black hair and blue eyes stood there, looking at a tablet in his hand. He looked up at them.

"Oh, hey, Coop, I was just on my way to your office."

Cooper ushered her into the elevator. "Anita, this is my colleague, Benjamin."

"Nice to meet you."

"Likewise," Benjamin said, then looked at Cooper. "Just got the sketch."

He pointed to the tablet, and Anita sidled up to him, and looked at the black-and-white drawing of a man. Cooper looked over her shoulder at the tablet, and she heard him suck in a breath of air.

"Ginger saw this man?"

Anita stared at the drawing, her heart beating out of control, her palms sweating, everything before her eyes blurring. This couldn't be. This couldn't be the man.

She'd seen him before. Many, many years before. So why was he still so young? He would be much older by now. Twenty-one years older to be exact. She focused on the man's face. He was handsome, with very short hair, a straight nose, piercing eyes, and a square chin. It was him, there was no doubt. When she looked at his mouth and saw the tips of two sharp canines peek past his lips, she knew she wasn't wrong. It was him.

Reno, Nevada, twenty-one years earlier

Anita shot up from her bed. Around her it was dark. Only the nightlight near the door was casting a little light on the carpeted floor meant to help her find the bathroom if she needed to pee in the middle of the night.

Something had woken her. A sound. She heard two voices, one was that of her mother, the other she didn't recognize. It wasn't her father's. He was on duty at the sheriff's department and wouldn't be home until it was time for her to go to school. Or had her father come home earlier?

There was no clock in her bedroom, and she had no idea what time it was. Only dressed in her nightgown, Anita got out of bed and walked toward the door. She turned the knob and opened the door by only a sliver, when a man's voice drifted toward her.

"You have no choice!" he ground out, the menace in his voice impossible to ignore.

Anita shivered despite the warm temperature in the house.

"No, please, take all the money and go," her mother begged, her voice laden with tears. "There's more hidden in the bedroom."

A growl sounding like that of an animal came from the living room, and despite the fear Anita felt, she had to help her mother. On tiptoes, she left her room and walked into the dark corridor. At the bend, she stopped and peered past the corner.

"I don't want your fucking money, bitch!"

The angry words came from a tall man, a stranger she'd never seen before. He had dark hair and a chiseled face, but she barely looked at that, because what captured her attention was the fact that he'd snatched her mother by the throat, lifting her in the air, his face only inches from hers.

He glared at her mother, his eyes like red beacons, his teeth sharp like those of a lion or a tiger. Frightened, Anita reared back, slamming her hand over her mouth to stop herself from screaming.

"I'm taking you, and there's nothing you can do about it!" He hissed like a beast warning its prey. "And if you don't come quietly, I'm taking your girl too."

Anita's heart thundered in her ears, and tears filled her eyes. No! She had to save her mother from that beast, that monster. Frantically, she thought of how to help, and remembered that she had a baseball bat in the bedroom. She rushed back to her room, and grabbed it, then hurried back to the hallway. When she went around the corner, ready to charge the intruder, she heard the front door slam shut. She rushed to the door and ripped it open, only to see a white van race away.

Her mother was gone. A monster had taken her. A monster with glaring red eyes and sharp, white teeth. A monster that shouldn't exist. A creature that only existed in lore and myth, in fiction and on TV: a vampire.

San Francisco, today

Anita was still staring at the black-and-white drawing. As far as police sketches went, this one was as accurate as they came. The only thing that she couldn't explain was the fact that the man hadn't aged. After two decades, he should look more like a man in his fifties. But perhaps even that could be explained, now that the old memory of her mother's abduction finally resurfaced with every detail. She'd suppressed the horrifying incident because her father hadn't believed her, no matter how often she'd told him. He'd claimed that she was making up this story because she didn't want to face the fact that her mother had left them without a word.

But now she was certain: her mother had been abducted. She'd been taken by the same man who'd taken many other women looking like her mother, and killed them. Everything about the victim profile matched. Her mother was blonde, blue-eyed, tall, and she'd been a school principal of a small elementary school in Reno, a woman in a position of power.

"Anita? You okay?"

Cooper's voice drifted to her, and she ripped her gaze from the sketch. "Yeah, yeah, it's just..." No, she couldn't say that she suspected the man of being a vampire. Cooper and his colleague would think she was crazy. And she certainly wasn't ready to tell him about what she'd seen when her mother had been abducted. After all, she wasn't sure she could trust Cooper right now. He was keeping secrets from her. But she needed to know if she was the only one who looked at the drawing and saw the face of a vampire. "Bad teeth, what do you think?"

Cooper exchanged a look with Benjamin, then both shrugged as if they were performing in a synchronized swimming contest.

"Maybe a little," Cooper agreed. "Could also be that Ginger was scared and projected her fear onto him. Happens."

"Yeah, that sounds about right," Benjamin agreed.

"Well, let's get copies of this sketch out to everybody, and send a few teams canvassing the neighborhoods. Let's concentrate on the neighborhoods around where Janet's body was found."

"I'll take care of it."

"Send me a copy to my cell," he instructed Benjamin and added, "Anita and I will take North Beach east of Columbus Avenue up to Telegraph Hill."

When the elevator opened, they exited, and Cooper turned to her. "I'll bring you to the lounge, where you can eat a bite, while I'll quickly check in with my boss. Won't take long. Then we can head out."

Anita was about to protest, when she thought better of it. She was hungry, and she needed some time to herself to contemplate her next steps.

22

———

After dropping off Anita at the H lounge, the Scanguards lounge that served food for humans, Cooper contacted Benjamin, and they met in Cooper's office.

"What now?" Benjamin asked.

"Whose brilliant idea was it to send you the sketch without editing out the fangs?"

"Sorry, the sketch artist who did the drawing just followed Ginger's lead and sent me exactly what she claimed she saw. I hadn't had a chance yet to alter the drawing when you showed up with a human in tow."

"Bad timing." It was his own fault for bringing Anita. "What's done is done."

"At least we know the guy is definitely a vampire."

"True. But we can't show the drawing like this when we're canvassing the neighborhoods. Edit out the fangs, and then send it to me, and distribute it to everybody else at Scanguards to be on the lookout. Whoever else is not on assignment needs to get out there to ask around if anybody's seen the guy."

"I'll get it done," Benjamin agreed. "And Anita? You haven't told her yet?"

"It's not exactly an easy thing to work into a conversation."

Benjamin smirked. "Yeah, from what I hear you don't have a lot of conversations with her."

"What's that supposed to mean?"

"Well, according to Wes, you guys have been shagging like rabbits."

Cooper huffed. "Wes is the worst gossip I've ever met."

"So you're not denying it. And I figure since you're risking exposure by having her stay with you at Wes's house, this isn't just sex."

"Has anybody ever told you that you're nosy?" Cooper deflected.

"No." Benjamin slapped him on the shoulder and laughed out loud. "Looks like another one bites the dust, huh?"

Cooper rolled his eyes. "Wait until it hits you broadside. Let's see who's laughing then."

Benjamin winked. "Not gonna happen for a while."

"That's what I thought too. But in an ideal world, I wouldn't be hunting a serial killer vampire either, while trying to figure out how to tell Anita what I am. Any suggestions?"

"Bro, you're on your own when it comes to that. But good luck anyway!"

Shaking his head, Cooper left and went back down to the H lounge. Several of the human employees were in the lounge taking a break. Anita sat on a sofa, a plate of food on her lap, looking lost in her thoughts.

Cooper sat next to her and put his hand on her shoulder. "Hey, Babe."

She shrieked and stared at him, but caught herself quickly. "Sorry, sorry, you startled me... I didn't notice you. I must have been daydreaming."

"Thinking about the case?"

"Yes, the case."

"How's the food?"

"It's excellent. But I didn't see where to pay for it."

"Oh, it's free to all employees and visitors."

"Wow, that's quite generous of the company." She glanced around. "I'm surprised there aren't more people here eating."

"Everybody's working different shifts. It's never too busy in here." He pointed to her empty plate. "You want some more?"

"No, I'm done. But you haven't eaten. Aren't you hungry?"

He wasn't, because he'd gulped down two bottles of blood, but he couldn't very well disclose that. "I'll eat something later. I'd rather go out there and see if anybody saw the guy from the sketch."

"Where do we start?"

"There's an apartment building overlooking the alley where Janet's body was found. Somebody might have seen something from their window."

On their way to the parking garage, Cooper noticed that Anita didn't walk as closely next to him as she'd done before. She was quieter too, and it didn't feel like the companionable silence that they'd shared before. But he didn't want to ask her if anything was wrong. Maybe she was exhausted. And why not? They'd had marathon sex, and while he as a vampire hybrid had pretty much endless energy for lovemaking, a human like Anita needed more sleep than he'd allowed her.

Damn it, he was a selfish bastard for not letting her rest when she'd needed rest. He hadn't even tried to rein in his insatiable need for sex and just assumed that she wanted the same.

When they were in the car, driving toward North Beach, his guilty conscience didn't let him remain silent. "I'm sorry, Anita."

She glanced at him. "Sorry for what?"

He sighed. "For not letting you rest last night. I'm sorry I'm so demanding when it comes to sex. My only excuse is that you're an amazing woman, and I just can't keep my hands off you."

"Oh."

"I promise you I'll let you sleep in the other guestroom tonight if that's what you need to get some rest from me. I'm afraid that if we're in the same bed, I won't be able to restrain myself."

There was a moment of silence, and for a second, he wondered if he'd said something wrong.

"Are you always like this? I mean with other women?"

"Not really. I mean don't get me wrong, I do love sex, and I've had my fair share of pretty women..." He shrugged. "But they never got under my skin. Not like you."

"So I fit your type, hmm?"

"That's not it. I actually don't have a type. No, it's something else about you. When I talk to you, when I'm with you, I want you to know everything about me."

ANITA'S HEAD WAS SPINNING. How could he play the open and honest man so convincingly while at the same time keeping a secret from her? And how was she going to find out what he was hiding from her? She couldn't exactly ask him directly. If it was something worth lying about, he might lash out if confronted with the truth.

The silence was stretching between them, and she knew she had to say something, or he would eventually realize that something was wrong.

"I feel I already know a lot about you," she finally said.

After all, she'd met his uncles and aunts, and his baby cousin, and saw how they lived. On the surface, they were a normal family—well, a *rich*, normal family, because the house his Uncle Wesley lived in was a massive Victorian that had to be worth several million. But what was lying beneath the surface? What secrets were they hiding? Was it something that would change how she felt about him?

She suddenly felt Cooper's warm hand on her thigh. "We're here."

They got out of the car, and Cooper pointed to the apartment building he'd spoken about earlier. They cut through the covered parking of a commercial building, crossed the street, and headed for the entrance door, which wasn't locked, and entered.

"Let's start with the flats that overlook the alley," Cooper suggested, and they began knocking on doors.

Cooper took the lead, and introduced himself to the tenants that opened their doors. "We're investigators working with the SFPD and are looking for this man." Cooper turned his cellphone so the tenant could see it. "He may have been in this area two nights ago. Do you recognize him?"

The woman who'd opened the door shook her head. "Sorry, doesn't look familiar."

"He may have been hanging around in the alley behind you," Anita added to help jog the woman's memory.

"Sorry, I can't help you. I have better things to do than look out the window all night." She shut the door.

They moved to the next flat and continued questioning the other tenants in the same manner. Anita had to admit that Cooper had excellent manners and treated everybody he spoke to with courtesy, never getting impatient or frustrated. She felt herself involuntarily relax in his presence. Would her body really react like this if he was a bad guy? At the moment, she couldn't trust her own judgement. When she and Cooper had made love, she'd felt loved and understood, cherished even, and desired. No man had ever taken care of her the way Cooper did, the way he made sure to give her the same pleasure he took for himself. She couldn't imagine a more selfless lover. But was the old adage true? *If something sounds too good to be true...* Or was she simply focusing on some minor inconsistencies to sabotage this relationship? She pushed the thoughts aside, concentrating on the task at hand.

By the time they found a person who had indeed noticed something the night of Janet's murder, it was already dark outside. The older man invited them into his flat and motioned them to the bedroom from which he'd seen something in the alley.

He opened the window and pointed to the alley. "I heard a vehicle idling out there, so I came to close the window. I didn't want those fumes in the bedroom, you know."

"Absolutely," Cooper said. "Did you look outside?"

"Sure did. It was some van."

"Did you notice the color?"

"It was already dark out, but I think it was white."

Anita nodded to herself. A white van—it agreed with what she'd seen in Elko. "You didn't by chance see the license plates?"

"No, sorry, ma'am."

"What did you see the man doing?" Cooper asked.

"I saw him lower something to the ground. But I couldn't see what it was. I figured he was dumping trash, you know, 'cause he didn't wanna call the city for a pickup, when they charge you for it. Wouldn't be the first time that happened here..."

"Did you see the man's face?"

"Just for a second. Can I see the picture again?" the old man asked.

"Of course." Cooper turned his phone so the man could see the sketch.

This time, Anita stood next to the old man and saw the sketch too. She sucked in a breath. The face of the suspect was still the same, but the protruding teeth the sketch on Benjamin's tablet had shown, were gone. Either Benjamin or Cooper had changed the sketch. Why? Why hide the fact that the suspect had pointy canines?

"Yes, that looks like him," the old man confirmed.

"Thank you very much, sir," Cooper said politely, put his cellphone back in his pocket, and added, "We appreciate your help."

They left the apartment building and started walking to where Cooper had parked the SUV. The cool night air made her shiver.

"At least, we know for sure that the man Ginger saw following the female bank employee, is the same one who dumped Janet's body in the alley," Cooper said, walking past a large truck.

"Yes, it's a start." But the doctored sketch still bothered her. Now was as good a time as any to grab the bull by the horns. "About the sketch of the suspect. Why did you edit out the teeth? Don't you think that's a pretty prominent feature by which to identify the killer?"

Cooper was almost at the car and looked over his shoulder. "Benjamin and I figured that it would just confuse people."

The answer didn't satisfy her. "Confuse? Confuse how?"

She noticed him hesitate, then suddenly glance in a different direction, remaining silent as if he'd heard something. But there was no sound. Was he stalling to find a suitable answer that she would accept?

"We want people to concentrate on the face, not be distracted by his crooked teeth." He motioned her to approach. "Come, we've got more ground to cover."

But Anita remained standing where she was. The tiny hairs on her nape prickled, and it felt as if a cold snake slithered down her back. She'd felt like that once before, and she remembered the moment: it had happened when she'd seen a man abducting her mother, and she'd stood by helplessly.

"Anita, get in the car, now!" Cooper suddenly ordered, a dangerous undertone in his voice as he glanced around the parked cars as if looking for something.

Anita didn't move, because what she saw now sent a shock wave through her body, paralyzing her. Cooper's eyes were glowing red, and this time it wasn't a play of the light, because something else had changed at the same time. Two long pointy teeth were protruding from Cooper's mouth.

Two fangs.

Snippets of the past two days with Cooper flashed before her eyes. Everything fit together now: the blood splatter on his shirt, the golden shimmer in his eyes when they'd made love, the incident where he'd nicked her lip with his teeth and claimed it had been accidental. And other things came back now too. The two puncture wounds on Janet's neck had been made by fangs. That's how she'd been drained of her blood. An image of Cooper's cousin Jacob with his two sharp teeth appeared before her mental eye—he'd bitten her. She was sure of it. Yet Cooper had played it down. Just like he'd glossed over the fact that the sketch of the suspect had shown fangs. He'd removed them—evidently to protect somebody. If not the killer, then at least himself. The secret he and Wesley had whispered about was so obvious now. Vampires existed. They weren't just myth or lore. They were real.

And Cooper was one of them.

A vampire.

"How could I have been so blind?"

23

"**F**uck!" Cooper cursed.

He'd sensed somebody in the shadows, and had briefly seen the aura of a vampire, even though he hadn't seen the man's face, but he'd perceived him as a threat. The stranger had watched them, maybe followed them from the apartment building. As a result, his fangs had descended, and his eyes were glaring red. He was ready to defend Anita against any hostile vampire. Too late, he'd realized that by allowing his protector instinct to take over, he'd revealed to her what he was.

The shock of it was painted on her face. She stared at him, horrified, and he could see her chest heave from the effort of pumping more oxygen through her body.

"Anita, don't be afraid." He stretched one hand out. "I'm not gonna hurt you. But we have to leave. Now." Because the stranger was still lurking somewhere, though Cooper didn't know exactly where.

"Don't come any closer!" she warned, her voice breaking.

"Anita, please, listen to me. We've gotta leave. There's somebody here, watching us."

"I'm not going anywhere with you."

"Please, you're in danger." He made a step toward her. "You'll be safe with me."

She let out a bitter laugh and shook her head. "No." She reached into her handbag.

"Damn it, Anita," he ground out and marched toward her, intent on dragging her to the car kicking and screaming if he had to.

Anita aimed her gun at him. "Stop."

He heard a sound from a few yards behind Anita but couldn't tell what it was. Had the vampire left? Was it just another pedestrian walking to their parked car?

"I'll explain everything at home," he said and made another step toward Anita.

The sound of a gunshot echoed in the night, and something struck him, making him lose his balance for a moment. Stunned, he looked at his chest. There, just below his right clavicle, a blood stain was spreading.

"You shot me!" Pain seared through him, and for an instant he paused and stared at her in disbelief. "What the fuck, Anita!?"

She continued to aim the gun at him. However, he knew that he couldn't be killed with a regular bullet and rushed toward her. She pulled the trigger a second time, hitting him in the chest, before he reached her. Despite the pain caused by the two gunshot wounds, he wrestled the gun from her. She fought him, kicking him in the stomach, making him stumble backwards. He fell, the blood loss clearly weakening him.

Not knowing whether the stranger was still in the area, he couldn't risk being unable to protect Anita and himself, so he reached for his cellphone. Time to call in the cavalry. He punched in his emergency code and hit send. Just in time, because Anita lunged for him, trying to snatch the gun from his hand. But he tossed it behind him and instead, grabbed Anita and wrestled her down to the ground.

"Damn it! Will you stop?" he hissed, while he finally managed to pin her beneath him.

She tried to free herself, and punched him in his chest wound, making him cry out in pain. Just because the bullet couldn't kill him—

only a silver bullet could do that—didn't mean that it didn't hurt like a bitch.

"Let go of me!" she cried out.

"Not a chance. I'm not gonna let you run into danger."

"Oh, that's rich!" She glared at him. "You're the danger! You're a vampire!"

"Vampire hybrid actually, half vampire, half human."

He pressed one hand to his chest wound, trying to stem the flow of blood, because the more blood he lost, the more likely it was that he lost consciousness.

She pushed against him, trying to free herself, but he continued to pin her, though he could feel his strength waning. He had to last a few more minutes. The distress call he'd sent out would automatically go to those Scanguards employees who were closest to his location—a task that was accomplished automatically by pinging all Scanguards owned cellphones.

He suddenly tasted his own blood in his mouth. "Oh, fuck!" His next breath was labored. "You... you punctured..." His voice broke.

He was losing his strength and eased off Anita. She freed herself from beneath him, while he braced one hand on the ground, trying to keep his torso upright. He looked at Anita, and with his last ounce of strength he snatched her wrist.

"Don't leave..."

"Cooper? Sweetheart?"

The female voice was accompanied by footfalls approaching fast. A moment later, Yvette Montgomery, his mother, came into view. She rushed toward him.

"Oh my God, my baby." She crouched down and pressed her hands on his wounds. "You were shot?"

He nodded, then managed to turn his head toward Anita. "Don't let her leave."

Yvette shot Anita a quick, assessing look, before she turned her attention back to him.

"Blood," he said.

Yvette's eyes widened, and with a quick move of her head she made an indication in Anita's direction.

"She knows."

Immediately, Yvette pulled a small flat bottle from the inside of her leather jacket and unscrewed the top of it. She set it to his lips, and he drank greedily. It was only a quarter pint, much less than the amount of blood in one of Scanguards standard bottles, but it would be enough for right now so he could at least be moved to another location.

Yvette stroked her hand over his head. "I'll take care of you now, sweetheart. I'll take you home. And then we can get the bullets out. Can you stand?"

He nodded, his hand still around Anita's wrist. He noticed that Anita had gone quiet and watched him and Yvette carefully. Was she planning to escape?

"And you're coming with us," he said with a look at Anita, taking a few steadying breaths. "You owe me that for having shot me. Twice."

Yvette's head whirled in Anita's direction. Simultaneously, her fangs extended, and she growled at Anita. "You shot my son? I'm going to—"

"Mom, don't hurt her. I love her."

24

———————

Anita's heart thundered out of control. What had she gotten herself into? When she'd seen Cooper transforming into a vampire before her eyes, she'd reacted out of instinct, protecting herself in a way her mother hadn't been able to so many years ago. Helen Diaz had fallen prey to a vampire, but Anita was determined not to follow in her mother's footsteps. She'd seen only one way to stop Cooper from attacking her: to shoot him. When he hadn't gone down after the first shot, she'd shot him a second time, but then he'd managed to wrestle the gun from her and overpowered her.

And just as she'd freed herself from him when he seemed to weaken due to his gunshot wounds, a beautiful woman in tight pants and a leather jacket had appeared. When she'd called him sweetheart and baby, Anita had assumed that she was Cooper's girlfriend—which would have added another lie to the mountain of lies he'd already dished up. But it was even worse: the woman was his mother, though she looked barely a couple of years older than Cooper. And as if that wasn't enough, she was a vampire too, and clearly a tigress bent on protecting her cub. Anita had never been as afraid as when the woman had glared at her, bloody murder in her eyes, her fangs extended as if she was ready to rip her throat out.

Yet Cooper had stopped her from inflicting bodily harm by announcing to his mother that he loved her. How could he love her? She'd just shot him twice. Besides, how could a creature who drank human blood love anybody? And she'd seen him drink blood. He'd asked his mother for it, and she'd given him a bottle. Was that what they did? Drain humans and fill their blood in bottles for them to consume whenever they needed it? It would certainly explain Janet's exsanguinated body, and also those of the other women who'd been killed in the same way.

"Fine. We'll talk about that later," Cooper's mother said with an annoyed look at her. "We've gotta go, before we draw attention to ourselves."

She helped Cooper up, and Anita rose with him, his hand still wrapped around her wrist.

"You can let go of her arm," Cooper's mother said to Cooper. Then she lashed a glare at Anita. "You won't run away, will you?"

The threat was clear. One move in the wrong direction, and the woman would take her down like a pack of coyotes took down a doe.

"No, I won't run," Anita assured her, and Cooper finally let go of her wrist.

Cooper motioned to the SUV, and moments later they were inside it, Cooper on the passenger seat, his mother driving. Anita was sitting in the back. She didn't even try to escape, too intimidated by the black-haired beauty. It was clear from whom Cooper got his looks.

Nobody spoke during the car ride, but she could hear Cooper's pained breathing, evidence that she'd punctured his lung with one of her bullets. How would they explain this to the hospital staff? In cases with gunshot wounds, they were obligated to call the police. And then the shit would hit the fan. Nobody would believe her that she'd acted in self-defense, because now that they were in the car, neither Cooper nor his mother showed any sign that they were vampires. They looked one hundred percent human.

When the car turned into a short driveway in front of a cottage near Coit Tower—which she could see on top of the hill—she was stunned, and for some reason, she had to make her concern known.

"He needs to go to a hospital." Anita leaned forward in the gap between the two front seats. "They have to take out the bullets, or he's gonna die." Why did she even care? Cooper was a vampire, or vampire hybrid, like he'd claimed. She shouldn't care what happened to him, but for some reason she did. How was that for hypocrisy?

Cooper turned his head to look at his mother. "See? She does care about me." His voice was weak, but he smiled.

"Could've fooled me." His mother's dry remark fit her skeptical facial expression.

"Mom, you fell in love with a vampire hunter," Cooper said. "And it all turned out okay in the end."

"Hmm."

It appeared that Cooper knew how to handle his mother. However, that didn't diminish the fear Anita felt every time Cooper's mother looked at her. Reluctantly, she got out of the car and followed the two to the pretty cottage that reminded her of a fairy tale. But she wasn't living in a fairy tale. By all accounts, she was entering the lion's den or, more aptly, the vampire's lair. She braced herself, expecting the interior to be furnished like a gothic crypt. But the interior was more *Town & Country* and less *Nosferatu*.

Inside the house, a dog barked excitedly, and a moment later, an excited golden retriever jumped up at Cooper.

"Lestat!" Cooper's mother admonished. "Down!"

Had she really called him Lestat like the vampire from Anne Rice's books?

"Into the kitchen. Sit down there, sweetheart."

With his mother's help, Cooper sat down on a kitchen chair.

"Make yourself useful and help him take his jacket off. What's your name?"

"A-Anita," she stuttered.

"I'm Yvette," she introduced herself as she turned to the kitchen counter and opened a drawer.

Meanwhile, Anita approached Cooper, hesitating when she saw that his face was distorted by pain. She'd done this to him. Hesitantly, she put her shaking hands on his windbreaker, when he turned his face fully to her and looked into her eyes.

"Don't worry, I'm not gonna bite," he said, his voice still breathy.

As gently as she could, Anita freed him of his jacket, then went for the buttons of his shirt, when Yvette stepped next to her.

"It's ruined anyway," Yvette said and ripped the shirt into pieces to take it off Cooper without him having to move his shoulder.

Anita gasped. With horror she stared at Yvette's fingers that were now topped with sharp barbs. She realized that these deadly tools could kill her in an instant, and the thought that Cooper had the same claws if and when he transformed into a vampire made her shudder. She'd been in bed with him the last two nights, and had let him touch her and make love to her with those hands. She'd even allowed him to handcuff her, not knowing that he could have easily killed her with those sharp claws.

"Mom, you're scaring her," Cooper said.

"Well, she should be scared! She hurt you!" Yvette gave her a sideways look then motioned to something behind her. "Get me a bottle of blood from the fridge. He needs to heal."

Anita followed the command instantly and opened the refrigerator. It was stocked with bottles and bottles of blood. They were all labeled with letters like A, AB and so on, and either a plus or a minus sign: blood type.

She looked over her shoulder. "Which blood type?"

"AB positive is his favorite."

Anita took a bottle with the label *AB+ bottled by Scanguards* from the shelf. AB positive was also her blood type. Was that why Cooper had slept with her? Because he was drawn to her blood?

When she turned on her heel, she saw that Yvette was using a sharp knife to cut open Cooper's chest wound, the one that had most likely pierced his lung. Cooper's face was a mask of pain.

"Without anesthesia?" Anita rushed to him.

"Doesn't work on vampires. Give him the blood," Yvette ordered.

Anita twisted off the cap and handed Cooper the bottle, but noticed that his hand was shaking from the pain, so she held the bottle to his mouth and helped him drink it. As he drank, she saw his fangs elongate and peek past his lips. Fascinated, she watched him swallow, saw how the pain seemed to seep from his features, and how his breathing normalized.

When she swept her gaze up from his lips to his eyes, she realized that Cooper was looking at her. His brown eyes shimmered golden, and she couldn't tear herself away from the sight. Whoever had coined the phrase that the eyes were the windows to the soul wasn't wrong, because what she saw in Cooper's eyes now was more than just his desire for her. She saw a part of Cooper now that he'd hidden from her.

When the bottle was empty, Anita set it down on the kitchen table. Then she suddenly felt Cooper take her hand and lead it to his lips. She held her breath. Would he bite her now that he'd regained his strength?

"This is gonna hurt." The words came from Yvette and were directed at Cooper.

Anita shot her gaze to Yvette, who had widened the entry point of the gunshot wound and was now pushing pliers into the opening.

"Fuck!" Cooper hissed and dropped her hand.

"Hold still!" Yvette applied more force to the crude make-shift medical tool. "Anita, either hold him down, or distract him."

It was easier said than done. She wasn't strong enough to hold down a vampire. Had Cooper been human then she could have managed, but even in his weakened state Cooper was still stronger than a human male. It left her only one other choice: to distract him.

Against her better judgement, she cupped his face with both hands and sank her lips onto his. Cooper gasped and jolted for a brief second, before he swept his tongue into her mouth and kissed her. She felt an instant surge of pleasure charge through her body, heating her as if he was infusing her with hot lava. Her head was spinning again. She was clearly going crazy. Less than a half hour ago, she'd shot Cooper, and now she was making out with him as if they were two teenagers on the backseat of his parents' car.

"I came as quickly as I could."

The male voice made her sever the kiss. The man who'd entered looked like a more rugged version of Cooper and couldn't be more than five or six years older than him.

"Haven, thank God!" Yvette said. "Help me with getting this bullet out."

"Hey, Son, you okay?"

Cooper nodded.

Haven turned his gaze to her. "So first you shoot him, then you kiss him? Looks like you two have issues."

Anita didn't know how to reply. She looked at Cooper for help, but Cooper simply smirked. No help there. When Haven assisted Yvette in digging the bullet out of Cooper's chest, Anita perused him more thoroughly. So this was Cooper's father. She would have never believed it before tonight. No wonder his uncle and aunt and their spouses had all looked so young. That was the secret he and Wesley had whispered about: the secret that they were all vampires. But how did Haven already know that she'd been the one to shoot Cooper? Neither Cooper nor Yvette had made any phone calls on the way to the house.

Cooper suddenly let out a loud grunt.

"First one's out," Yvette reported and let out a long breath.

"Let me handle the second one, Baby," Haven offered. Then he looked at his son. "Have you had enough blood?"

"Yes, I'm good, Dad. I can already feel my lung healing. It's easier to breathe again."

Anita had to agree with Cooper's assertion. His voice was stronger again, and he breathed evenly. Was that how quickly vampires healed?

This time, Yvette held Cooper down, while Haven cut into the gunshot wound below his clavicle and proceeded to dig the bullet out. Anita had to look away, feeling queasy, though blood had never before bothered her. But seeing somebody she cared about being operated on without anesthesia was a little too much even for her strong stomach.

She didn't understand why she wasn't more disgusted by the fact that Cooper was a vampire. She still had feelings for him, and it was hard to admit that to herself. But right now, when she looked at how vulnerable he was, she regretted that she'd shot him.

"Bullet's out, Coop," Haven said.

"Thank God." Yvette sighed and proceeded to wipe the blood off his chest with a wet towel. "You should rest until you're fully healed. Sleep for a couple of hours."

"Mom, I'm fine," Cooper protested.

Anita caught his gaze on her, before he looked back at his parents. "I think I owe Anita an explanation."

Anita swallowed hard, anxious about the things she would learn about him now. What if she didn't like the truth? What if the truth was too difficult to swallow?

25

Cooper caught Anita's apprehensive facial expression. She'd surprised him tonight. And not just because she'd shot him. She'd also surprised him when she'd expressed her concern about his health, wanting him to be brought to a hospital. And she hadn't tried to flee. Yvette was undoubtedly the reason for that. She'd probably scared Anita sufficiently so she didn't even try to run. But the biggest surprise had been when she'd kissed him while his mother had dug out the bullet from his chest. At that moment, he'd assumed he'd passed out and was merely imagining Anita's lips on his.

After drinking the bottle of blood, he felt better, and he could feel his body starting to heal with the help of the bottled human blood. While he wasn't ready to physically exert himself, he had enough energy to talk. It was time to tell Anita everything she needed to know so she could—hopefully—accept him for what he was. But he also wanted some privacy.

"Mom, Dad, why don't you give us a little time alone, so I can talk to Anita?"

Yvette shook her head. "Not gonna happen! She shot you. Twice! What if she hurts you again?"

Haven put his arm around her. "Baby, she doesn't look like she's gonna hurt him again. Didn't you see them kiss?"

"Hmm! She wouldn't be the first woman to kiss a man, while stabbing him in the back."

Haven shrugged and grimaced apologetically. "Sorry, Son, I tried. But you know your mother. She's not gonna leave your side until she knows you're safe."

"I guess I already knew that." Cooper motioned to the door. "Can we at least go to the living room, so I can sit on something a little more comfortable while I recover?"

Hearing no objections, Cooper got up. He nodded to Anita. "Come, let's talk." Looking over his shoulder at his parents, he added, "With two chaperones."

In the comfortably appointed living room, Cooper sat down on the sofa. Lestat, the golden retriever his parents had gotten after their second dog had died, jumped onto the couch and put his head in his lap.

Automatically, Cooper petted him. "Hey, Lestat, miss me?"

The dog looked at him with adoring eyes. Cooper watched as Anita sat down in one of the armchairs, and his parents took their seats. For a moment, there was silence.

"Anita," he started, "this wasn't exactly how I wanted you to find out that I'm not human."

Anita swallowed visibly. "That makes two of us."

"Well, let me start with the most important thing: you're safe with me and my family. We don't hurt people."

She glanced at Yvette and Haven. "What about the blood? Is that what you all do? Drain humans and then fill up bottles with their blood? I mean I saw the puncture wounds on Janet's body. They fit your fangs—"

"Not mine per se," Cooper interrupted quickly so the conversation didn't go down the wrong path. "But it was a vampire who killed Janet. As for my parents and myself, and our friends at Scanguards, we don't drain humans. And we certainly don't kill them."

"Then how do you explain all those bottles of blood in the fridge?" She pointed in the direction of the kitchen. "That's several gallons."

"It comes from a blood bank." He looked at his parents. "Dad? Wanna jump in here?"

Haven nodded. "How much do you want her to know?"

"Everything."

"All right. Anita, it's true. The blood is procured through a medical shell company owned by Scanguards, the company we all work for. It's distributed to us free of charge to discourage us from feeding directly from humans and risk exposure."

Cooper noticed the perplexed look on Anita's face. "Are you saying that everybody at Scanguards is a vampire?"

"Many of them are," Cooper replied, making her look back at him. "You've met two: Benjamin and Vanessa are both vampire hybrids."

"And the young woman in the morgue? Buffy?"

"She's human."

"And she knows? Is she not afraid of... you know..." She made a motion toward him and his parents.

"Her stepfather is a vampire. And she has a half-brother who's a vampire hybrid, half human, half vampire."

For a moment, Anita's forehead furrowed. "You said earlier that you're a vampire hybrid. But..." She pointed to Yvette and Haven. "Wouldn't that mean that either your father or your mother had to be human? I've seen your mother's fangs, which would only leave your father, but he looks almost as young as you."

"We're both vampires," Haven confirmed. "But vampire females are infertile—"

Yvette put a hand on Haven's arm. "I had a treatment with human stem cells so I could give birth to Cooper. That's why he's half human. But that's not important."

Anita nodded. "Okay. So, you all are saying that you don't bite people." She looked at each of them in turn, until her eyes landed on Cooper. "Is that true?"

Cooper cleared his voice. He didn't want to lie to her. "Mostly."

"Mostly?"

"Ahm, there are times when a vampire bites somebody..." He looked at his parents and he added, "I wouldn't mind a cold glass of water."

"I'll get it for you," Yvette said quickly and jumped up.

"I'll help you," Haven added and followed her in the kitchen.

They were alone. Cooper looked back at Anita. "A vampire or a vampire hybrid will bite his lover during sex. It heightens the pleasure."

Anita huffed. "For whom? The vampire?"

"For both of them." He tipped his chin in the direction of the kitchen. "My parents do it all the time. I've bitten women during sex before, humans and vampires."

"Against their will?"

He shook his head. He wasn't a cad. "Never. Though I have to admit I've been tempted with you. More than ever before. But I kept myself in check."

Anita's hands trembled visibly, and she clasped them over the arms of the armchair. "But you were close to doing it, weren't you? That's why you grazed my lips with your fang. You almost bit me."

"Yes, I almost did. I can't deny that. But I didn't want to do it without your permission." Just thinking about it right now made him salivate. "You have my word that I won't do anything against your will."

Slowly, she nodded, but didn't show any outward sign of what she was feeling. She'd slipped into her role of the sheriff's deputy again, stoic, strong, and emotionless. "I understand. Tell me about the serial killer. He's a vampire. Are you protecting him?"

Cooper vehemently shook his head. "No! Why would you even think that? I have no idea who he is."

"You knew all along though, didn't you?"

"When I heard about the exsanguinated body, I knew it, and seeing Janet's body only confirmed it."

"So how were you able to keep this from the police? Is the chief of police a vampire?"

"Mike? No, he's human. But he's worked with us since he was a detective and discovered our existence. He funnels all vampire-related crimes to Scanguards so we can take care of them."

"Take care of them? Do you mean that in a mafia kind of way?"

He chuckled. "What I told you about Scanguards is the truth. We investigate crimes that are too complex for the SFPD. All I left out is that these crimes always involve a vampire. We're better equipped to deal with them. Officers from the SFPD wouldn't know how to fight them. There would be many needless deaths. We keep the city safe."

"Safe from your own people?"

"Trust me, those *people* have nothing in common with us. A rogue vampire puts us all in danger. We eliminate them, or if we believe they can be rehabilitated, we'll incarcerate them in a vampire prison."

Her eyes widened. "You kill vampires?"

"To keep humans and everybody at Scanguards safe, yes."

Cooper looked toward the kitchen, where his parents were talking quietly. It appeared that Haven was trying to convince Yvette to give them more privacy.

"So, what happened tonight? Why did you try to attack me?"

"I wasn't trying to attack you."

"Could've fooled me. Your fangs were out, and your eyes were glaring red. You were coming toward me." Her chest heaved as if she was reliving the incident.

"I smelled somebody near you in the parking lot. I couldn't see his face, but I know he was a vampire."

"That doesn't make sense." Anita leaned forward, becoming more the combative woman he knew. "If you couldn't see his face, you couldn't see his fangs either."

"That's true, but I recognized by his aura that he was a vampire. And by his smell."

"Aura?"

"It can only be seen by preternatural creatures. It's invisible to the human eye."

"And you're telling me that you could smell him from afar?" she asked with a good deal of skepticism.

"Yes, a vampire's sense of smell is extremely sensitive. Better than a dog's. I smelled the vampire. I didn't know who he was, but I was worried. He was lurking, and considering that a vampire who's a serial killer is loose in this town, I decided to be careful and get you out of there quickly. But my adrenaline was spiking, and I realized too late that I showed my vampire face to you."

Haven and Yvette entered the living room. Yvette set two glasses of water on the coffee table.

"Your dad and I have to go to work." Yvette looked directly at Anita. "And Anita, I'm keeping your gun. And I took the liberty to check your handbag for any other weapons. Know this: if you hurt my boy again, I *will* come after you."

"Yvette," Haven admonished. "Cooper can look after himself."

"Thanks, Dad."

When they left the house, and the door fell shut behind them, Anita let out an audible sigh.

"Has anybody ever told you that your mother is scary?"

"She can have that effect on people who don't know her." He smirked. "Luckily, Dad knows how to handle her. And now that they've finally left us alone..."

Instantly, a panicked look crossed Anita's face. She jumped up, and Lestat woke from his slumber and jumped off the couch. He barked. Anita gasped as if she expected the dog or Cooper to attack her.

"Lestat, go to bed!"

The dog looked at him, then trotted to the soft dog bed in the corner near the fireplace.

"Please sit down again, Anita. I'm not going to hurt you. I was just going to suggest that we talk about more personal things, since we have some privacy."

"Oh." Anita slowly sat back down. She folded her hands in her lap, then took a deep breath. "I've encountered him before."

"Whom?" Cooper asked, not following her rapid change of subject.

"The serial killer."

26

———————

Anita wasn't ready to talk about something personal with Cooper. She was fully aware of the elephant in the room: Cooper had said that he loved her to make it clear to his mother that he wouldn't allow Yvette to hurt her. A vampire loved her? Even though he'd told her the previous night that he was falling in love with her, she hadn't expected to hear him tell his mother of all people. Anita had no idea how to react to it. Therefore, she opted for changing the subject and discussing the case further. She needed more time to digest what she'd learned about Cooper so far, and what it meant for her, and for the case. Could she really trust him?

"You saw him when Janet Fillmore disappeared in Elko?"

"No, I didn't see his face then. It was too dark, and I was too far away. But I saw his face when he took my mother twenty-one years ago. I saw his fangs and his glowing red eyes."

"You saw his fangs? You knew he was a vampire? Why didn't you tell me?"

"Probably for the same reason you didn't tell me that you're a vampire. You wouldn't have believed me." She shrugged. "Had I known you were a vampire, I would have told you right away that I recognized his face from the sketch."

Would she? Or would she have thought the worst and assumed that Cooper was helping the serial killer? In fact, she had acted exactly like that when she'd shot him, assuming he was bad because he was a vampire. But what if vampires were just like any other species? Some were bad, and some were good. Just like humans.

"I'm sorry that your mother was taken by a vampire," Cooper said, his voice soft and full of compassion. "I know it was a long time ago, but it must hurt nevertheless."

Anita nodded and tried to suppress the tears. "Nobody believed me that she was taken." A sob tore from her chest. "My father thought she'd left us."

"Did you tell him that you saw the man?"

"Yes. Many times. But he thought I was lying." Another sob, and the tears streamed down her face, blurring her vision. "And all these years, I pushed those memories back, because maybe I had made it up. I was only nine. But now..."

She felt a hand on her shoulder and looked up. Cooper pulled her up into an embrace. "I know, Baby, you were right all along. We'll get him, and he'll pay for what he's done. I promise you that."

Anita rested her head on his shoulder and allowed the tears to flow and Cooper to console her with his embrace and his comforting words.

"Scanguards and I will make sure that he can't hurt anybody else."

Anita sobbed, but she finally knew that she would get justice for her mother, and for all the other women who'd met with the same fate. And maybe it was her fate to do this with the help of a man like Cooper, a man who wasn't human, a man who had preternatural strength to take the killer down.

She was suddenly fully aware of the fact that Cooper wasn't wearing a shirt. She felt his warm skin against her cheek, and his heartbeat reverberate against her palm that was resting on his chest. It beat much faster than hers. Worried, she lifted her head.

"Your heart is beating so fast. Are you okay?"

He met her gaze and smiled. "I'm better than ever. A vampire's heart beats twice as fast as that of a human to give us our superior strength and speed."

Cooper used his thumb to wipe away her tears. Then he pointed to the bullet wounds. "See? The skin has already closed, and I'm healing inside."

Fascinated by the rapid healing process, she brushed her fingers over the wounds. "Does it still hurt?"

"A little." He put two fingers under her chin to tilt it up. "So, about that apology..."

"What apology?"

"The one you haven't given me yet for shooting me." He smirked.

"I'm not gonna buy you a drink right now. I don't think you should be having alcohol."

Cooper chuckled, and the dimples in his cheeks made him look younger and so innocent that she could barely believe what he really was. "Alcohol actually has no effect on me. But I'm not interested in you buying me a drink... However, I wouldn't say no to a kiss."

Anita sucked in a breath of air, searching for an answer. Did she want to kiss him? She hadn't been disgusted when she'd kissed him to distract him from the pain. On the contrary, it had felt just as wonderful as when they'd made love. But she knew what a kiss would lead to. They were alone, and once she kissed him, they would both want more. Was she ready for that? For sleeping with a vampire?

"I know you're not afraid of me."

Cooper brushed his lips over hers in a featherlight kiss. The tenderness surprised her.

"What if you can't control yourself?"

"Do you have your handcuffs on you?"

"In my handbag."

He kissed her tenderly for just a few seconds, before severing the contact. "Why don't you cuff me to the bed in my old room?

Her breath hitched. "Why?"

Cooper's hand was on her nape now, gently caressing her and making her shiver with pleasure, his mouth only an inch from hers.

"You could explore my body, without me being able to stop you."

With his other hand on her lower back, he pressed his groin to hers.

She could feel the hard outline of his cock beneath his pants. Cooper was seducing her, and she had no defenses against him. She was putty in his arms, and the fact that he was a vampire didn't matter right now, because what she felt was the man, the lover who'd given her pleasure before.

"I mean, now that you know that I'm a vampire hybrid, wouldn't you want me to submit to you? Wouldn't you want to be in charge and find out what it feels like to have power over somebody?"

Heat shot into her cheeks. What he was offering excited her. "Just like when you handcuffed me."

"Yes."

Cooper sucked her upper lip into his mouth and licked over it. The touch sent a delicious shudder down her spine, and her eyes closed.

"I loved making love to you when you were handcuffed," he murmured. "Now do the same to me."

She opened her eyes and kissed him, unable to resist the draw he had on her any longer. Maybe it was reckless of her to do this, but Cooper had had so many opportunities to hurt her, yet he hadn't. She put both arms around him to press herself closer to him and felt him intensify the kiss.

For a brief second, he drew his head back. "Oh, Babe." Then his lips were back on hers, and he delved into her mouth, dueling with her tongue, while farther below, he rocked his pelvis against hers, and his hand slid down to her ass, grabbing her possessively.

This was the man she knew, the passionate lover who put her pleasure before his. The man who made her feel desired and cherished. Did it really matter that he was a vampire? Did it matter that he drank human blood? What if he wanted hers? Could she allow that?

There were still so many questions she had. Questions about immortality, blood, and relationships. Questions about love, and how long a love between a vampire and a human could last. And she could see the future heartbreak already: a human aged, and a vampire didn't. The end was already programmed in.

But right now, she didn't want to think about that.

Breathlessly, she ripped her mouth from his. "I'm so sorry, Cooper. I nearly killed you."

He pressed his forehead against hers, breathing just as hard. "Not likely. The bullets weren't silver."

"I thought silver kills werewolves. That is if they exist too."

"How about we talk about all that later? I'll give you a crash course on vampires."

Anita didn't protest. His lips were back on hers, and he was virtually devouring her, kissing her with such fervor that she let go of the anxiety of the past hours. There was no doubt in her mind that he desired her and would never hurt her. Cooper's kiss was all-consuming, maybe because the secret he'd kept from her was out now. Nothing stood between them and the desire they felt for each other.

Was it love that she felt? Love for a vampire? She pushed the thought back into the recesses of her mind. She would examine her feelings later. Right now, all she wanted was to feel the physical pleasure Cooper could give her, and she him.

They staggered rather than walked into Cooper's childhood room, snatching her handbag in passing. She barely noticed her surroundings. All that was important was that there was a bed. Freeing herself from Cooper's arms, Anita gave him a little shove so he fell onto the bed. She pulled the handcuffs out of her handbag and bent over him.

He kissed her neck, while she took one arm, clicked a handcuff around the wrist, then looped it around a metal rod of the headboard.

"Give me your other arm," she demanded.

"In a second." He palmed her breasts with his free hand, squeezing them through the fabric of her shirt. "You're not wearing a bra."

"Because I'm on vacation."

"I like it." He slipped his hand underneath her top and caressed her naked skin, before he took one nipple between thumb and index finger, teasing it.

A moan escaped her, before he removed his hand and reached for the headboard. Finally, she was able to handcuff him properly. She tugged on the cuffs. They held.

Anita swung herself over him, straddling him. He looked up at her, his eyes suddenly shimmering golden.

Curiosity made her ask, "Your eyes... why are they golden now?"

"Because I'm aroused. Can't you feel it?"

He thrust his hips upwards, and Anita became aware of the hard bulge in his pants.

"Hard to overlook."

He cast her a seductive look. "Very hard."

"Then I guess I'll need to give you some relief. I don't want you to suffer needlessly."

Anita scooted down on him. With every inch she moved, she kissed other parts of him. First his neck that he so obligingly offered as if he wanted *her* to bite *him*. At the thought, everything female inside her awoke. She slid farther down on him, caressing his muscular, hairless chest, and sucked one nipple into her mouth.

Cooper arched off the bed, thrusting his chest toward her. A strangled moan issued from his lips, making her smile. She had power over him, over a vampire, a creature so strong he could easily crush her with his hands. A thought hit her, and she lifted her head.

"How strong are you actually? Can you break the handcuffs?"

A sheepish grin traveled over his face. "They're not made of silver, so... yes, I could. But I don't want to. I'm enjoying this too much."

She rolled her eyes, smiling nevertheless. "You could've said so earlier."

"And rob us both of the illusion that I'm at your mercy?" He shook his head. "Now, let's pretend I can't get out of the handcuffs, and do what you want with me."

She lifted herself onto her knees and moved farther down on him, until she could rest on his upper thighs. She placed her hand on the front of his pants, feeling the hardness of the bulge there.

Cooper hissed in a breath.

"I haven't started yet," she murmured, before she opened the button of his pants, and pulled the zipper down as far as she could.

Again, she lifted herself on her knees, and Cooper helped her by lifting his butt off the mattress so she could pull his pants and boxer briefs down sufficiently to free his cock and balls from their prison. She lowered herself back onto his thighs and wrapped her hand around his cock while cradling his balls in the palm of her other hand.

"Fuck, Babe!"

She noticed him clench his jaw and press his head into the pillow, while his cock pulsed in her hand. "Definitely very hard," she murmured. "Are all vampires like you?"

"How?"

"Always hard, with endless stamina, skillful, and adventurous?"

"Probably. Everything we feel and do is more intense. We have more stamina, and getting hard with you in the room is just automatic. I've been hard from the moment I first saw you."

She pulled her lower lip between her teeth, his confession sending a spear of heat through her core. "So that's why you didn't free yourself when I arrested you."

"Yes." He glanced down at his erection. "'Cause I was hoping that maybe you and I could pleasure each other."

She tugged on his cock, moving the thick shaft up and down in her hand.

"I guess I was right," Cooper added on a moan, his long, dark eyelashes fluttering.

"I'm glad I arrested you," Anita whispered and lowered her head to his groin. "So I get to do this."

She licked over the head of his erection, before she closed her lips around it and slid down on him as far as she could.

"Fuck!"

Cooper's curse was accompanied by his hips jerking. She put one hand around the base of his shaft, before she lifted her head a few inches, until only the thick head of his cock was still in her mouth. Then she took him deep again and began sucking him in a slow and steady rhythm, holding him firmly at the root and brushing her fingers over his balls. Cooper's moans bounced off the walls in the small room, accompanied by the sound of the rattling handcuffs fastened to the metal headboard.

The sound of a door opening, and somebody gasping made Anita release Cooper's cock and whirl her head in the direction of the door. A young woman stood there frozen, staring at them in stunned surprise.

27

"Lydia!"

In shock, Cooper stared at his sister, while Anita scrambled to pull on the duvet and managed to cover his midsection with a corner of it, her face as red as the blood that thundered through her veins. Her embarrassment was impossible to overlook. Cooper didn't care about his sister seeing him half-naked and in the middle of a sexual act, after all, vampires had a high sex drive, and his sister knew that better than anybody else. For a while, she'd gone through men like underwear, trying on a new one every day. But Anita had probably grown up with other sensibilities when it came to sex.

"I'm not sure why Mom asked me to check on you." Lydia motioned to him and Anita. "By the looks of it, you're doing just fine." She smirked. "Better than fine."

It was no surprise that their mother was responsible for this rude interruption. "It appears Mom still has trust issues."

Lydia tipped her chin toward the handcuffs. "I can see why."

"That's just for fun." He looked at Anita. "Anita, this is my older sister, Lydia. Lydia, this is my, uhm..." He rattled on the handcuffs. "... my keeper."

"Hey, Anita," Lydia said with a grin. "Don't mind if I don't shake your hand, but..." She tossed a pointed look at the spot where the duvet covered his groin.

Anita's face turned even redder if that was possible. "Uhm, hi, Lydia, nice to meet you."

"How about you tell Mom that I'm perfectly fine, and she doesn't need to worry about me," Cooper suggested. "As you can see, I'm in good hands."

"Do you want me to give her all the details?" Lydia asked, still not making a move.

"Not necessary. Bye, Lydia. I would say, stay and chat, but as you can see, this is not a good time. I'm a little tied up right now."

Chuckling, Lydia looked at Anita, giving her a once-over. "I hope my brother isn't behaving too selfishly." She winked and turned on her heel. "Have fun, guys."

He heard Lydia leave the house. Anita was already jumping off the bed.

"Oh my God," she cried out, breathing irregularly and fanning herself with both hands. "Your sister saw me give you a blow job. Oh my God! What are we gonna do now?"

"Continue?" Cooper asked with a smirk.

"Are you crazy? What if your mother interrupts us next? No, no! I have to get out of here."

"Easy, Baby. Breathe. Nothing happened. My sister doesn't care." He pulled on his restraints. "But if you don't want to stay here, then uncuff me, and we'll go back to Wesley's house."

Anita looked as if she didn't know what to do, turning on her own axis twice, before she seemed to realize what she needed to do. She pulled a key out of her handbag, and unlocked the handcuffs. When he was free, Cooper rose and pulled his pants up and zipped up. Then he put his arms around her.

"It's okay."

"This has never happened to me." Slowly, Anita's breathing settled into a steadier rhythm. "Your sister is beautiful."

"You're more beautiful," he murmured into her ear and pressed a kiss to her cheek.

"She doesn't look like you or your parents at all."

"She's adopted."

"Oh. Does that mean she's human?"

Cooper shook his head. "No, she's a vampire hybrid like me. Her parents were murdered the night she was born. So my parents raised her as their daughter."

"That's so sweet of your parents to do that."

"They are good people. You'll see when you really get to know them. My mother is a very loving woman. She almost lost my father when they first met. That's why now when something happens to the people she loves, she's like a tigress."

"What happened with your dad?"

"He, Wesley, and Katie were the three children of a witch. They were supposed to be the three most powerful witches in the world: the power of three. But another witch captured them and was about to harness the power for evil. So my father decided to kill himself to destroy the power."

Anita gasped, staring at him wide-eyed. "Oh my God!"

"He stabbed himself, hoping that my mother would reach him in time to save him. She did. She had to turn him into a vampire."

"So he's now a witch slash vampire?"

Cooper shook his head. "The powers of a witch can't live in a vampire's body." He opened the closet and pulled an old T-shirt out of it and slipped it over. "Wesley is the only one who still has his powers and practices witchcraft. He's actually very accomplished."

"And your aunt, Katie?"

"She's almost completely human." He motioned to the door. "Let's go."

In the kitchen, Cooper grabbed his jacket, snatched his car keys from the table, and took Anita's hand.

"Are you okay to drive?" Anita asked.

He leaned closer. "Baby, I was well enough to have sex. I'm well enough to drive."

In the car, Cooper made a call to headquarters to check in and report that he'd seen an unknown vampire lurking in North Beach. None of the other staff on canvassing duty had reported anything of note yet. Nobody had seen Janet or the suspect.

Cooper disconnected the phone and gave Anita a sideways look. "There's no need for us to go back to HQ tonight. It's best if we rest for a while. It's late anyway. You must be tired."

"Just a little. So much happened tonight. I'm too wound up to sleep right now. Tell me more about your family. You said that Katie is human, but if she's your father's sister, I assume she's much older than she looks."

"She still has the genes that identify her as a witch. That's why she ages only incrementally. But even if she were one hundred percent human, she wouldn't age at all, because she's blood-bonded to a vampire."

"Blood-bonded? What does that mean?"

"Luther, her vampire mate and husband, shares his immortality with her." He glanced at Anita, wondering how much about the blood-bond she was ready to hear.

"Are you saying he turned her into a vampire like your mother did with your father?"

"No, not at all. Katie's still human, but there's a ritual that bonds a vampire to his mate. They drink each other's blood, and through this bond, Katie stays young and won't age, unless Luther dies."

For a moment, Anita contemplated his words. "Wow. I never thought there's such a thing. I mean, in the lore, a vampire always has to turn the human to bestow immortality... But if that's not the case... If you don't need to turn somebody... and you can still be with that person..." She looked at him from the side, suddenly silent.

Cooper took her hand and squeezed it, glad that he'd told her that there was a way they could be together, while not putting any pressure on her to make a decision. He pulled Anita's hand to his lips and kissed her knuckles.

When he gazed into her eyes, he saw affection shining back at him. There was no fear left in them, no apprehension, no horror. The Anita who looked at him now was the woman who understood him. The woman he wanted to be with.

"Yes, a human can be with a vampire and be very happy. I have friends, other vampire hybrids, who're bonded to human women. I'll introduce you to them, if you want to talk to them... you know, to find out what it's like to live with a vampire hybrid."

Anita took a deep breath. There was a short pause, before she spoke. "You said to your mother that you loved me."

Cooper slowed the car and turned into the driveway of Wesley's house, before looking at her. "It shouldn't come as a surprise to you. I told you before that I'm falling in love with you. But I don't want you to feel that you have to make a decision about me, about us..." He pressed the garage door opener and waited for the gate to lift. "I would have chosen a more romantic situation to tell you that I love you, but I had to make sure my mother knew not to hurt you."

Anita leaned over the divide between their seats and put one hand on his nape, pulling his head to her. "I'm glad you said it. It helped me be less afraid." She brushed her lips over his in a featherlight touch. "And more hopeful."

"Hopeful about what?"

"That we might have something... that this is developing past a one-night stand."

He smiled. "Anita, this was never a one-night stand to begin with. At least not for me. Any man lucky to have you in his bed just once, is a fool if he lets you get away. And I don't mean that in a stalker kind of way."

"I get that."

She pressed her lips to his, and he accepted the invitation and kissed her tenderly, before he severed the kiss. "We'd better go inside."

He drove into the garage, and the gate lowered behind him. They got out of the car, and Cooper took Anita's hand as they walked into the corridor from where a staircase led up into the house. At the bottom of the staircase, Anita suddenly stopped and turned to him.

"Something wrong?" he asked and glanced around to ascertain if they were still alone. They were.

"Yesterday, when you brought me here, I'd forgotten my handbag in your car. When I came down to get it, I thought I saw Virginia disappear in front of my eyes. There." She motioned to the end of the corridor. "Is that a vampire skill? To disappear into thin air?"

Cooper chuckled. "Virginia isn't a vampire. She's a Stealth Guardian."

"A what?"

"A preternatural creature sworn to protect humans from demons. She can make herself and others invisible, and she can walk through walls. That's probably what you saw."

He didn't elaborate why Virginia had walked into the room at the end of the corridor, where a portal was located that allowed her to teleport to other locations in the world within seconds. It wasn't his secret to share, and the existence of the Stealth Guardian portal had to be kept a secret from outsiders. However, he hoped that Anita would soon become a trusted member of their extended family. Sometime very soon.

28

Anita could barely digest the news that vampires and witches existed, but the fact that creatures who could make themselves invisible and walk through walls lived among them, was on a whole other level of out-of-this-world unbelievable. Yet, she had to believe it, because that's what she'd witnessed: Virginia using her Stealth Guardian powers.

Anita looked in the mirror in the bathroom between her room and Cooper's. She didn't look any different from this morning, yet she felt different. She was falling in love with a vampire. Tonight would be the first time she slept with him with the full knowledge of what he was, and the thought both excited and scared her.

She opened the door and walked into his room. Cooper sat in bed, his chest naked, the duvet covering his lower half. He turned his face to her, and she noticed how his eyes began to shimmer golden as he gazed at her. She wore a thin, very short nightgown with spaghetti straps and a plunging neckline that reached halfway to her navel, barely covering her breasts.

"You look gorgeous," he murmured, his words beckoning her to approach.

Barefoot, she walked to the bed, her chest lifting with every inhale. She was fully aware of her body now. Her nipples were hard, and she felt the fabric chafing, while Cooper's gaze dropped to her breasts as if they were powerful magnets meant to draw a man's attention.

"Lift the duvet," she demanded.

Cooper complied instantly and pulled the duvet to the other side of the bed, laying himself bare. Anita sucked in an audible breath. His cock stood erect, hard and beautiful, the head almost purple from the amount of blood in the veins snaking around the shaft.

Anita pushed one spaghetti strap off her shoulder, causing the fabric that had covered one breast to drop. Cooper's cock jerked in response.

"Tease," he murmured.

She smiled and pushed the other spaghetti strap off her shoulder, making the nightgown slide down her body and pool around her feet. Cooper ran his eyes over her naked body, before their gazes met. Slowly, without haste, she slid onto the bed and straddled him. His hands were on her waist instantly, and she lifted herself on her knees and reached for his cock.

He let out a moan, and she brought his cock to her center, its tip already nudging at her moist folds, before she let go of it. She lowered herself by half an inch, and felt the bulbous head part her nether lips.

"Fuck!" Cooper hissed, while he held her hips in a vise grip.

"Too much for my sensitive vampire lover?" she asked, bringing her face to his, enjoying a surge of power. The power a woman had over a man.

"I'm trying my best not to lose control," he gritted through clenched teeth.

Anita brushed her lips over his. "Tell me what that's like... to lose control..."

He let out a ragged breath, while he thrust his cock an inch deeper into her. "Don't toy with me, Anita. I'm seconds away from my fangs emerging."

A spear of heat charged through her core, and she realized that it wasn't fear but excitement that filled her.

"Why don't you show them to me?" She could barely believe what she was asking him. Had she lost her mind?

"Are you sure?"

Was she? "Yes."

They locked eyes, and slowly, his lips parted, and she saw two beautiful rows of even white teeth. She blinked, and his two canines lengthened and changed their shape, turning into two razor-sharp fangs.

Anita swallowed hard, unable to tear her eyes from the sight. She lifted her hand to his face, wanting to touch them to confirm that she wasn't hallucinating, when Cooper suddenly snatched her wrist, stopping her. The action made her drop her hips, and she impaled herself fully on his cock.

Anita gasped, and Cooper echoed her.

"Fuck!" he cursed, pressing his head against the headboard, breathing raggedly.

"I'm sorry," she murmured. "I only wanted to t—"

"—touch them?" he asked, completing her sentence. "I know."

Something akin to disappointment flooded her. "You don't want me to?"

He let go of her wrist. "I do, but you should know first what that does to me."

Curious, she drew her head back. "What do you mean?"

"If you were to touch my fangs..." He hesitated. "Or lick them, it would feel to me as if you were sucking my cock. That's how intense a pleasure it is."

Anita stared at him, fascinated. "Your fangs are erogenous zones?"

He nodded. "Do you still want to touch them?"

She shook her head. "I want to lick them."

"Fuck, Babe. This is gonna kill me for sure."

But Cooper didn't push her back. Instead, he placed his hand on her nape, caressing her skin and making her shiver, while he pulled her to him gently. She moved her face closer until her lips were hovering over his.

"Be careful," he murmured, "they're very sharp."

She heard the warning, but it didn't matter. She wanted to experience this, wanted to know what it felt like to lick a vampire's fangs, to play with fire. Because that's what she was doing: tempting fate. But she couldn't back away now. She wanted this.

Cooper remained motionless, his breath shallow, waiting for her to take action. Anita cupped his face, and licked her tongue over his right fang. Cooper's cock jerked inside her, and a moan dislodged from his chest. Encouraged by his reaction, she licked over the other fang, eliciting the same reaction. A feeling of power surged through her at the knowledge that she could give this powerful man pleasure by simply licking his fangs.

Without thinking, she began to kiss him, not caring that his fangs were still extended, and that she could easily cut her tongue and lips on the sharp instruments. Cooper moaned into her mouth, kissing her back, his fangs grazing her lips. All of a sudden, she felt herself being lifted off him, and before she knew what was happening, she lay on her stomach, and Cooper pulled her hips up. Before she could brace herself, he plunged his rock-hard cock into her from behind, the sheets beneath her absorbing her surprised gasp.

"See what you're doing to me?"

His voice sounded different now, much gruffer, but she wasn't afraid of him or of the ferocity with which he took her. On the contrary. She loved feeling the untamed beast in him, the vampire who was all powerful. She loved how he thrust deep and hard, how he gripped her hips with his hands, so she couldn't escape.

She managed to lift her head just long enough to answer him, "I love it when you lose control."

"Goddamn it, Anita!" he cried out, and pulled out of her.

Before she could protest, he rolled her on her back, pushed her thighs apart, and plunged back into her. Breathing hard, she wrapped her legs around him, and put her hands on his ass to force him deeper into her.

Cooper slowed his thrusts and brought his face to hers. "I will never get enough of you."

He didn't give her a chance to reply and kissed her. His fangs were gone, but his kiss wasn't any less tantalizing. Combined with his relentless thrusts into her drenched pussy, he showed her the desire he felt for her. When he shifted his angle slightly, she felt the approach of her orgasm. She tensed, and a moment later, her entire body seemed to float on an ocean of bliss. She moaned into Cooper's mouth and felt his cock spasm inside her. The warm spray of his semen that followed only intensified her pleasure.

Cooper severed the kiss and braced himself on his elbows and knees. He brushed a few strands of her hair from her face. She looked into his eyes, eyes that were still shimmering golden.

"I'm sorry I was so rough with you."

"Don't be. I loved it. I've never felt anything so intense," she said almost breathlessly.

"That makes me very happy."

Cooper smiled at her, and the dimples in his cheeks made him look young and innocent, the polar opposite of what he looked like in his vampire form. She lifted her hand to his face and traced it with her fingers, marveling at his flawless skin, his perfect bone structure, his masculine beauty.

"I could get used to this," she confessed.

"You'd better." He smirked and moved his hips back a couple of inches, before sliding back into her, making her realize that he was still hard and ready for more. "'Cause you're not leaving this bed anytime soon."

"Promise?"

"Promise."

29

It was well past noon, when Cooper walked next to Anita toward the kitchen in Wesley's house, showered and dressed, a bottle of blood in his hand. He was fully healed, and he had no scars from the two bullet wounds. In fact, he'd never felt better in his life. Anita had accepted him for what he was, and had shown no fear of his vampire side. On the contrary, she'd been curious and explored him without hesitation. It wouldn't take long until she would allow him to bite her, making their lovemaking even more perfect than it already was.

He'd answered many of the questions she'd had about vampires, explained a vampire's capacity to heal a human with his saliva and his blood, and confessed that his baby cousin Jacob had indeed bitten her with his tiny fangs. He'd also explained that as a vampire hybrid he could be outside in the sun, whereas the sun would kill his pure-blooded vampire parents if they were to brave it. The relief he felt at being able to tell her the truth about himself and his family and friends, was freeing, and it had brought them closer, not just physically, but emotionally too.

"Smells like somebody's making lunch," Cooper said with a glance at Anita, before he pushed the door open, and they entered the kitchen.

Wesley was cooking, and Virginia was setting out plates. Both turned their heads.

"Hey, guys," Cooper greeted them and motioned to Wesley at the stove. "Are you making enough for all of us?"

"Good morning," Anita said, addressing Wes and Virginia.

"Morning," both of them replied.

Wesley added, "Yeah, I made plenty. You guys hungry?"

"Famished. Virginia, let me help you with setting the table." Cooper placed the bottle of blood on the counter.

Virginia looked up. "Here—" She stopped herself and sucked in a breath of air. Her gaze shot from the bottle of blood to him, and then to Anita.

Wes turned at the same time.

"It's okay," Cooper said quickly, pointing to the bottle. "Anita knows."

"I found out last night," Anita added.

Wes put a hand on his wife's arm. "Sorry, Babe, totally forgot to mention this. Cooper got shot last night. By Anita." He smirked.

"How do you know about that?" Cooper asked.

"Haven called me, of course. Everybody knows about it."

"Everybody but me," Virginia said.

Wes pressed a kiss to her cheek. "You were busy at the council, and when you got back, we had something better to do than talk..." He winked at Virginia.

Virginia rolled her eyes, then looked at Anita. "You shot Cooper? What did he do?"

While Anita filled Virginia in on what had happened the previous night, Cooper set the kitchen table for four people, and Wesley put finishing touches on the stew and the potatoes. Cooper opened the bottle of blood and gulped it down.

Wes pointed to the empty bottle. "You sure you wanna eat with us after this?"

"Trust me, I could eat a cow right now." He looked over his shoulder to Anita, who was still talking to Virginia, before he looked back at

Wesley and dropped his voice. "Some women can really take it out of a guy."

His uncle chuckled. "Like you would have it any other way."

Cooper smiled to himself, and his gaze drifted to Anita. No, he wouldn't change anything about Anita and their relationship. She was absolutely perfect for him.

"You've got it bad," Wes whispered.

"I know."

"Let's eat!" Wes announced and set the pot of stew in the middle of the table, while Cooper placed the bowl of roasted potatoes next to it.

Everybody helped themselves to the food and dug in. Cooper was happy to see that Anita didn't just pick at her food, but ate with gusto. She, too, had burned a lot of calories the night before, and they'd both barely gotten any sleep. Holding her in his arms all night and into the morning, had put him in a constant state of arousal, one he could only relieve by making love to her again and again. It was a wonder that she wasn't complaining that she was sore after he'd relentlessly thrust his cock into her. Instead, she'd welcomed him even when she was half asleep.

Wesley pulled him out of his reverie. "I heard you guys got a sketch of the suspect. So, a serial killer, huh?"

Cooper nodded. "Yeah, we know what he looks like, and thanks to Anita, we know his modus operandi." He kissed Anita on the cheek.

She swallowed her food and looked at him. "Which reminds me: we should set a trap for him. With me as bait."

Cooper nearly choked on the piece of meat he was chewing. "Excuse me?"

Anita set down her fork. "You promised if I could defeat you, you'd let me do this."

He remembered only too well how she'd *defeated* him: by caressing his cock. But he also remembered what he'd promised her. "It's too dangerous. Now that you know the killer is a vampire, I thought you'd changed your mind about wanting to be bait."

Anita shook her head. "Now it's even more important that he's caught. Just think of all the women he's killed. How many more will he take? And they have no way of fighting him. But you do. You and your friends—only another vampire can defeat him. And we have to catch him here, in San Francisco, before he moves on."

"She's got a point," Wes said with a shrug.

"Thanks for your support," Cooper said dryly. "You could have backed me up."

"Coop, you've gotta know when to fold." He cast a sideways look at Anita. "As a Montgomery, you should know by now that the women we pick don't cave easily."

Anita smirked and put a hand on Cooper's arm. "Your uncle is right."

"She's a trained law enforcement officer, Cooper," Virginia added. "Besides, she didn't fall apart when she found out you're a vampire. She's stronger than you think. She can handle this."

"*Et tu*, Virginia?" Cooper shook his head, but he knew he'd already lost this argument. He took a deep breath and clasped Anita's hand. "All right, we'll work on setting a trap with you as bait." And he hoped he wouldn't regret that decision.

The doorbell rang. Wesley looked at his wife. "Are we expecting anybody?"

"I'm not," Virginia replied. "If it were somebody from the council, they would use the portal not the door."

Wesley rose. "I'll check." He left the room.

"What's a portal?" Anita asked, her gaze directed at Virginia.

Virginia hesitated. "Uhm..."

"Oh," Anita said quickly. "If it's a secret to do with you being a Stealth Guardian, you don't have to tell me. I didn't mean to be nosy. There's just so much that's new for me."

"It's all right, Anita," Virginia said with a smile. "It's just there are still a few things we need to keep to ourselves until..."

Cooper caught Virginia glancing at him and knew what she was referring to. If and when Anita truly became a part of their family by blood-bonding with him, there would be no more secrets.

He was saved from giving Anita an explanation, when the door opened, and Wesley entered followed by a tall Hispanic man in his late fifties or early sixties, dressed in casual clothes. His cowboy boots made a loud clacking sound on the hardwood floor.

Anita jumped up from her chair, staring wide-eyed at the newcomer.

"Dad?"

30

———————

"Dad!" Her heart beating like a jackhammer, Anita stared at her father in disbelief. "What are you doing here? How did you even find me?"

"Your cellphone GPS," he said in a clipped tone. "But that's not important right now. Is this Cooper Montgomery?"

Cooper had already jumped up from his chair. He extended his hand toward her father. "Yes, I'm Cooper Montgomery. Nice to meet you, Sheriff Diaz."

He ignored the offered hand, and instead, glared at Cooper. "I wish I could say the same thing, but you, Mr. Montgomery, are a liar."

"Excuse me?" Cooper asked, his voice colored in stunned disbelief.

"I don't know what kind of scam you're running here, and what you're trying to do with my daughter, but you're not a police officer like you claimed."

"Uh..."

But Sheriff Diaz cut him off with an impatient wave of his hand. "And don't try to deny it. I called SFPD, and you're not working for them!"

"Dad! Stop it," Anita interrupted.

He turned his gaze on her. "You, young lady, are coming with me.

I'm not leaving you here with a con artist who's trying to reel you in with lies."

"Sir," Cooper started. "I can clear this up."

"Oh, I'm sure you can. I'm sure you've got plenty of lies lined up. But I'm not as naïve as my daughter."

"I'm not naïve!" Anita ground out. "And Cooper isn't a con artist! He's an investigator."

"Didn't you hear what I just said?" Sheriff Diaz asked, his jaw tight. "I called SFPD. He doesn't work for them!"

"I never said I did," Cooper interjected. "I said I worked *with* the SFPD not *for* them."

Her father huffed. "Bullshit!" He made another step closer to Cooper, going almost nose to nose with him. "What the fuck do you want from my daughter, huh? What game are you playing? You're pretending to believe in her crazy serial killer theory to do what? Use her? What's your endgame?"

Anita noticed how the cords in her father's neck bulged, and his face turned red, while Cooper looked like he was trying to restrain himself from lashing out at him.

"First of all," Cooper said, inhaling a deep breath, "it's not a crazy theory. We have a serial killer on the loose. And secondly, I've been working with your daughter to find him. I didn't lie to you or to Anita about what I do. And the chief of police will be able to confirm that what I'm telling you is the truth."

"Right!" He thrust his chin up. "Next you're gonna make a phone call to one of your cronies and pretend he's the chief of police. Nice try!"

"Goddamn it, Dad! How can you be so stubborn? I spoke to the chief of police myself to verify Cooper's identity."

He cast her a sideways look. "Don't mind if I verify that myself. You haven't exactly shown the best judgment lately."

Anita gasped.

"Sir, I'd suggest you stop insulting your daughter," Cooper said tightly.

"How about we all relax a little?" Wesley asked. "Would you like some lunch, Sheriff?"

He turned his head to look at Wesley. "And you are?"

"Wesley Montgomery…"

"His brother?"

"His uncle." He pointed to Virginia. "And that's my wife, Virginia."

Anita could firmly see the wheels in her father's head spin as he looked at Wesley and Virginia who looked almost as young as Cooper.

"Hmm," he grunted.

Virginia spoke for the first time. "Coop, why don't you take Sheriff Diaz to see Chief Donnelly at the police station?"

Anita nodded at Virginia. "I think that's an excellent idea. That's the only way to get past his boneheaded, stubborn—"

"I heard that!" her father proclaimed loudly.

She shot him an annoyed look. "You were supposed to!"

"Now I can see from whom you get your doggedness," Cooper said with a smirk, before he looked back at her father. "I'll call the chief to let him know that we're coming to see him."

Shaking her head at her father, Anita walked toward the door. "I'll get my jacket and handbag from upstairs."

She pushed the door open and walked into the hallway. Her father followed.

"You're staying here?"

"Yes, if you must know."

But she wasn't going to tell him about her misfortune with the Airbnb, or he would only use that as another example that she was gullible or naïve. It was bad enough that he had accused Cooper of being a conman, when Cooper had been the first to believe in her and support her in her theory—a theory that had turned out to be correct.

"Anita, I'm just looking out for you," her father said as he walked up the stairs next to her. "I was worried about you, so I tried to call Mr. Montgomery to ask him how you're doing, and then found that he'd lied to me about who he is."

Anita snapped her head toward him. "He didn't lie to you. He's a private investigator the police hires for...uhm..." She couldn't very well tell him vampires existed. "...difficult cases."

She marched toward Cooper's room, where she'd left her things.

"Well, what was I supposed to think, huh? Put yourself into my shoes."

Anita entered the room, and glanced at the unmade bed. There was no evidence that she'd not been the only one sleeping there. Cooper had tossed his dirty clothes into a hamper in the bathroom, and the closet that held his clothes was closed. Before she'd taken a shower this morning, she'd brought her suitcase and anything she'd unpacked into Cooper's room, leaving the other guestroom as pristine as it had been before.

She snatched her handbag and her jacket and turned on her heel, when she noticed that her father looked around the room as if it was a crime scene.

"It's a nice place, this house."

Surprised at his complimentary assessment, she nodded. "It is."

"Why are you staying here? Didn't you book a hotel?"

There it was, the question she'd been dreading, so she decided to lie. "Only for the first week. But when I identified Janet's body and Cooper asked me to work with him on this case, I decided to stay longer. But the place I'd stayed was booked solid." Which wasn't exactly a lie. "So he offered me a place to stay."

"Hmm."

"Sort of for compensating me for my help. Hotels are expensive here." She thrust her chin up.

"Still odd that he would offer you a place with his relatives."

Her father was fishing, but she wasn't going to volunteer more information. If he wanted to know why Cooper had really offered her a place to stay, then he'd have to find the courage to ask her directly.

"Shall we go?" she prompted and left the room, pulling the door shut behind her.

"Looks like your future father-in-law is quite stubborn," Wes said grinning.

Cooper didn't even make an effort to dispute Wesley's assumption that he wanted to make Anita his. The fact that he hadn't wiped her memory when she'd discovered that he was a vampire, made it clear to everybody that his intentions were serious.

"Can't choose family," Cooper said instead.

"Don't worry," Virginia interjected. "He'll change his tune once you have Donnelly vouch for you."

"I'd better call him quickly." Cooper navigated to Mike Donnelly's number. "Thanks for lunch, guys." When Donnelly picked up, Cooper filled him in on what he needed to know, including the fact that Anita knew of the existence of vampires, but that it had to be kept a secret from her father.

Half an hour later, an assistant ushered him, Anita, and Sheriff Diaz into the chief of police's office in the Hall of Justice on Bryant Street. Donnelly greeted them, and Cooper could instantly see that Sheriff Diaz was relaxing when Donnelly shook his hand.

"Cooper tells me you're the Sheriff of Elko County," Donnelly said.

Diaz nodded. "And I was a little worried when I couldn't verify who Mr. Montgomery really is."

"Well, let me assure you, he's indeed working with the SFPD. In fact, he's leading the investigation into the serial killer who's currently roaming San Francisco."

Diaz nodded, then turned to Cooper, extending his hand. "My apologies, Mr. Montgomery, for treating you the way I did."

Cooper shook his hand. "Please call me Cooper. We're not very formal here."

"Thank you, Cooper. Then please call me José."

"Now that that's cleared, do you have any updates on the case?" Donnelly asked with a look at Cooper.

"I do. We've got a sketch of the suspect. My people already did some canvassing last night, but we can only cover so much ground. I need your help, Mike."

"What do you need?" Donnelly asked.

"Distribute the sketch to every police officer in the city, unis, undercover, detectives, even the administrative staff. I want everybody to know what he looks like. But give them strict instructions not to approach him under any circumstances, even if they're armed. He's extremely dangerous."

Since Donnelly already knew that the suspect was a vampire, Cooper didn't have to make it any clearer that a human wasn't equipped to fight a dangerous vampire.

"Got it. You want them to report to Scanguards' command center if they see him?"

"Yes, make sure that everybody has the number. They can send a text to the same number, in case they can't speak without being overheard. Thanks, Mike."

"Not a problem. The sooner that guy is off the streets, the better. Any other plans I should know of?"

Cooper looked at Anita. When she nodded firmly, he sighed. Apparently, he couldn't change Anita's mind about playing bait.

"Actually yes," Cooper started. "Since we know that the suspect was trying to abduct another woman a few days ago, we know he's looking for a new victim. We've decided to give him what he's after: a woman fitting the victim profile." He tipped his head toward Anita. "Anita has agreed to play bait."

For a moment, it was completely silent in the room. Nobody breathed, and only Cooper could hear the three humans' heartbeats. But the silence lasted for only a second.

"You're out of your mind!" Diaz protested loudly. "My daughter will not play bait! I won't allow it." He glared at Cooper. "How dare you even make such a suggestion to her?"

"José, please, I know exactly how you feel," Cooper said, trying to calm him.

"No, you don't!"

Cooper was about to reveal to him that he was in love with Anita, when Anita gave a light shake of her head, so he took a breath, before adding, "I was against it too, but I'm afraid your daughter has a very stubborn streak." And that was one of the many things he actually loved about her: her tenacity. She was no pushover.

"What Cooper is trying to say, Dad, is that it was my idea," Anita said.

Diaz whipped his head in Anita's direction, glaring at her now. "Are you crazy?"

"She's not," Cooper interrupted. "Let me assure you that Anita will be protected by myself and a team of my colleagues. If the suspect gets within five yards of her, we will take him down. He'll never lay a hand on her."

He would make sure that the most experienced bodyguards would be taking part in this sting.

Sheriff Diaz grunted with displeasure, while addressing Anita, "Why would you do this?"

Anita took a visible breath. "Dad, maybe you should sit down for this."

"I don't need to sit down."

Cooper caught Anita's look, and knew instinctively what she wanted to tell her father.

"Dad, I recognized the serial killer suspect. I saw him once twenty-one years ago..."

Something in Diaz's face changed. It was as if all blood drained from it, but he remained silent.

"I saw him the night Mom disappeared. I woke up. He was in our house. He took Mom. She didn't want to go, but he threatened her... He said he'd take me instead, if she didn't go with him..." Tears suddenly welled up in Anita's eyes.

Cooper registered her last sentence with shock. Anita hadn't mentioned this to him before. Her mother had sacrificed herself for her daughter to live. He could only imagine what that knowledge did to Anita, and why she'd kept it to herself until now. No wonder she wanted to take the killer down. This was even more personal than he'd known.

"You were only nine..." Diaz said, his voice shaky.

"He's the same man… He took her. And he killed her. She protected me. She loved us, Dad, she loved us both."

Cooper wanted to take Anita into his arms to console her, but this wasn't his moment. This moment was for her and her father. Finally, Sheriff Diaz bridged the distance between himself and his daughter, and wrapped his arms around her.

"I'm so sorry I didn't believe you. I'm so sorry, honey. Please forgive me."

Anita sobbed into her father's chest.

Cooper motioned to Donnelly. "Let's give them a minute."

He and Donnelly left the room and remained in the ante office.

"No wonder she wants to play bait," Donnelly said. "How are you gonna keep her safe?"

"I'm bringing in the big guns: Zane, Amaury, Gabriel, Mom and Dad, Orlando, maybe even Samson. This asshole won't get away, I swear."

"I hope you're not gonna scare him away before he's in the net."

"You and me both."

But Anita would be protected heavier than Fort Knox, because she was much more valuable than all the gold in the world. Anita was his, and he wouldn't allow anybody to hurt her.

31

———

Anita's tears dried, and for the first time since her mother had disappeared, she felt that her father understood her, and they were pulling in the same direction.

"Thank you, Dad." She lifted her head from his chest.

Cooper and the police chief entered the room. She caught Cooper's gaze, and smiled at him, thanking him silently for giving her and her father privacy.

"Sheriff," Donnelly said, "as you can see, we have the situation under control. We'll be running the sting tonight. Or rather, Cooper and his men will. They know what to do."

"If you say so. But I'm going to take an active part in the sting," her father insisted.

It was a terrible idea. She wanted her father nowhere near the crazy vampire who'd abducted and killed her mother. And she couldn't very well tell him that the killer was a vampire. And that Cooper was too. She looked at Cooper for help.

"Sir, uhm, José," Cooper corrected himself. "Trust me when I tell you that this isn't the first time I and my team have dealt with a brutal killer like this one. We're a well-oiled machine and know what we need to do. There's no need for you to put yourself in danger."

"That may well be, but you're not gonna change my mind. I wasn't able to save my wife from this killer, but I'm gonna make damn well sure my daughter won't become his next victim. So save your breath, 'cause I'm not going anywhere."

Cooper hesitated, meeting her eyes. Anita shrugged. There was nothing she could do. Once her father's mind was made up, there was no way of changing it.

"Fine," Anita said, resigned. "Dad, why don't you get a hotel, and then we can organize the sting?" It would give her and Cooper some time to talk in private.

"All right, honey, I'll get us a two-room-suite. There's no need for you to wear out Cooper's hospitality."

Fuck! That wasn't the plan. She had no intention of staying in a hotel with her father. She wanted to stay with Cooper.

"José, it's really not necessary for you to book a hotel," Cooper interrupted, clearly having the same reaction. He wanted to be with her just as much as she wanted to be with him. "There are plenty of guestrooms in my uncle's house. You'll stay with us. Please, I insist."

Her father hesitated. "I don't know. I don't want to be a burden."

"It's not a burden," Cooper said quickly. "It'll be much more comfortable than in a hotel."

He cast her a stolen glance, and she read the promise in his eyes. Yes, it would be much more comfortable for her and Cooper to sleep in the same bed.

"All right then," her father conceded. "Thank you for the offer, Cooper."

Cooper nodded. "Let me make a few phone calls to apprise my team that we're on our way to HQ, and get a few things prepped." He nodded to Donnelly. "Mike, maybe you and the sheriff could look over the sketch I sent you a few minutes ago, while Anita and I use your assistant's office to make the calls?"

"Yeah, sure, let's do that," Donnelly said instantly.

"Excuse us for a few minutes," Cooper said and motioned to Anita to follow him outside.

When the door shut behind them, and they were in the ante office, where an assistant was typing on a computer, Cooper took her hand and opened another door, and led her into an even smaller office used for storage. He closed the door, and they were finally alone.

"Okay, so we have a little issue," Cooper said.

"You mean the fact that my father wants to be part of the operation? Yeah, I'd say that's more than just a little issue. How are we gonna keep him from finding out that we're hunting a vampire? And that you and your team are vampires too?"

"I'll make sure that everybody knows to be extra careful around him."

Anita rolled her eyes. "Famous last words."

"Don't be so pessimistic," he said, chuckling. "It'll turn out fine." He put his arms around her and drew her into an embrace. "So, the other little issue..."

"What little issue?"

"The fact that you don't seem to want him to know that we're together. What's that about?"

Anita took a long breath. Would Cooper understand? "My dad is kind of old-fashioned. I don't think he would approve of you if he knew that you got me into bed so quickly, you know, without us really knowing each other. He would think that you're just using me." But there was something else too. She sighed. "And he would think that I'm reckless for trusting a man I barely know."

"All right. We won't tell him yet. But just so you know, I will not spend the night without you in my arms."

She leaned closer, her lips only an inch away from his. "Nor will I."

"I'll tell Wesley to give him the guestroom at the other end of the hallway, so he won't hear us."

He'd barely finished his sentence, when his mouth was on hers, and he was kissing her deeply, his tongue dancing with hers, their breaths mingling, while he thrust his groin against her, one hand on her ass to press her closer.

Within a second, Anita lost all coherent thought and didn't even know where they were. Cooper's kiss and touch were all-consuming, and if they'd had time, she wouldn't have objected to him taking her in this storage room, her back pressed against a filing cabinet, while he thrust his cock into her. But they didn't have the luxury of time.

Reluctantly, she freed her lips from his and pressed her forehead to his, breathing hard. "You'd better make those phone calls…"

Cooper breathed raggedly. "Yeah, I'd better." He took her hand and pressed it over his fly, where his cock was already hard and big. "And later, I need you to take care of this for me."

"Oh," she murmured, squeezing him through the fabric. "That'll be my pleasure."

He slid his other hand between her thighs and rubbed over her pussy, making her gasp. "And it'll be mine when I take care of you."

THE SUN HAD ALREADY SET, when they reached Scanguards' headquarters in the Mission. Cooper had made phone calls to arrange for everybody necessary for the sting to assemble in one of the smaller conference rooms on the first floor, just opposite the H lounge. He'd also notified Wesley that Anita's father would be staying with them until the killer was caught, and not to let it slip in front of Sheriff Diaz that Cooper and Anita were lovers. He would find out soon enough.

"This way," Cooper said, ushering Anita and Sheriff Diaz into the conference room.

Inside, several vampires were waiting for them. Cooper was pleased to see Samson among them. As the founder and owner of Scanguards, Samson had many responsibilities, yet he was always ready to jump in where he was needed most. Cooper made the introductions.

"José, Anita, this is my boss, Samson Woodford. Scanguards is his company. Samson, these are Sheriff José Diaz and Anita Diaz from the Elko County Sheriff's Department."

As Samson shook hands with the guests, Cooper noticed Sheriff Diaz peruse Samson, before looking at the others assembled in the room. Was he wondering why everybody looked so young? Even Samson, who was well over 250 years old looked like he was in his early to mid-thirties.

"It's a pleasure," Samson said and turned to introduce the other vampires in the room. "Have you met Cooper's parents yet? Yvette and Haven Montgomery."

They greeted each other, before Cooper introduced Orlando, a massive vampire who could scare the shit out of anybody. Next to him stood Zane, the bald vampire who had a decidedly mean streak, even though he'd softened over the years, thanks to his mate, Portia. Amaury, Samson's best friend and a director at Scanguards, was almost as big as Orlando, and nobody would guess that he was tightly wrapped around his mate Nina's little finger, and that he was like a big soft teddy bear when in the company of Nina.

"Meet Orlando Carlisle, Zane Eisenberg, and Amaury LeSang. They'll all be taking part in the sting." Cooper motioned to the large table for everybody to sit down.

"Luther is joining us later," Haven announced.

"Good," Cooper said. "Then let's start. We've got a lot to discuss to bring everybody on the same page. And we have to pick the right spot where to set the trap."

"Yeah, about that," Diaz interjected. "No offense, but San Francisco is a large city. How are you gonna figure out where he's gonna show up?"

Cooper looked at Diaz, then at Anita, who sat next to him, close enough to touch. But he refrained from doing so. "We've been working with our IT team to run Janet's photo and the suspect's sketch through facial recognition. We're cross-referencing this with sightings of white vans and—"

"There must be hundreds if not thousands of white vans," Diaz interrupted.

It wasn't difficult to guess that Diaz wasn't keen on his daughter playing bait, and that he was trying to pick the plan apart so Anita wouldn't be put in the path of the killer.

"José, you need to trust us," Cooper said. "We know what we're doing. We have decades of experience dealing with cases like this."

"Decades?" Diaz shook his head. "If anybody has decades of experience, it's me. Look at yourselves: you're barely out of college."

He gestured to the others in the room, breathing hard, clearly readying himself for coming up with more protests, when Anita put her hand on his forearm.

"Dad, please. Let them explain what they're trying to do. This is not their first rodeo."

"Well, it sure looks like it."

Cooper exchanged a look with Samson.

Samson nodded. "Sheriff Diaz, let me assure you that Chief Donnelly would have never assigned us this case if he didn't think we could handle it better than the SFPD. You've met Mike. He's a very level-headed man, and he trusts us. I hope you can too."

Before he could respond, there was a knock on the door, and it opened. Vanessa popped her head in.

"Sorry to disturb you, guys," she said with a smile. "Anita, you wanna come with me? We need to get you ready."

"Doing what?" Anita said with a surprised look on her face.

Cooper turned to her. "They'll put a wire on you, and put you in the right outfit."

"All right," Anita said. "But won't you need me here?"

"I'll catch you up on the operation just as soon as we've decided on where and how to run this," Cooper assured her, leaning in, ready to give her a kiss on the cheek, when he stopped himself in mid-movement. "Uhm, so, take your time with Vanessa."

Anita rose. Her father put his hand on her forearm. "You can still change your mind."

She shook her head and leaned down to him, kissing him on the cheek. "I have to do this, Dad."

She pivoted, and followed Vanessa out of the room.

32

———————

The room Vanessa led her to was located a floor below the conference room. It looked like a cross between the prop room of a midsize theater and the dressing room of a transvestite. A young woman with dark hair sat on an armchair in a corner and jumped up when she saw them.

"Scarlet, hey," Vanessa greeted her, before turning to Anita. "Anita, this is Scarlet, my sister-in-law. She's blood-bonded to my brother Ryder."

"Hi, nice to meet you," Anita said and stretched her hand out.

Scarlet shook it. "Likewise. So you're with Cooper."

"Yes, it's just... you know... we've only seen each other for a few days," she said, feeling a little awkward about Scarlet mentioning her relationship to Cooper.

"Cooper wanted to give you a chance to talk to one of the humans blood-bonded to a vampire hybrid," Vanessa explained. "And you can't very well do that while your father is hovering."

She wasn't wrong. Her father had eagle eyes, and it would be difficult to keep things from him. "I appreciate it."

"Scarlet is human, and my brother is a vampire hybrid like myself."

"And I'm happy to answer all your questions," Scarlet offered.

"Oh." Anita ran her eyes over Scarlet, her gaze zeroing in on her flawless neck. There was no sign of bitemarks at all. Hadn't Cooper said that a vampire bit his lover during sex?

She caught Vanessa and Scarlet exchange a conspiratorial look.

Vanessa chuckled. "I'll leave you guys to it. Nicholas will stop by shortly to bring you the wire."

"Bye, Nessie," Scarlet called after her as Vanessa turned on her heel and left the room.

When the door closed behind her, Anita took a deep breath. "Uhm... so, uh..." Her throat felt like sandpaper. She'd never had a girlfriend with whom she talked about guys and sex, and now she was supposed to ask this stranger about the mating habits and sex practices of vampires?

"I've been where you are now." Scarlet motioned to the two armchairs in the corner. "Let's sit down. I'm on my feet all day, running after two boys that have more energy than their father and I combined."

Anita took the proffered seat, and Scarlet sat down too. "You have kids with Ryder?"

Scarlet smiled, and her eyes lit up. "Twins. And they're already a handful at seventeen months!" Then she leaned forward in her chair. "But you don't really want to talk about kids, do you? You want to know what it's like to be bitten."

Anita gasped. "How did you—"

"Because that was my first question too when I found out what Ryder is."

"You don't mind telling me? I mean... Cooper said it's part of the sex between vampires."

"It is. And not just because Ryder has to feed from me, otherwise he would starve, but—"

Anita shot forward on her seat. "What?"

"Well, when a vampire blood-bonds with a human, he can only drink that human's blood. In Ryder's case, he can only drink mine. If he ever drank from another source, he would get sick."

"Are you saying, he's dependent on you? But what if..." There were so many what ifs, so many scenarios where things could go wrong. So many what ifs that contradicted Scarlet's statement.

"What if his human mate left him?" Scarlet prompted. "He would die. But I haven't heard of a single case where that's happened. Vampires mate for life. And they'll do everything to make the woman they're blood-bonded to happy."

"But what if the woman dies? That must happen. Or what if they are mated to a vampire, like Cooper's parents? You can't tell me they can only drink from each other. That can't work. It's like a closed system... there's no nutrition coming in... no..."

Scarlet took her hand. "Anita, breathe."

Anita took a breath.

"Okay," Scarlet started calmly. "There are a few exceptions to this rule about blood. If the human mate dies, there's a change going through the vampire, and he will once again be able to drink any human blood. It happened to Luther, Cooper's uncle. Katie is his second mate. And in the case of Cooper's parents, vampires mated to each other don't undergo this change within their bodies that would restrict them to the blood of their mate only. They can drink any human blood."

Anita listened carefully. "Okay, that makes more sense." But she still hadn't asked what she really wanted to know. It was time to stop beating around the bush. "What's it like, the bite? Does it hurt? How often does he have to... feed from you?"

Scarlet looked into the distance, a contented smile around her lips. Her chest rose, and her cheeks looked flushed all of a sudden. "It's out of this world. The connection the bite creates, it's as if you're not just physically connected, but also on an emotional and spiritual level. It's addictive. It's a high I've never experienced before I met Ryder. And to make love while he drinks from me... it's a pleasure only few people will ever experience."

Anita noticed the sparkle in Scarlet's eyes, and she looked almost as if she was glowing. The sight increased her longing for Cooper. They could have what Scarlet and Ryder had, the same kind of connection.

"And when I hear his voice in my head, it feels like he's touching my heart." Scarlet rose and walked to the clothes rack. "We should find you something to wear."

Anita shot up from her seat. "His voice? What do you mean?"

"Every blood-bonded couple has a telepathic connection, a way to communicate without speaking."

"That's how they did it."

"What?" She pulled a pencil skirt with a matching jacket from the rail and looked at it.

"Cooper's parents. After I shot Cooper, and his mother brought him home to take out the bullets, his father arrived, and he already knew that I had shot Cooper. But nobody had called or texted him."

Scarlet nodded. "Yvette probably told him via their bond what had happened." Then she grinned. "So how are things with Yvette? I heard she was livid about you shooting him."

"Does everybody know about what I did?"

"Yep, gossip like that spreads faster than a wine stain on a white carpet." She held the navy-blue suit up next to Anita and tilted her head. "I think that color works on you. Makes you look very authoritative."

"Who am I supposed to dress up as?"

"Cooper said to make you look like a businesswoman, maybe in finance." She motioned to purses and high heels, scarves, and jewelry. "We'll need to accessorize." Then she reached for another suit in a different color. "Try the grey one too. Should be your size."

Anita took both hangers, and Scarlet pointed to a screen. "You can change behind there."

While she slipped behind the privacy screen, and got undressed, she asked, "How long did you date Ryder before you guys blood-bonded? That's what it's called, right?"

"About a week."

Anita nearly choked on her own saliva. "A week?"

"I know, it seems short," Scarlet admitted. "But when a vampire falls in love, it happens practically overnight. And it's hard to resist that kind of intense connection. Besides, he saved my life, and that of my father.

Ryder would have died for me. But even before that, I think I knew instinctively that he was the one for me."

Did that mean what Cooper felt for her was as intense as Scarlet described Ryder's love for her? And did it mean that what she was starting to feel for him wasn't as crazy as she thought? Wasn't reckless at all, but natural?

"Were you never afraid of what he's capable of? That he could hurt you?"

Scarlet sighed. "Ryder was defending me against another vampire, when he transformed, and I realized what he was. I was scared at first, but Ryder gave me a choice. He said he'd let me go if I didn't want anything to do with him now that I knew. All he wanted was the chance to explain. And he did. And the more he told me who he was, the more I realized that vampires aren't so different from humans. They are capable of love, of friendship, of loyalty. And I was already so in love with him that it really didn't matter in the end what he was. Do you understand that?"

Anita felt tears sting her eyes. "Yes..." She understood it, because she felt the same for Cooper. And tonight, after this was over, after they'd caught the killer, she would tell him that she loved him no matter who or what he was.

"I thought you might," Scarlet said softly. "Now let me see you in the suit."

Anita sniffled and walked out from behind the screen. "Thank you for talking to me so openly."

"Any time."

There was a knock at the door.

"Come in," Scarlet said.

A young man with dark hair entered, a small box in his hand. "Hey, I'm here with the wire."

"Hey, Nicholas," Scarlet greeted him. "Give me the bug, and I'll put it on Anita."

"I'm supposed to do that," Nicholas protested and marched toward her. "You don't know what you're doing."

Scarlet stepped aside, and folded her arms over her chest, while Nicholas stopped only a foot away from Anita and grinned at her.

"As you wish," Scarlet said. "Just thought I'd warn you not to touch what belongs to Cooper. He's gonna rip your head off if you touch her."

"Cooper?" Nicholas immediately stepped back as if bitten by a hornet. He looked her up and down appreciatively. "Fuck!"

Anita caught Scarlet winking at her. "Yep, so, you'd better not touch. And don't look down her cleavage either."

Nicholas's head shot up, and Anita realized that Scarlet was having fun chastising him and felt sorry for him.

"Nicholas? I'm Anita. I'm sure Scarlet is only exaggerating."

"No, she isn't."

Anita whipped her head in the direction of the door from where the familiar voice had come. Cooper stood there, a smirk on his face.

She shook her head at him. "You're terrible."

Cooper shrugged, the reprimand pearling off him like water off Teflon. Then his expression turned serious. "We've got a plan."

33

———————

Cooper sat in the driver's seat of one of Scanguards' black-out vans, Sheriff Diaz in the passenger seat. On the dashboard, a tablet showed live-streams from different cameras in a three-block radius Scanguards had set up. The car was parked half a block from the spot where Anita had just exited a large office building, dressed in a navy business suit and high heels, a briefcase in one hand. She looked up and down the street, pretending to wait for an Uber like they'd discussed.

"And you really think he's gonna show up here?" Sheriff Diaz said skeptically, glancing at him briefly before looking back in Anita's direction.

"It's our best guess. Janet Fillmore's body was found a quarter mile from here, and two nights before that, he tried to abduct a woman only two blocks from here. That, together with sightings of white vans, makes this area his most likely hunting grounds."

"I still don't like it," Diaz grunted. "What if he gets to Anita and slips through your net?"

"Very unlikely. We have somebody on every block, plus the cameras. If he enters this three-block radius, we'll see him."

And hopefully the killer wouldn't see the vampires who'd hidden themselves at strategic spots. While there were civilians around, it was imperative that their suspect didn't see any vampires, or he would suspect a trap.

"I didn't see any of your colleagues." Diaz motioned to the cameras.

"That's the point. If you can't see them, neither can the suspect."

"Easy for you to say. You're not the sitting duck. My daughter is."

There was no convincing Diaz that Anita was safe short of telling him that the people from Scanguards were vampires and would be able to come to Anita's aid within seconds.

Cooper tapped his microphone. "Anita, turn to your right, and walk to the next block, then cross the street."

Anita didn't answer, but she turned like he'd instructed, and walked toward the intersection.

"Samson, she's coming toward you."

A moment later, Samson replied, "I have her in my sight."

When Anita crossed the intersection and disappeared from Cooper's view, he looked at the tablet and saw her show up in one of the feeds.

"Anita, wait at the bus stop. Pretend to look at the bus route," Samson instructed through the earphone.

Cooper tapped on his mic to mute it. "José, I know you're worried." He continued looking at the live feed of Anita standing at the bus station a block away. "Trust me, I'm the last guy who would want your daughter to get hurt."

Diaz turned his head to give him a long look. "You've got a funny way of showing that. You should have talked her out of this."

"You know better than I that once your daughter has made up her mind about something, she can't be dissuaded."

Diaz let out a huff. "Yeah, well, she gets that from me, I guess. Damn stubborn. That's what she is."

"It's a good trait for an investigator. If she hadn't been so stubborn then we would still not know that we're dealing with a serial killer." And they would have never met, depriving him of the chance to be with the woman he wanted as his mate.

"Samson, the bus will be turning onto your street in a couple of moments," Yvette said via the earpiece.

"Anita," Samson said, "move five steps to your left otherwise I'll lose sight of you when the bus stops."

Cooper kept his eyes on the live feed and saw the bus approaching. When it stopped at the small hut, it blocked the camera, and all he could see were several people standing on the bus, ready to get off.

Cooper's heart pounded out of control. "Samson? The camera lost her."

"I've got her," Samson confirmed.

Suddenly, the bus driver rose from his seat.

"What's happening?" Diaz asked.

"A wheelchair user has to get off," Samson replied.

"There's a white van approaching," Orlando suddenly announced. "Coming toward you, Amaury. Turning now."

Cooper looked at the live feeds covering Orlando's and Amaury's blocks, and saw the white van as it drove past Amaury's block.

"Samson, he's heading for you," Amaury said. "He's slowing down."

"Who's got eyes on Anita?" Cooper asked.

"I've got her," Samson confirmed.

"Shit, the white van is stopping behind the bus," Diaz said, pointing to the tablet.

Cooper tried to zoom in on the driver in the van, but the image was too dark, and a camera couldn't capture the aura of a vampire.

"I'm heading over there," Haven said. "Keep your eyes on Anita."

"Fuck!" Samson hissed.

"Samson?" Cooper asked, panicked.

"I can't get to her. She's trapped between the wheelchair platform and the people getting off the bus from the back door."

Cooper reached for the handle and opened the car door. He jumped out, and heard Diaz doing the same. He raced toward the intersection, then turned. The bus driver was helping the wheelchair-bound passenger safely reach the sidewalk. The people who'd exited from the back door were already dispersing.

"False alarm," Haven said through the earpiece. "The driver of the white van is an Asian man. Back to your positions."

Diaz reached Cooper, just when Cooper spied Anita, who'd stepped behind the covered bus stop to get out of the way. Relieved, he let out a sigh. Anita was okay.

"You're mighty fast," Diaz said to him. "You a sprinter or something?"

Cooper turned his head. "I was on the track team in high school." Which was a lie. Every vampire ran faster than the fastest human.

"Pretty impressive speed."

"Like I told you, my colleagues and I will keep Anita safe at all times."

Diaz nodded. "I can see that."

"Let's get back to the car," Cooper suggested. He tapped on his mic. "You heard Haven. Everybody back to their positions. Anita, count to ten, then head across the street and turn right onto the next street. Orlando, she'll be coming toward you."

By the time they were back in the blackout van, Anita was on the move again, walking within the circle of blocks they were surveilling with cameras and Scanguards staff. Cooper looked at the clock. It was still early, not even ten o'clock yet.

"What if he doesn't bite?" Diaz asked into the silence.

"Then we'll have to stake out a different area tomorrow night." He cast him a sideways glance. "Don't worry. We've got a lot of people out there who've seen the suspect's sketch. SFPD sent out a bunch of their people in plain clothes, and we're running registrations for all white vans in the Bay Area. We'll find him."

Diaz nodded. "The company you work for, they're an interesting bunch."

"What do you mean?"

He tipped his chin up. "Pretty young, all of them. Your parents must have had you when they were ten."

Cooper shrugged. "Just good genes."

"Hmm. I'm still not sure why the police chief lets Scanguards run this operation. No private company should be responsible for a case like this. No offense, but it's totally against police procedure."

"That's San Francisco for you," Cooper deflected. "We do things differently here." It was best to change the subject, before Diaz found even more things strange. "Is this your first time here?"

"Actually, no. My first wife, Helen, Anita's mother, and I spent our honeymoon here." He let out a breath. "That was a long time ago. Never thought her killer would lead me back here." He rubbed his neck. "Well, until earlier today I didn't even believe that she was dead. Doesn't exactly make me a brilliant cop, does it now? I can't even imagine what Anita went through all these years because I didn't believe her. What kind of father am I not seeing that my child wasn't lying?"

"Don't beat yourself up, José. Anita is a strong woman, maybe because of what she went through. All that matters is that you believe her now."

"Hmm. Those are very wise words for somebody so young."

Cooper's cellphone suddenly chimed with an alert, and a corresponding message flashed on the screen. He tapped on it and read the message.

"Fuck!" Cooper slammed his hand on the steering wheel.

"What?" Panic infused Diaz's question. "Is it Anita?"

Cooper quickly shook his head, then tapped on his mic. "Abort mission. The suspect was seen abducting a blonde woman near the Ferry Building. He got away in a white van."

Several curses came through the earpiece.

"Who's closest to Anita?" Cooper asked.

"I am," Yvette said, "I'll escort her back to your car."

"Thanks, Mom." He tapped on his cellphone, connecting to the command center at Scanguards.

"Coop?" Sebastian answered.

"Got your alert. What other details do you have? I'm with Sheriff Diaz. You're on speaker."

"An administrative assistant working for the SFPD recognized the suspect when she came out of a restaurant across the street from the

Ferry Building and was walking to her car on Steuart Street. She saw him drag a blonde woman into a white van and drive off."

"Did she get the license plate?"

"No, she had to duck down between two cars so the perp wouldn't see her. But she noticed that the woman had dropped something. She picked it up. It was her handbag, so we have an ID on the victim."

"And the van? Did she see which direction it went?"

"No, by the time she felt safe to look around, the van was gone. But around that area it's mostly one-way streets. There aren't that many directions he could have gone."

"Okay, get Thomas and Eddie and their team to comb through the traffic cams in the area. See if they can pick up the van and figure out where it went. We have a good chance to catch him before he has a chance to hurt the woman."

"I'm already on it."

"Good. Samson and the others will be heading back to HQ in a few minutes. I'll drive Anita and her father back home. Expect me at HQ in about an hour. It will take IT longer than that anyway to get any leads on the van. If you need me before that, call me."

"Okay. See you later."

Cooper disconnected the call just as Yvette opened the side door to the van. He looked over his shoulder. Anita got into the van.

"He got another woman? Are they sure it was him?" Anita asked.

"I'm afraid so. But we have a lead. We'll find him. I'll take you and your father back to Wesley's." He cast a grateful smile at his mother. "Thanks, Mom."

"I'll see you at HQ shortly," she said, nodding, and closed the door.

"I'll come to HQ with you," Diaz said.

Cooper shook his head and started the van. "No. You've had a long day. You drove all the way from Nevada this morning. It's best if you and Anita stay at the house and rest. We've got this."

"But—"

"He's right, Dad." Anita leaned forward between the seats and put her hand on her father's shoulder. "You're probably dead tired. Let them do this. There's nothing you can do right now anyway. Once they find where he's taking the woman, we'll see if you're needed."

He looked over his shoulder, remaining silent for a few long moments, before he finally nodded, "Fine. I'll grab a couple of hours of sleep."

34

———

Anita watched her father set down his travel bag next to the bed in the guestroom Wesley and Virginia had prepared for him.

"You have your own bathroom through there," Cooper explained and pointed to a door.

"Thank you. I really appreciate your hospitality," he replied.

"Have a good night."

"Sleep well, Dad," Anita added, and walked back into the hallway, while Cooper pulled the door shut.

She slipped her hand into Cooper's, and motioned him toward the room they'd shared the previous two nights, putting her finger over her lips as a sign to remain quiet. She opened the door, and entered. Cooper followed her and closed the door behind them.

"I don't have much time," he murmured and pulled her into his arms. "But I need to hold you in my arms for a few minutes. You being out there, waiting for the killer, scared me. And I hate feeling scared."

Before she could say anything in return, his lips were on hers, and he kissed her passionately, while he pressed her against the wall. She welcomed his passion and pulled him closer. Within seconds, she was breathless. Reluctantly, she allowed Cooper to take his lips from hers.

"Damn, Anita, you keep this up, and I won't make it into the office."

"Me? You started the kiss."

"Yeah, but you rubbed yourself against me." He chuckled softly. "I wish I could stay, but I only have enough time for a bottle of blood, and then I have to leave."

She nodded. "About that."

"About what?"

"The blood."

"What about it?"

"I want you to bite me and drink my blood instead of what's in the bottles."

She'd made the decision after speaking to Scarlett—or maybe even earlier. Maybe as early as she'd found out that vampires bit their lovers during sex to heighten the pleasure. Scarlet had only confirmed what she'd hoped for. And now that she knew what it was like for a human to be bitten, she couldn't wait for it to happen.

"Anita..." Cooper's eyes turned the color of a river of gold. "You want me to taste your blood?"

She nodded. "Yes. Wasn't that what you hoped for when you arranged for me to talk to Scarlet?"

He ran a hand through his short hair, and Anita noticed that it was trembling. "Yes, but I hadn't expected you to say yes so quickly... Damn it, Babe."

He pressed her back against the wall and rubbed his groin to hers. Beneath his pants, she felt the familiar hard outline of his erection, and her breath hitched at the thought of how quickly she could arouse him. It sent a surge of power through her core.

"Just a quick bite, just so I have something to look forward to until you're back" she murmured, brushing her hair away from one side of her neck, while tilting it in invitation.

He growled, and the sound went through all her cells, making her tremble with anticipation.

"Not like this." Cooper shook his head. "When I drink from you for the first time, I want to do it while I make love to you." He stepped back and pulled his shirt over his head and tossed it on the floor. "Guess my colleagues will have to wait a little longer. I'm sure they can handle things without me for a half hour."

Anita smiled and pulled her shirt over her head, before she kicked off her shoes. Moments later, they were both naked. She let her eyes roam over Cooper's perfect form, drinking in his gorgeous physique. His cock stood proudly like a flag pole, and his chest rose with every breath he took. She would never get enough of this sight of an aroused male who looked at her with such desire in his eyes.

Cooper sat down on the bed, his back against the headboard, and pulled her onto him so she straddled him. His hands locked on her hips and with one thrust, he was inside her, the forceful invasion making her gasp loudly. At the same time, she welcomed his cock, loved the way he took her. And while she'd never liked possessive men, it was different with Cooper. She craved his possessiveness.

"No time for foreplay tonight," he said and sank his lips onto her breasts to lick them.

Anita tossed her head back and arched into his caress, while she followed his hands guiding her hips up and down on his cock. He seemed to be even bigger tonight, and stretched her pussy to its capacity. With every second his tempo increased, and the way he licked and sucked her breasts gave her a preview of what it would be like to feel his bite. Her nipples were hard little pebbles, and her entire body was already covered in a thin sheen of perspiration. Cooper moaned, and his breath ghosted over her flesh, making her shiver with pleasure.

She rode him faster now, taking over the rhythm he'd set. She caressed his nape and ran her fingers up his scalp, feeling him shudder. He released her hips and lifted his head to kiss her, while he kneaded her breasts with both hands. She responded to his kiss, stroking firmly against his tongue, and explored him. Like she'd done once before, she swiped her tongue over his canines, tempting them to come out of hiding.

Cooper moaned into her mouth, and then she felt them: his fangs were extending to their full length. He severed the kiss and looked into her eyes. Their golden hue was more beautiful than anything she'd ever seen.

"I love you," she murmured.

A breath rushed over Cooper's lips. "I love you more."

He tilted his head and brought his face to the crook of her neck. The next thing she felt was his hot tongue licking her, making her skin tingle pleasantly. Then the sharp tips of his fangs pierced her skin and drove deep into her. There was no pain, only the feeling of anticipation. When he began to suck, her entire body began to vibrate from the waves of pleasure that shot through her. Without warning, she climaxed so hard she feared she would pass out from the intense pleasure. But she remained conscious, while her climax ebbed and flowed, only to start all over again a moment later. Inside her, she felt Cooper's hot semen fill her tight sheath, while he continued to thrust deep and hard.

ANITA'S BLOOD filled his mouth and ran down his throat, fulfilling not just his need to feed, but also his need to connect on a deeper level with the woman he loved, the woman he'd give his life to protect. She tasted like the richest dessert on any menu. Her blood was smooth and seductive, tempting and rewarding. She was everything he'd ever dreamed of in a woman. Her wish to feel his bite had been unexpected, and come much earlier than he'd hoped. He'd been unable to resist the temptation to take her, even though he knew he didn't have time for a long night of lovemaking. But he needed this bite. He needed to taste her sweet blood now that she'd offered it to him.

When he felt Anita's interior muscles clamp around his erection while she climaxed, he couldn't stop his own climax. But despite the satisfaction that spread within him, he couldn't stop making love to her. He remained hard, and continued to plunge into her silken sheath. And even though he wasn't gentle tonight, Anita welcomed him nevertheless, her pussy gripping him on each withdrawal as if she didn't want him to leave. Just like he didn't want to end this, even though he knew he had to.

"Yes, yes, oh yes."

Her words spurred him on, and the more blood he took from her, the more his need for her increased. Cooper palmed her responsive breasts, caressing her hard nipples, teasing more moans and sighs from her. He loved the way she rode him, the way she let herself go in his arms, the way she was willing to give him everything he craved. And he craved her, now and always. They would be perfect for each other. He could already see the life they'd have together, the family they would have, the love that would grow deeper with each day.

A foreign sound drifted to his ears, and his vampire instinct took over. With a jolt, Cooper withdrew his fangs from Anita's neck and snapped his gaze to the origin of the sound. It took him almost a second to see who was standing in the open door, the image tinted red because of his glaring eyes.

Sheriff Diaz stared at him, his eyes wide, his jaw dropping. "You monster! Get away from my daughter!" He put his hand to his hips as if wanting to grip his gun, but luckily, he wasn't armed. "Anita!"

Cooper snatched a pillow and used it to cover Anita's nakedness as best he could, while Anita finally looked over her shoulder.

"Dad!"

Diaz made a few steps into the room. "Damn it! He's hurting you! Let go of her!"

"José, please, it's not what it looks like." He held Anita pressed to him, and stretched one arm out in attempt to stop Diaz from coming any closer.

"I'm gonna kill you!" Murder in his eyes, Diaz approached.

"No, Dad! Don't! I love him."

"No! He's a monster! Don't you see that?" He glared at Cooper. "What have you done to her?"

He motioned to the blood that was still seeping from Anita's neck, because Cooper hadn't had a chance to lick over the incisions to close them.

"I'm fine, Dad, please, we'll explain everything to you."

"José, not a step closer. I know you're Anita's father, but that doesn't give you the right to violate her privacy! She's naked, so at least give her the curtesy of allowing her to get dressed. Please leave the room."

"So you can suck her dry?" Diaz yelled, shaking his head, his face a mask of disbelief and distress. "Damn it, Anita, have you no sense of self-preservation? Don't you see what he's doing to you?"

"He loves me!" Anita yelled.

"He's hurting you!"

"I would never hurt Anita! She's going to be my wife, my mate for eternity."

Anita whirled her head back to him. "Your wife? Are you saying..." Tears suddenly brimmed in her eyes.

"Of course, I want you as my wife. Anita, Baby, I want a life with you, a family, children..."

"You can't be serious!" Diaz spat. "You're a monster! You're just using her."

"What's going on here?"

Cooper looked past Diaz and saw Wesley enter the room. He was dressed in only a bathrobe, his skin covered in a golden sheen. Great! There was another thing he had to add to his list to explain to Sheriff Diaz: the mating habits of Stealth Guardians.

"The cat's out of the bag," Cooper said with a shrug.

"I can see that," Wesley replied dryly, pointing at him. "Coop, your fangs are still dripping with blood, and you might wanna close the incisions on Anita's neck."

Diaz's gaze ping-ponged between Wesley and Cooper. Cooper quickly licked over the puncture wounds his fangs had left in Anita's neck, licking up the blood, while resisting the temptation to drink from her again. His saliva healed the wounds immediately, leaving no visible sign of the bite.

"What the...?" Diaz stared at Anita's neck.

Wesley put his hand on Diaz's forearm. "Why don't we give these kids a few moments to get dressed?"

"Thanks, Wes."

Wesley managed to lead Diaz outside, and shut the door.

Cooper took a deep breath. "That's not exactly how I'd hoped me drinking your blood would end."

Anita sighed. "Guess we have to face the music."

"You sure you want your father to know that I'm a vampire?"

"I can't see how we can hide it now."

"I could erase his memory, if that's what you want."

"You can erase people's memories?"

He nodded. "Yes. Though I only do it when it's absolutely necessary. It's your choice."

Anita's inhaled and exhaled slowly. "He needs to know. It'll make everything in the future easier." Then she put her hands on his nape and leaned in. "About what you said to him... that you want me to be your wife..."

He smiled back at her, and moved his hips, thrusting his still-hard cock deeper into her. "I would have proposed in a more romantic setting, but I needed to make sure your father knew that I'm not just using you for your blood." He chuckled. "Though your blood tastes better than anything I've ever had before."

"I'm happy to hear that, because from now on you'll only drink from me." Her eyes sparkled with affection.

"My love," he murmured and kissed her.

35

———————

Fifteen minutes after her father had interrupted them so rudely, Anita walked downstairs, Cooper by her side. They were both fully dressed.

Cooper squeezed her hand. "Don't worry, Baby. It'll turn out fine."

"I hope so." She lowered her voice even more. "What's wrong with Wesley?"

His golden skin had shocked and worried her.

"He's fine. I'll explain everything in a minute."

They entered the living room. Her father was standing near the fireplace, his entire body tense. To her shock, Anita noticed that he was now wearing his gun belt with his gun. Wesley stood leaning against the backrest of the sofa, and straightened immediately when he saw them enter the room.

"Hey, guys, there you are. I'd better get back to my insatiable wife." Wesley smirked.

Cooper nodded. "Thanks for the help."

Wesley disappeared into the foyer, and Anita walked toward her father.

"Why don't we sit down?" she asked and motioned to the large sofa.

"I'd rather stand." Her father demonstratively rested one hand on his belt.

"You won't need that," Anita said, pointing to his gun. "I know firsthand that these bullets can't kill a vampire."

He tipped his chin in Cooper's direction. "So you're not even denying it. You're a fucking vampire."

Cooper nodded, his demeanor calm and collected. "I have no reason to deny it. Yes, I'm a vampire. A hybrid actually, half vampire, half human. And I was drinking your daughter's blood."

"Just like I thought." He pointed his finger at Cooper in accusation. "You're using her. You're a monster! You're forcing her—"

"He isn't forcing me to do anything, Dad," Anita interrupted. "I asked him to bite me. I wanted this."

Her father's forehead furrowed, and he shook his head in disbelief. "Why on earth would you allow that? Why would you allow him to hurt you?"

"Because it doesn't hurt." She stroked her hand over the spot where Cooper had bitten her and exchanged a look with Cooper. She'd never felt such an intense connection with anybody than when Cooper had bitten her.

"The bite is painless when it's done right," Cooper confirmed. "It doesn't leave any scars. Between lovers the bite increases the pleasure."

Anita felt her cheeks heat. She'd never discussed sex with her father, and was glad that Cooper was the one explaining this to him.

"A vampire would never hurt the woman he loves. And I love your daughter. I'd give my life for hers."

At the passionate declaration, Anita inhaled and put her hand to her lips, holding back the tears of joy. She leaned her head against his shoulder, and felt his arm around her back pulling her closer.

"But... but..." Her father ran a shaky hand through his full hair. "How? Why? How did this happen? How can this even be true?" It was almost as if he was talking to himself to try to come to grips with this new reality.

"Earlier tonight, when you ran to get to Anita..." He looked at Cooper. "You were so fast."

Cooper nodded. "Vampires are incredibly fast. And I was scared that the killer would get to her. So I just ran. I didn't care if you saw it. Because if anything happened to Anita, it would kill me." He pressed a kiss to her temple. "It would break my heart."

With wide eyes, her father stared at them as if he was only now truly seeing them. "You do love each other. I should have seen that. So that was the reason why you're staying here with him."

Anita stretched her hand out to him. "Dad, I would have told you earlier that Cooper and I are together, but I knew how you'd react. You would have said that I only just met him, and thought I was reckless. But I know him. I know what's in his heart."

"Aren't you afraid of him?" He pointed at Cooper. "I've seen his fangs. He could rip your throat out with them."

Anita shook her head. "Dad, Cooper would never do that. I shot him when I saw him in his vampire form for the first time, and even then, when he had every right to defend himself and hurt me for hurting him, he didn't lash out. He's a good man."

Her father directed his gaze at Cooper. "Anita really shot you?"

"Yep, she did. One bullet hit my lung, the other lodged just below my right clavicle. She's a pretty good shot, actually."

"When did that happen?"

"Last night."

"You don't look like you're injured."

"My parents got the bullets out quickly. I'm already healed." Cooper shrugged. "It's a pretty neat trait to have."

"Hmm." He studied them in silence, before he added, "Your parents? Are you talking about Yvette and Haven? Are they the vampires who turned you?"

"Turned?" Cooper shook his head. "I was born a vampire. Yvette and Haven are my biological parents.

"So what, Yvette gave birth to you, and then Haven turned her into a vampire? Otherwise, she wouldn't look that young."

It was clear that her father had a hard time wrapping his head around these revelations. Anita stretched her hand out toward him once more.

"Dad, maybe we could sit down now?" She gestured to the sofa.

Finally, he nodded, and they all sat down.

"To answer your question, when my mother gave birth to me, she was already a vampire. And she was the one to turn my father to save his life, when he was mortally wounded."

"Oh." He glanced at Anita, then back at Cooper. "Is that what's gonna happen to Anita? Are you planning to turn her into a…?" A visible shudder went through him, and it was evident that the thought disgusted him.

"If Anita wants to bond with me, she'll remain human. But she won't age."

"How?" The word was more a bark than a question.

"She'll occasionally drink my blood."

Her father jumped up. "So you *are* turning her into a vampire!"

"No, I'm not. It's an unbreakable bond between a vampire and a human, or between vampires." Cooper squeezed her hand. "And if you must know, once Anita and I blood-bond, my life will be in her hands."

Her father narrowed his eyes, looking more quizzical than suspicious now. "What do you mean?"

"Her blood will be the only one I'll be able to drink. If she leaves me, I will starve."

He gasped, but Cooper continued, "As you can see, I have every interest in your daughter being happy with me so she'll never have a reason to leave me."

Anita leaned closer to Cooper. He turned his face to her.

"And I know she'll make me as happy as I'll try to make her."

Anita pressed a kiss to his lips, not caring that her father was watching. "I love you."

"I love you more."

When she turned her head back to her father, she saw him sit down again, slumping against the backrest of the armchair.

"This is crazy. Absolutely crazy. How am I ever gonna explain that to anybody? Nobody will believe me. They'll think I'm nuts."

Cooper leaned forward. "Actually, I have to ask you to keep our secret. It's better that way. For everybody's safety. Scanguards can only work the way they do and help people, because nobody knows what we are. We can't afford a bunch of wannabe vampire slayers descending onto San Francisco and distracting us from our task."

"Which is?"

"Right now?" Cooper asked. "Catching the serial killer just like Chief Donnelly ordered us to do."

"Does he know?"

"He does. He's known about us for three decades. So, getting back to the killer..." Cooper exchanged a look with her.

Anita nodded. "Dad has to know." She looked at her father. "The killer is a vampire too."

"Oh my God!"

All color seemed to drain from his face, and she could see in his eyes what was going through him. He thought of Helen Diaz, her mother, and the monster that had taken her. But Anita didn't want him to go down that dark road right now. There would be time to grieve later.

"That's why the police chief ordered Scanguards to handle this investigation," Anita continued. "The police aren't equipped to fight a vampire. Cooper and his friends are."

Her father stared at Cooper. "But he's one of your own. You must know him."

Cooper let out a bitter laugh. "Do you know every Latino in this country?" He didn't wait for an answer, but continued, "Just like we don't know every vampire. And a rogue vampire who kills people and sucks them dry, hurts us all. He has to be taken down."

"No offense, Cooper, but you can't tell me that you've never snatched a human off the street to drink his or her blood."

"I've bitten humans before. That's true. But never without their permission. Never to hurt somebody. My parents raised me and my sister on bottled blood. Scanguards purchases it through a medical supply company, just like any hospital does."

"Hmm." Slowly, he nodded. "So everybody I met at Scanguards and here at your uncle's house... they're all vampires. I knew something was off. But I couldn't figure out what. I should have known."

"It's not an easy thing to figure out," Anita said.

"And, uhm, Wesley is not a vampire. He's a witch," Cooper added.

"A witch? What else is new? Is that what caused his golden skin? Something went wrong with a magic potion?"

Cooper chuckled. "No, nothing went wrong."

"Then what?" Anita urged, because she was curious too.

"Okay," Cooper said, lowering his voice. "Just keep it to yourselves please."

Her father huffed. "Who would I tell even if I wanted to?"

"Wesley's wife is a Stealth Guardian, and let's just say that their mating rituals are a little different from ours. The partner of a Stealth Guardian will shimmer golden when they have sex, and for many hours afterwards. It..." Cooper cleared his throat. "...uhm, extends the pleasure."

"Oh." Her father suddenly stared at his shoes, clearly uncomfortable.

Anita whispered to Cooper, "You mean like the bite?"

"Yes, like the bite." He smiled at her, his eyes shimmering golden now too as if in response to the memory of what they'd shared only half an hour earlier.

Cooper leaned in for a kiss, but his cellphone rang and he pulled it from his pocket. "Nicholas?"

For a moment, he was silent, then he said, "I'm on my way."

Cooper disconnected the call and jumped up. "We've got a lead on the suspect. You both need to come to HQ with me."

36

The command center at Scanguards was teeming with people. Nicholas was sitting at the main console, while Yvette and Haven stood talking with Samson and Amaury. Zane was hovering over Nicholas, talking quietly to him, while Luther sat next to Thomas, Scanguards' resident IT genius, and both were scrolling through video footage.

"What do we have?" Cooper asked, approaching Nicholas.

Nicholas looked up, and clicked on something with his mouse, then pointed to the large wall of screens. "We were able to backtrack the serial killer from where he snatched his latest victim."

Cooper looked at the video feed on the large screen, where a man in dark clothes dragged a well-dressed blonde woman into a white van.

"He was careless, parking only a few yards away from a traffic camera," Nicholas explained. "From here we were able to follow the van. We pieced together where the white van disappeared to."

He switched to a different video feed, where the van could be seen entering a building. "That's on 22nd Street and Tennessee. We've got eyes on it via the feed from a business across the street, and he hasn't come back out yet."

"Okay." Cooper nodded and turned around to look at everybody.

"We've got about four hours till sunrise, which means we have to act now. It gives us more flexibility as to who can take part in the mission, but it also gives the perp a chance to slip out without risking getting burned to a crisp. So—"

"Cooper," Haven interrupted with a quick sideways glance at Sheriff Diaz.

"It's okay, Dad, Sheriff Diaz found out earlier tonight. He's aware of what we are, and that the serial killer is also a vampire."

Several pairs of eyebrows rose. Cooper shrugged. "Couldn't be avoided. But he's good with it, right, José?"

"Do I have a choice?" Diaz asked laconically and shrugged. "So, what's the plan?"

"Thomas and Luther, you'll continue the electronic surveillance, and make sure he doesn't slip out before we get there."

Thomas nodded. "No problem. I've already got a drone in the air."

"Good thinking," Cooper praised. "Nicholas, you'll stay in the command center with Sheriff Diaz and Anita. Alert Charles to be ready in case we need to apply witchcraft. And call Wesley to come in as well just in case. He and Virginia are home right now."

Then he looked at the others. "We'll go in three cars. Zane, go with Samson. Dad, go with Amaury, and Mom, you're coming with me. Nicholas, make sure Maya follows in the Scanguards ambulance, but have her on standby two blocks from 22nd and Tennessee. Have one of the hybrids drive. You have your weapons?"

Several affirmative replies could be heard in the room.

"Do we shoot to kill?" The question came from Zane, which was no surprise. He was the most cold-blooded amongst them.

"Only if you can't avoid it. But I'd rather get this asshole alive, if we can." He took a breath. "Okay, let's roll out."

As the teams started leaving the command center, Cooper approached Anita and took her hand. "You and your dad have to stay here. Under no circumstances can you leave this building. We've had instances where the bad guys tricked some of us, pretending that something happened to one of us. It happened to Blake's wife, who was tricked, thinking she was helping Blake, and she wasn't the only person that's happened to. It happened to Katie too. So, don't believe anybody, if they say that I got hurt, and you need to come and save me. It'll be a lie. Stay here with Nicholas. You can trust him."

Anita nodded, her body visibly tense. "All right. But you'd better come back in one piece."

"Promise." He pressed a quick kiss to her lips, nodded at Diaz, and left the command center.

THE BUILDING on 22nd Street and Tennessee was a residential home undergoing a major renovation after what looked like extensive fire damage. The gate to the double garage was closed. Many of the windows on both floors were either missing or covered with plywood to keep the elements out.

Cooper drove past it and parked around the next corner. He killed the engine and looked at Yvette. "Rock 'n' roll."

"Let's gets this bastard."

They jumped out of the SUV, and Cooper locked the car. When they came around the corner, he already saw his colleagues approach the building from the other side.

Cooper touched his earpiece. "Thomas, any new developments?"

"It's all quiet. No changes. I can see all six of you."

"Any heat signatures in the building?" Cooper asked.

"Negative. There might be a basement or something the drone can't penetrate."

"Okay. Guys, we're ready. Zane and Samson, tradesmen entrance. I'll pick the lock," Cooper offered, and approached the front door, where Amaury and Haven were already waiting.

"Not necessary," Amaury whispered. "Door's unlocked."

"Careful," Cooper cautioned. "Could be a trap."

Gun in one hand, he reached for the door handle, but Haven stopped him.

"I'll go in first, Son. Stay behind me," Haven ordered, and was already swinging the door open, rushing into the dark interior.

Cooper was behind him. They covered each other, going from room to room, Amaury and Yvette on their heels. When a sound came from the back of the house, Cooper aimed his gun in that direction, but it was only Zane who appeared, followed by Samson.

"All clear in the back," Zane confirmed.

"Upstairs?" Cooper motioned to the stairs, ready to ascend, when he realized that the stairs only led halfway up to the top floor. The remainder had been destroyed by a fire. He stopped in his tracks. "Thomas? Can your drone see what's going on on the second floor? There's no access from the first floor; stairs are damaged."

"Give me a sec."

Meanwhile, Cooper motioned toward the others. "Garage?"

Amaury turned to a door and opened it by a sliver, peering inside. A second later, he swung the door open and rushed inside, Yvette on his heels. By the time Cooper followed them, Amaury was already giving the sign for the all-clear.

"White van is empty," Amaury reported. "No sign of the victim or the serial killer."

"There's a door," Yvette announced.

Cooper approached. "No lock." He turned the knob and eased it open. Before him was a flight of wooden stairs, and beyond that, only darkness. He turned his head and noticed a light switch. He flipped it, and a single light bulb illuminated the stairs. They led down into a basement.

Cooper heard a sound drifting up. He turned his head and raised his hand to ask for silence. There it was again, a grunt.

Then Thomas's voice came through the earpiece. "No sign of anybody on the second floor."

"We're going down to the basement," Cooper announced, and descended the stairs, gripping his gun firmly and staying vigilant. He sniffed. The further he descended, the stronger the aroma of blood became. Human blood.

At the bottom of the stairs, he turned to his left. There, a blonde woman was bound to a wooden support post, her mouth taped with duct tape, her eyes shining with fear, blood residue crusting along her neck.

"She's here," Cooper called out over his shoulder, where Yvette was already appearing. "She's alive."

He put his gun away and approached the frightened woman, crouching down next to her. "We're here to help you. We'll take care of you now."

He removed the tape from her mouth, and she cried out in pain.

"I'm sorry," he said in a calm voice, not wanting to scare the woman even more. "The man who kidnapped you. Where is he?"

Tears started streaming down her cheeks. "I don't know. He brought me here, then he bit my neck... and, oh God, it was terrible..."

"When did he leave you?"

"I don't know." She sobbed. "I must have passed out."

"I'll take care of her," Yvette offered and untied her. "Honey, let's get you out of here."

Cooper tapped on his earpiece. "Maya, please bring the ambulance around. We have the victim, but the perp is gone. He must have slipped out the back via one of the houses behind us."

By the time Yvette had helped the victim up the stairs, the Scanguards ambulance was already parked outside, and Maya was ready to examine the woman's injuries. Cooper approached his colleagues.

"This was too easy," he said.

"Way too easy," Samson agreed. "First, we can't find his white van anywhere in the city, nor him, for that matter, and suddenly we find his lair less than two hours after he abducted his latest victim?"

Cooper rubbed his neck. "He wanted us to find her."

"That's what I think too," Amaury said. "He led us here. Why?"

"It doesn't fit his pattern at all." Cooper touched his earpiece again. "Nicholas, are we sure that this woman was abducted by our suspect?"

There was a crackling in the line, then Nicholas replied, "A hundred percent. On one of the traffic cams after he abducted the woman, you can clearly see his face. He didn't even try to disguise it. In fact, it's kind of odd, but now that I'm looking at it again, it looked as if he was purposely looking up at the traffic cam."

"Thanks." Cooper let out a grunt. "We gotta get back to HQ. He's planning something else. And I'm not gonna let Anita or her father out of my sight."

"Agreed," Samson said and looked toward the street. "Ambulance is leaving. Let's all get back now. We'll regroup at HQ."

While Haven, Amaury, Zane, and Samson headed in one direction, Cooper and Yvette headed into the opposite one to get to the car.

"There's no way he can get into HQ," Yvette said, clearly in an effort to reassure him.

"That's what we always think. And then somebody manages to penetrate our defenses nevertheless. And I can't allow that."

He unlocked the car and jumped into the driver's seat. Yvette got in on the passenger side and slammed the car door shut.

"She's the one, isn't she?" she asked with a sideways glance at him, just as he put the car in drive.

"Yes. She offered me her blood earlier tonight." He smiled at her. "I'm a very lucky guy."

"Then let's make sure nothing happens to her."

Yvette had barely finished her sentence, when there was a loud popping sound, while the car slowed down. Before Cooper could figure out what had gone wrong, smoke came out from under the hood, and penetrated the interior of the car.

"Fuck!"

He exchanged a quick glance with his mother.

"Out, now!" Cooper ordered, worried that the car might catch fire and they'd be trapped inside. He yanked his door open, and heard Yvette do the same on her side. The smoke around them temporarily impeded his vision.

"Mom, you okay?" he called out. "Where are you?"

"Here, honey," she replied.

He followed her voice, and approached her, until he could finally see her again, just reaching the sidewalk. Yvette was already pulling her cellphone from her jacket pocket, when the muffled sound of a bullet whizzing past him made him gasp in horror.

Yvette was hit, and the impact slammed her back, making her fall backwards onto the sidewalk.

"Mom!"

In the same instance, he was yanked back, and the cold metal of a silver chain wrapped around his neck. His skin sizzled, and pain seared through him, almost paralyzing him for a moment.

"Mom, no!" Cooper tried to kick his elbows back, but his attacker was stronger, and he couldn't free himself from the iron grip. When the attacker slammed him against the car, Cooper got a quick glance at him. It was the vampire they'd been looking for.

"Gotcha, pretty boy!" his attacker hissed. "Shame I'm not into guys, but you'll do nicely as a bargaining chip."

Two thoughts went through his mind in a flash. Would his mother survive the gunshot wound? Since the attacker was a vampire, he was certain that the bullet was silver, and the silver would spread inside her body, eating away her flesh, if it wasn't removed in time. His second thought was of Anita. Would his friends at Scanguards be able to keep her safe?

37

The command center was getting busier again. After Cooper, his parents, and his colleagues had left to catch the serial killer, Anita and her father had been alone with Nicholas, Thomas, and Luther for a short while. Virginia had joined them shortly after, and told them that Wesley had gone straight to his lab to meet with the other witch in Scanguards' employ in case anything went wrong, and their skills were needed.

Over the next half hour, more people had joined them, among them Vanessa, who she'd met the night she and Cooper had questioned the prostitutes and homeless in the city. Anita had listened in on the communications between the members of the rescue team and the command center staff.

"Thank God the woman is alive," Anita said with a sigh of relief, though she was disappointed to hear that the killer had escaped.

Nicholas looked over his shoulder. "The ambulance is about six minutes out."

Anita exchanged a look with her father.

He sighed heavily. "He got away. I thought that finally, tonight, we'd get closure."

She squeezed her father's arm. "So did I. But they'll find him. If not tonight, then another night."

He nodded slowly, then addressed the Scanguards staff. "I must say I'm impressed with the setup you people have here. Looks like state of the art. Can't say that at my station we're as well equipped as you."

Luther rose and stretched his legs. "If you're impressed with this here, you should see the vampire prison."

"There's a vampire prison?"

He didn't get a reply to his question, because in that moment, an alarm sounded and a photo flashed on one of the monitors on the wall. It was a photo of Yvette.

Instantly, everybody in the room was on high alert, and several curses echoed against the walls.

"What's going on?" Anita asked, her heart beating like a jackhammer.

"Yvette's sending a distress signal," Nicholas said quickly, then turned with his chair and addressed Thomas, "Haven's car is closest to her."

"Got him," Thomas confirmed and typed frantically on his keyboard.

"Not Cooper?" Anita asked as people started to talk over each other. "He's driving back with her in the same car." She gripped her father's arm for support. "Dad?" Her chest heaved, and panic choked off her air supply. "Where's Cooper?"

"Haven and Amaury are making a U-turn," Thomas confirmed, calling out over his shoulder. "ETA to Yvette's position: ninety seconds."

"Where's Cooper?" Anita yelled, finally managing to be heard over the din in the room.

Nicholas looked over his shoulder. "I can't ping his cell. The car and Yvette are two blocks from the place where they freed the woman, but—"

"His phone is off, or somebody disabled the GPS," Thomas confirmed.

"How about his comms?" Virginia asked.

"Offline," Nicholas replied. "Thomas, the drone."

Thomas hit his fist on the desk. "Damn it! The drone was too low. It didn't see anything farther than fifty yards from the house. Redirecting it now."

Anita felt fear grip her, making every breath painful. It seemed to take forever until Thomas finally projected an image onto one of the wall monitors.

"That's the live footage of the drone. The car's there. Fuck!"

When Thomas zoomed in, Anita could see it too. Not only was there smoke coming from the car's engine, and the doors were open, but Yvette lay on the sidewalk, her body twisting in agony, blood drenching her clothes.

Anita pressed her hand on her mouth to stop herself from screaming. Her father put his arm around her, holding her, just when two men entered the drone's field of vision: Haven and Amaury. They rushed to Yvette, and Haven crouched down.

A moment later, Haven's voice filled the command center. "Yvette's been shot with a silver bullet. Maya, turn the ambulance around. We've gotta get it out now before it's too late."

"And Cooper?" Anita choked out, tears welling up in her eyes. "Where's Cooper?"

On the monitor she saw Haven cradle Yvette in his arms and bring his face to hers. "Baby, where's Cooper? What happened to him?"

Anita couldn't hear what Yvette said, or if she managed to say anything, and the seconds ticked by like hours. She couldn't lose him. She couldn't lose the man she loved. He had to live.

"She said the suspect from the sketch shot her, then overpowered Cooper and dragged him away, a silver chain around his neck. She couldn't see the car he used to get away."

For a moment, Anita felt relief. Cooper was still alive. But for how long? What was the killer planning to do with him?

"We'll find him," Thomas promised and hammered away on his keyboard. "Command center to all units in the vicinity of 22nd and Tennessee..."

Anita tuned out Thomas's voice as he gave instructions to

Scanguards staff to start the search for Cooper and the vampire who'd snatched him.

"Anita?" Vanessa said and put a hand on her shoulder.

Anita turned away from her father, and Vanessa put her arms around her. Overwhelmed by her kindness and sensitivity, Anita let the tears flow.

"We'll find him," Vanessa assured her. "That's what we're good at. Trust me, the reason the perp didn't shoot him like he shot Yvette means that he needs him alive."

Anita sniffled and nodded, trying to convince herself that Vanessa was right. "And Yvette? Will she make it?"

Vanessa sighed. "A silver bullet is very dangerous. It burns a vampire's body from the inside out, like acid. She's got about thirty to forty minutes to get it out, or the progression can't be stopped."

She didn't have to ask what that meant.

"Haven is with her now," Vanessa continued, "and my mother, Maya, has all the equipment to cut the bullet out. She just has to get there in time."

Anita looked back at the main screen where Haven crouched next to Yvette, slicing away the clothing around her gunshot wound with his claws, evidently prepared to cut the bullet out with his bare hands.

38

———

The smell of the brackish water of the San Francisco Bay drifted into Cooper's nose, and he knew they were only a few yards away from it. The vampire who'd captured him had tossed him in the trunk of a car, his hands bound by silver and a silver chain around his neck. The metal bit into him like acid, eating away the top layers of his skin to get to the sensitive flesh beneath. The physical pain was excruciating, but the emotional one was worse. The attacker had shot his mother, Yvette, and Cooper had no idea whether Scanguards had gotten to her in time to save her.

At least fifteen minutes had passed since the ambush. He wasn't sure where exactly he was. The attacker had dragged him out of the trunk moments earlier inside a building, and all Cooper could see was that they were in a large warehouse or hanger that appeared abandoned. A large window provided a view of the road leading to the building, and by the looks of it, it was the only way to reach it. He assumed that only water and maybe a pier were behind the building. It gave his opponent the upper hand: should anybody approach, he would be able to shoot them like fish in a barrel.

Cooper was tied to a pipe at one wall, propped up against the damp surface of the brick for support. Defiantly, he glared at the vampire as he approached. He was indeed the man Ginger had described to the sketch artist, and the one Anita had recognized as her mother's abductor.

"What do you want with me?" Cooper ground out, forcing himself to ignore the pain. He wasn't defeated yet. He trusted Scanguards to come for him, even though his attacker had taken his cellphone from him, and either discarded it or removed the chip so Scanguards couldn't track it. They'd have to find him by different means. He just had to buy himself enough time to give them a chance to locate him.

"I'm not really interested in you per se, just what you can do for me." An evil chuckle echoed in the empty hall. "I don't swing that way, if you get my meaning."

Cooper didn't care either way. "I don't see that there's anything I can do for you." He shrugged, tilting his head slightly toward his bound hands. "Given that I'm a little tied up."

"So you wanna play the funny one. Your moods change quickly, considering that you screamed for your mama not too long ago."

"Fuck you!" Cursing made him move his head, resulting in the silver chain chafing more violently against his neck. A pained grunt made it past his lips.

The killer smiled. "Well, let's get down to business then, now that we've established who's in charge." He pulled a cellphone from his pocket and punched in a number. Two yards away from Cooper, he pointed it straight at him. "We're doing a little video call, so smile for the camera."

Cooper clenched his jaw.

"Hello?"

He recognized Anita's voice instantly, even though she sounded choked up as if she'd been crying.

"Anita," the vampire said, "look who wants to say hello."

"Oh God, no! Cooper!" Anita cried out. A sob followed.

From the background noise coming through the line he deducted that Anita was still in the command center surrounded by Scanguards staff.

"I have a little trade to propose," the serial killer said. "I'll let him go.

Unharmed. Well, almost unharmed, but he'll be alive. Would you like that?"

"Let him go!" Anita demanded.

The vampire's grin sent a chill down Cooper's back. Before he even continued, Cooper instinctively knew what the man wanted. A trade, that's what he'd said. And he knew exactly what kind of trade the asshole would propose.

"Don't listen to him, Anita!" Cooper yelled. "Whatever he's offering you, don't—"

A gloved fist punched him so hard that his head whipped to the side, and the violent action made the silver chain slice even deeper into his neck. He cried out in pain.

"Don't touch him!"

"As you wish, my dear Anita," the vampire said. "You know, you're just like your mother in so many ways."

A loud gasp came through the line, and Cooper could only imagine what Anita was going through right now. "Don't listen to him, Anita!"

"Would you shut up for a minute or do I have to cut your tongue out? Goddamn it, your boyfriend is an annoying piece of shit. I can't wait to get him out of my sight. So, here's how it's gonna go: you, my dear Anita, will come to me, alone, and once you're here, I'll let him go. Simple as that. He in exchange for you. It's a pretty good deal."

"Don't, Anita!" Cooper yelled. "The moment you're here, he's gonna kill me anyway. You can't trust him!"

The vampire let out an annoyed huff and reached into the back of his waistband with his free hand, pulling a gun from it. He pointed it at Cooper. "I said, shut up!" He pulled the trigger.

The silver bullet hit Cooper's upper thigh, the impact and the resulting pain knocking the wind out of him. He screamed involuntarily, unable to clamp his jaw shut.

"No! Cooper, no!" Anita screamed through the phone.

"Now, listen to me, Anita! That was a silver bullet, and if you don't know what a silver bullet does to a vampire hybrid, ask his family, they'll tell you. He's got thirty minutes, maybe forty-five until the silver burns him from the inside, and he's gonna turn into a pile of ash. You wanna save him? I'll text you my location. Come alone. If I see anybody but you coming closer than a quarter mile, I'll stake your boyfriend instantly. Take a convertible and keep the top down. I wanna see that you're alone. No tricks. Now get moving. Clock's ticking."

He disconnected the call.

"I'm gonna kill you," Cooper pressed out through clenched teeth, the pain of the silver attacking his body from the inside making him delirious. He could only hope that his friends and family at Scanguards would stop Anita from going through with this exchange.

39

In shock, Anita stared at her cellphone, digesting what she's just seen and heard, when a message chimed: the location of where the suspect was keeping Cooper.

She showed the display to Nicholas. "Where is this?"

While Nicholas typed the location info into his computer, her father put her hand on her shoulder. "You can't possibly do what that perp is demanding! That's suicide!"

Her eyes tearing, she shook her head. "It's love. I'm not going to let him die."

"But he said himself that you shouldn't follow those demands."

"Your father is right," Luther interjected. "Nobody expects you to make the exchange. It's too dangerous."

"I'm already working on how else to get him out of there," Thomas said without looking over his shoulder, hacking away on his keyboard. "We'll find a way."

"Not in time!" Anita pointed to her cellphone. "You all saw it yourselves! He shot Cooper with a silver bullet." She looked at Vanessa. "Tell me the truth: will it really kill him in half an hour?"

Vanessa quickly glanced at the others in the room, but then nodded. "Yes, and it's not a painless death."

A sob tore from Anita's throat, but she choked it back down. "Then I have no choice. I love him. I have to save him."

"Damn it, Anita!" her father grunted. "Don't do this! Think what that monster did to your mother. And now you want him to do the same to you? No! I forbid it!"

"You don't have a say in this, Dad. It's my life." She looked at the other faces in the room. "Does anybody here have a convertible?"

Nicholas looked over his shoulder. "Amaury's 911 is in the garage. We have the spare keys." He already rose and hurried to a cupboard, ripping it open.

Anita nodded, then caught Virginia's gaze on her.

"You don't have to do this alone," Virginia said.

It took her one second to understand Virginia's words. Her heart beat excitedly. "You're right." She reached for the key that Nicholas was handing her.

"Level P1, right outside the elevator."

"How do I get the bullet out of Cooper's thigh?" Anita asked, looking at the assembled.

"Knife," Virginia said. "I have one on me." She pointed to her boot. "Where are the silver chains?"

Luther jumped up to open another closet. "Help yourself."

Virginia grabbed what she needed.

"Good." Then Anita thought of something else. Something that might help with actually pulling this off. "Does anybody have perfume I can borrow?"

"Perfume?" her father asked. "What the—"

"I do," Vanessa interrupted, and dug into her handbag, pulling out a small bottle. "This should do. Use double what you think will be enough."

Anita snatched it. "Virginia, let's go!" She was already hurrying to the door.

"By the time you're in the car, I will have programmed the Porsche's GPS system to lead you straight to the address," Nicholas called after her.

In the elevator, Anita sprayed a liberal amount of perfume all other herself, and Virginia did the same. It took them almost a minute to reach parking level P1.

"There it is," Virginia pointed out. "You've got this, girl."

Anita unlocked the car remotely, and jumped in. Moments later, the car shot out of the garage, and she followed the instructions the navigation system provided her with. She had no time to marvel at the efficiency with which every member of the Scanguards team had instantly jumped into action. Instead, she concentrated on the street ahead of her, and kicked the gas pedal down. There was virtually no traffic this time of night, and the further she drove, the more industrial the area became. Her heart beat into her throat, and her palms were covered in cold sweat.

"Cooper, I'm coming. Hold on a little longer. I'll be there," she murmured to herself.

What was he going through right now? What kind of pain did he have to endure?

"In two hundred yards you'll arrive at your destination. Your destination is on the right," the car's navigation system announced.

A moment later, she stopped the car. She was on a large area that looked like an abandoned shipyard or building yard. A large hanger-like building rose to her right: the place where the serial killer was holding Cooper.

Anita opened the car door and got out. She'd left her handbag and her cellphone at Scanguards, but she knew she wouldn't need it. Taking a deep breath, she rushed toward a door that was half open. She ripped it fully open and stepped into the dark interior.

"Well, there you are, Anita." It was the killer's cold voice.

It took her another few seconds before her eyes had adjusted to the darkness, and she could see well enough to see the man who'd spoken. She peered past him, her eyes searching for Cooper. She found him at the same spot where he'd been during the video call.

Anita approached, the clacking of her shoes and her purposely heavy footfalls echoing in the empty building, drowning out other sounds.

"I'm here. So, let him go," she demanded.

The killer chuckled.

"Anita, run," Cooper called out to her, his voice weak. "Please, save yourself."

But she wasn't here to save herself. She was here to save him. "Everything will be all right, Cooper. Even if you can't see it."

"How cute," the killer spat, then suddenly whipped his head in the direction of the door, his eyes narrowing. "Hmm." He sniffed visibly, then looked back at her. "You're wearing an awful lot of perfume."

"Don't like it?" He would like it even less in a moment, because the fact that the smell intensified, meant that Virginia was in position.

"Let's go, Anita. Time to make an exit," he commanded.

He grabbed her forearm, but was instantly yanked back, a surprised gasp dislodging from his throat. A second later, he landed with his back on the ground. The sound of a chain clanking echoed against the walls, and the perp suddenly screamed in pain. Anita stared at him as he struggled against his invisible attacker, when Virginia all of a sudden became visible, pulling on the chain that she'd wrapped around the serial killer's neck. She was pinning him down on the cold ground without effort, though the asshole tried to fight her—without much success.

"I'm good here," Virginia assured her. "Start cutting open the bullet wound." She reached into her boot and retrieved a knife. "While I tie this bastard up."

Anita snatched the knife and rushed to Cooper. She cupped his cheek. "I'm here, my love. I'm not gonna let you die."

"Anita," he murmured, his voice even weaker than before.

As carefully as she could without causing him any harm, she unwrapped the silver chain from his neck, revealing the raw flesh beneath. She couldn't fathom what pain Cooper was in, but she couldn't dwell on this right now. She had to get the bullet out.

Her hand shook when she directed the knife toward Cooper's thigh wound.

"It's gonna hurt, but I have to cut the bullet out," she said, more to herself than to him. She'd never done anything like this. Coopers head rolled forward, his eyes drifting shut. "Oh God, Baby, hold on."

"I've got you," Virginia suddenly said from behind her.

Anita looked over her shoulder, and saw that Virginia had secured the long silver chain around the perp's neck on a hook on a support post.

"Scanguards, you're clear to approach. Perp is subdued," Virginia said, pressing a button on her cellphone, before she kneeled down and took the knife from Anita's hands. "He needs blood."

Anita nodded. At least that was something she could do. While Virginia started to work on Cooper's upper thigh, Anita leaned over Cooper. She lifted his chin up and brought her neck to his mouth.

"You have to drink, Cooper, please," she urged him, putting her hand on the back of his head, careful not to touch his injured nape, to press his lips to her exposed neck. He didn't immediately react. "Please, Cooper, you need to be strong now." Tears started to run down her cheeks, and she could taste the salt on her lips.

"Cooper, please drink."

Finally, she felt his hot breath on her skin, and the sharp tips of his fangs drove deep into her flesh. She gasped at the initial pain, and realized why this time the incisions caused her to feel pain: Cooper hadn't licked the spot before driving his fangs into her neck. But it didn't matter. Now that he was sucking on her vein, drinking her blood, there was no more pain, just the knowledge that he was alive, and that, with her help, he was fighting to stay alive. Because she knew in that moment that a life without Cooper wouldn't be worth living. He was everything to her. Everything she'd ever dreamed of. The keeper of her heart. The vampire she trusted with her life and her happiness.

Behind her, she heard the sound of several car engines, then the opening and closing of car doors, followed by footfalls of a large number of people. The cavalry had arrived.

40

———————

Cooper felt the excruciating pain lessen all of a sudden, and realized that its origin, the silver bullet, wasn't lodged in his thigh anymore. Somebody had cut it out. The delirium he'd been in was clearing at the same time, and he was fully aware of the lifegiving blood that ran down his throat, strengthening him so breathing became easier again. He recognized the blood. It was AB positive, but it wasn't just any AB positive blood. It was Anita's. And the body pressed against his and the hand on the back of his head belonged to Anita. Against his orders, she'd come to save him, had put herself in danger—for him.

Slowly, his brain began to work again, and his body registered the amount of blood he'd already taken from her. It was enough for now. He withdrew his fangs from her neck and licked over the incisions, sealing them.

"Bullet's out, Anita," he heard somebody say and recognized the voice as Virginia's. "He should be healing now."

Anita drew her head back, and he was able to look into her face. It was tearstained. Virginia was kneeling next to him, wiping her knife on her pants.

"Thank you, Virginia." She acknowledged his words with a smile.

Then he looked back at Anita. "Baby, you came. You shouldn't have put yourself in danger for me." His voice sounded breathy in his own ears, and he realized the extent of the damage the silver had already done to his body.

She put a finger over his lips. "I had to. I love you."

"I love you more." He locked eyes with her for a second, before looking past her and seeing his friends and colleagues from Scanguards. Some of them were dealing with the serial killer, others walked toward him. He zeroed in on Samson, though his vision was blurry, his body too weak to supply all his senses with enough energy and blood.

"My mother?" Cooper asked, dread filling his gut, his heart clenching in pain.

Samson smiled and crouched down. "She's healing. Maya got the bullet out of her chest just in time. Your father is with her back at HQ."

Relief washed over him. "Thank God."

Samson turned to Anita and Virginia. "Nice touch with the perfume. Even I can't smell the difference between the two of you right now."

"The asshole didn't smell me coming," Virginia said with a smile. "It was Anita's idea though. You've got a smart cookie there, Coop." She rose.

Cooper looked past Samson. "Let's deal with that bastard." He tried to stand up, but searing pain shot through him at the attempt, and he sank back against the ground. He hated to be weak. "Fuck!"

"You're badly injured. You need help," Anita said and shook her head.

Samson reached for him, but before he could help him up, Sheriff Diaz appeared at his side. "I'll help him. Guess my daughter risking her life for yours means you'll be family pretty soon, Son."

"Yeah, you're not getting rid of me now," Cooper managed to say.

"And you and Anita are part of the Scanguards family now, Sheriff," Samson added.

With Diaz's and Samson's help, Cooper was able to get up. Diaz kept his arm around Cooper's waist, and Anita slipped her hand into his. He gave her a grateful smile. He'd thank her for what she'd done for him later when he was healed. Right now, all he could hope for was to remain upright until the hostile vampire was dealt with.

Supported by Diaz, Cooper was able to walk toward the post where the serial killer was tied up with a silver chain around his neck. Luther and Zane stood to his sides, restraining him. Still, the hostile vampire was fighting against his restraints.

Cooper stopped a few yards away from him, making sure that the bastard couldn't reach Anita or Diaz even if he kicked his legs toward them.

The vampire glared at him, his eyes glowing red, his fangs extended, his attitude promising violence. "It's that bitch's fault!" He tipped his chin toward Anita, even though the movement made the skin around his neck sizzle even more. "Your mother! It's Helen's fault! If she had stayed with me, I wouldn't have had to kill all the others! But no, I wasn't good enough for her! So I gave her what she deserved. I bled her dry slowly for stringing me along."

Next to him, Anita gasped, and released his hand in the same instance. She took a step closer toward the serial killer, and Cooper wanted to pull her back, but Diaz held him back.

"You little shit!" Anita faced the bastard, her body showing no signs of fear. "Don't you dare besmirch my mother's memory! She didn't want you. You took her against her will. And then you used her. She would have never loved a man like you! And you knew that all along, or you wouldn't have had to threaten her to take me too if she didn't come with you."

There was a flash of surprise in the vampire's eyes. "You were there…"

"I saw you," Anita continued, going toe to toe with him now.

Cooper glanced at Luther and Zane, giving them a wordless sign, and the two bent the bastard's arms farther back to inflict more pain and make it impossible for him to lash out at Anita.

"You're a fucking coward, blaming others for your shortcomings," Anita continued. "The only one who's responsible for the murders you've committed is yourself. If you were a man, you'd realize that. But you're not a man. You're a psychopath, and a sniffling little weasel on top of it." She spat in his face.

The vampire growled, but there was nothing he could do. Luther and Zane held him in an iron grip, and the silver chain around his neck weakened him. Still, the bastard was full of defiance, and glared at Anita.

"It took her a long time to die. And I made sure she knew that I'd come back for you, her daughter, when the time was right." He let out a sinister laugh. "And then I chopped up her body and burned the pieces."

Anita let out a sob, and Cooper's heart broke for her.

"You're a monster." Anita turned away from the bastard.

Cooper wanted to comfort her, but he was running on fumes, and could barely keep himself upright even with Diaz's help. While Anita's blood had started the healing process, the silver bullet in his thigh had done great damage, and he needed to rest so his body could fully heal. He leaned more heavily on Diaz, his strength waning fast.

"Let's take care of him here and now," Samson announced. "Cooper? Do you want to do the honors?"

Cooper shook his head, and the action made him feel lightheaded. "As much as I want to stake him myself, I believe two others have an older claim."

Samson looked at Anita and Diaz. "Anita, José, if you want to take justice into your own hands, you can execute him right now. If not, one of us will do it."

"How do I kill him?" Diaz asked immediately.

"A stake through the heart," Samson replied.

"I want to do it," Anita suddenly said.

Diaz shook his head. "No, honey, killing somebody, even a lowlife like this one, isn't something I want you to have on your conscience. I'll do it for the both of us. For your mother."

Samson reached into his jacket pocket and handed him a wooden stake. "Just aim for the heart."

"And step back quickly, unless you want to be covered in ash," Zane added.

Diaz removed his arm from Cooper's waist and cast him a quick look. "Can you stand on your own?"

"I've got him," Anita said quickly, putting her arm around his waist to hold him up.

Diaz stepped forward toward the vampire.

"Your wife was a great fuck," the serial killer hissed defiantly. "I bet your daughter would have been even better."

"You aren't worth the dirt under their shoes." Diaz slammed the stake into the vampire's chest.

Before everybody's eyes, the vampire turned into ash, and the silver chain fell to the floor, the sound echoing in the empty building. Luther and Zane jumped to the side in time not to get vampire ash on them, but Diaz wasn't as fast, and some of the ash landed on his clothes.

Diaz turned around and looked at him and Anita. "It's finally over." Tears welled up in his eyes, and Anita stretched her hand out to pull him into an embrace.

"Yes, it's over, Dad." Anita sniffled, pushing back the tears. "Let's go home."

Cooper looked at Samson, who nodded. "We'll clean up here. You need to rest."

"Yes, I need to—" Cooper took one step, when his knees suddenly buckled, and everything around him began to turn.

"Cooper?" Anita's panicked voice drifted to him.

Everything turned dark, and he tumbled. Somebody caught him, and he let it happen. Anita was safe, and so was he.

COOPER WOULD HAVE CRASHED to the concrete floor, had Samson not caught him in time. Anita had never seen anybody move so fast.

"What's wrong?" she asked, panic cutting off her air supply.

"He'll be all right," Virginia replied calmly. "He needs his regenerative sleep."

"It's a wonder he was able to stay on his feet for as long as he did," Samson added.

Anita looked at Cooper's pale face, and touched his cheek. "His skin is cold. Are you sure he'll make it?"

A hand on her shoulder made her turn her head to Virginia.

"I would be the first to tell you, if he won't recover. He's my family too. But this is normal. Your blood helped him over the first hurdle, but he'll need more, and he can only fully heal by sleeping."

Anita nodded slowly.

"He drank your blood again?" her father asked, his voice laced with concern, before he turned to Samson. "You can't let her give him any more tonight. He already bit her back at the house, when they... uhm... during...uhm..."

It appeared that her father still had problems mentioning the word sex in front of her.

"Don't worry, I understand," Samson said. "We'll make sure he gets sufficient bottled blood to let Anita recover."

"But I feel fine," Anita protested.

"You've already done more than anybody expected from you," Samson replied. "Cooper wouldn't want to weaken you any further. Let's get him back to HQ. We'll monitor him there."

Samson turned to his team. "Clean up here. We'll take one of the SUVs back to HQ. Amaury, you'll take your Porsche back."

Luther, Zane, and Amaury nodded.

Less than half an hour later, Samson and her father helped the unconscious Cooper lie down on a hospital bed in the mini medical center on one of the lower levels of Scanguards HQ. In the same room, his mother lay sleeping on another bed, Haven and Lydia by her side. Haven jumped up and rushed to Cooper, stroking his hand over his son's forehead.

"Thank God, he's alive," Haven said and turned to Anita. "Thanks to you."

He approached her, and put his arms around her, pulling her into a tight embrace. "Thank you for giving me my son back."

"I was so scared that I'd lose him," she admitted, tears welling up in her eyes again. In fact, she'd never felt so scared in her entire life.

Haven released her from his embrace, and Lydia put her arms

around her, squeezing her for a moment. "Thank you, Anita. You're so brave."

Anita tipped her chin toward the bed next to Cooper's. "And Yvette? How is she doing?"

"Mom will be fully recovered in twenty-four hours, maybe even earlier," Lydia said.

"In the meantime," Samson said, "you and your father should get some rest."

"But what if he wakes?"

"We'll take care of him," Samson assured her. "Maya, our physician, will monitor him and Yvette, and will make sure both of them have what they need. Besides, Haven and Lydia are here to watch over them both."

"Come, Anita," Virginia added, "You and I will quickly go to the lab. Wes can give you something for you to recover from the blood loss a bit quicker."

"All right," Anita agreed with another glance at Cooper, who appeared peaceful in his sleep.

When her father made a move to join her and Virginia, Samson put a hand on his shoulder. "José, I wonder whether I can have a word with you."

Her father hesitated, then he nodded. "Sure. What do you wanna talk about?"

"Let's go somewhere private."

Anita left the room with Virginia, and they walked down a long corridor.

"What was that about?" Anita asked.

Virginia shrugged. "Not sure. But whatever it is, don't worry. You're part of the Scanguards family now, and so is your father. Nobody will hurt either of you."

Anita smiled. She could feel a bond with all of them now; she could feel their gratitude for having helped save one of their own, even though she'd done it for herself, because she loved Cooper unconditionally. And she couldn't wait for their life together to begin.

41

"Chief Donnelly wants to see us now?" Anita asked, staring at Samson and her father. They were in Samson's office. "But Cooper could wake any minute. Maya said he's almost completely healed. And Yvette is already awake."

It was early evening again, and Cooper had been out for well over twenty-four hours already. According to Maya, he'd received several pints of human blood, which he'd consumed in a semi-conscious state. Now it was just a matter of time.

"It won't take long," Samson assured her. "Let's go."

Reluctantly, she followed Samson, her father by her side. In the garage, they got into an SUV with darkened windows, and left headquarters. It took her several minutes to realize that they weren't driving downtown to the Hall of Justice on Bryant Street, but farther north toward some of the fancier San Francisco neighborhoods.

"This is not the way to the police station," Anita said from her seat in the back of the car.

She noticed Samson and her father exchange a conspiratorial look.

"What's going on?"

Her father smirked and addressed Samson, "She's got quite an inquisitive mind. You sure about this? Hope you can handle her. Just saying she doesn't always play by the rules."

"Don't worry, José. She's just what we need. Besides, I won't be the one who has to handle her when she steps out of line. I leave that up to Cooper."

They were talking about her as if she wasn't even in the car. She leaned forward between the two front seats.

"I'm asking again: what is going on? And what does Cooper have to do with it?"

Both men chuckled. Her father looked back at her. "Relax, honey. We're almost there."

There was something they weren't telling her, and it made her nervous. However, since both men seemed to be in a good mood, whatever they were keeping from her, was probably nothing bad.

When Samson turned into the driveway of a large Victorian home, and the garage door lifted, Anita leaned forward again.

"That's not the police station."

"No, it isn't." Samson drove into the huge garage where several cars were already parked. "But then I didn't say that we're meeting Donnelly at the station."

Samson parked his car, and they exited. He ushered them to the stairs that led up into the house. When he opened the door on the first floor, Anita found herself in a large wood-paneled foyer. An open arch ahead of her led into a large living area, and a majestic staircase rose to her right. The living room wasn't empty. In fact, she recognized several faces. All the people who'd taken part in the take-down of the serial killer and Cooper's rescue, as well as others she hadn't met before, were present. She spotted Wesley and Virginia in the crowd, as well as Luther and Katie, who'd brought their toddler.

A beautiful petite woman with dark hair walked toward them. "Welcome to our home, Anita." She offered her hand, and Anita grasped it. "I'm Delilah, Samson's blood-bonded mate."

"It's so nice to meet you, Delilah."

When Delilah turned to her father to greet him, Anita noticed Chief Donnelly in the crowd. He smiled at her and approached.

"It's good to see you, Anita," he said with a smile.

She returned his smile. "So this was just a pretense to get me to come to a party?"

"Actually," Samson said from behind her, "it's more than that. Mike has a proposition for you."

Anita looked over her shoulder and noticed that her father appeared to smile proudly. She looked back at Donnelly. "What kind of proposition?"

"There's a job vacancy. The SFPD needs a liaison officer to identify and funnel cases involving vampires and other preternatural creatures to Scanguards. And we could really use somebody with your skills."

Anita's heart began to pound out of control. "You want me to work for you?"

"Actually, you'd be working both for the SFPD and for Scanguards. Ultimately, Scanguards would be paying your salary, but you'd have a police badge, and all the powers of a police officer. Your starting rank will be Detective. At the SFPD, you'd be reporting directly to me."

Anita turned her head to look at her father. "You knew about this?"

Her father nodded. "Cooper spoke to Samson about it a few days ago. And Samson talked to me about it. Considering that it's unlikely that you'll move back to Elko, I figured you'd need a job, and you'd be perfect for this. You're a great investigator."

"Oh, Dad." Tears welled up in her eyes at her father's praise. She sniffled.

"So, is that a yes?" Donnelly asked.

She took his hand. "Yes. When can I start?"

Donnelly's gaze drifted to the stairs behind her. "How about after your honeymoon?"

"Honeymoon?"

When Donnelly continued to stare at the stairs, and others in the crowd did the same, she turned to follow their gaze. There, coming down the stairs, was Cooper. He looked more virile than ever. He was fully healed and wearing casual clean clothes. Behind him, Yvette, Haven, and Lydia descended.

"Cooper, why didn't anybody tell me that you're awake?" She could barely get the words out, choking up all of a sudden, the joy of seeing him overwhelming her.

"I wanted to surprise you."

Cooper drank her in with his eyes. During his restorative sleep, he'd had vivid dreams about Anita, and the knowledge that she'd saved him and was waiting for him had helped him push through the physical pain. He was fully healed now, and ready to grab his second chance at life with both hands—and with Anita by his side.

At the foot of the stairs, Anita threw herself into his arms, and he welcomed her open display of affection—no, more than just affection: deep, everlasting love. He felt it in every fiber of his being. Not concerned that everybody at Scanguards was watching, he captured Anita's lips and kissed her deeply. He'd missed her smell and her taste, and the aroma of her blood that drifted to him now.

When murmurs reached his ears, he knew it was time to end the kiss. He drew his head back and released her, before reaching into his pocket. He felt the metal item there and pulled it out, keeping it hidden in his palm.

"Anita." He got down on one knee and looked up at her.

Anita's eyes widened in surprise, and her cheeks colored a pretty pink, while her eyes shimmered like the ocean on a white sandy beach. A breath escaped from her throat.

"Will you be my blood-bonded mate for all eternity?" He opened his palm and laid bare the gold ring with the sparkling blue sapphire that matched her eyes.

It was so quiet in the room that he could have heard a feather land on the floor.

"Yes, yes, I will," Anita said amongst tears of joy. "I love you, Cooper."

Rising, he slid the ring on her finger. "I love you more, Baby." He kissed her once more among cheers by his friends and family.

"Congratulations, honey," Diaz said. "Congratulations to both of you."

"Cooper, don't monopolize her," Yvette said from behind him.

Cooper released Anita and looked over his shoulder. "You do know she's mine, right?"

There were chuckles coming from the crowd.

"Do I at least get to hug her?" she asked. Yvette pulled Anita into a tight embrace, and even though she spoke quietly, Cooper heard every word. "Thank you, Anita, thank you for everything you've done. I can't imagine a better woman for my son than you. You're my daughter now too, and I'll always protect you."

Anita sniffled. "Thank you, Yvette. I'm so glad you're all right."

When Lydia and several others crowded around Anita to congratulate her, Cooper caught her gaze and smiled at her, then stepped back and turned to Diaz.

"I'll keep her safe," Cooper promised.

Diaz put a hand on his shoulder, squeezing it. "I don't doubt it, Son. Not for a second."

Samson and Haven joined them, both of them smiling contentedly.

"She's quite a catch," Haven said. "You're a lucky guy."

"Trust me, Dad. I know it." He glanced back to Anita, who was surrounded by his friends.

"So, when's the wedding gonna take place?" Diaz asked. "I wanna make sure that my wife and my sons can come."

Cooper exchanged a quick look with Haven. "Actually, the bonding is tonight. And it's a very private ceremony... uhm..."

"What Cooper is trying to say," Samson said with a grin, "is that they will blood-bond during sex tonight."

"Oh." Diaz suddenly feigned interest in his shoes.

"But we'll have a human wedding too," Cooper assured him. "I'm sure Anita will want that so our families and friends can attend."

Diaz nodded. "Good. Sorry. I guess I'm not used to people talking so freely about... uhm... you know... sex."

"I understand." Cooper exchanged a look with Samson.

Samson nodded. "And we'd like to give them some privacy at the house tonight. Since Cooper's flat is still under renovation, and Cooper is still staying at Wesley's, Wesley and Virginia are leaving for a quick trip to Baltimore tonight. And I would like you, José, to stay here, at my house, as my guest. Delilah has already prepared a room for you."

The news seemed to come as a relief to Sheriff Diaz. "Yeah, of course, great. That's perfect." He nodded at Cooper. "And I should leave tomorrow morning to drive home to Elko. I'd better let Anita know."

"She'll be sad to see you leave."

Diaz laughed. "I've seen the way she looks at you. Trust me, she can't wait until I'm back home, and the two of you are alone."

Cooper smirked. He couldn't argue with the truth.

42

―――――

Cooper pulled Anita into his room in Wesley's house and shut the door. They were finally alone.

"Are you sure Wes and Virginia are flying to Baltimore tonight?" Anita asked. "They were still at Samson's house when we left."

He grinned and pulled her into his arms. "I didn't say they were *flying* to Baltimore."

Anita's forehead furrowed, and she looked utterly delectable. "But how then?"

"Remember when you saw Virginia disappear downstairs in the basement?"

She nodded. "Yeah, but what's that got to do with them going to Baltimore?"

"There is a portal down there in the last room. It can only be opened by a Stealth Guardian. It's used to teleport to other portals the Stealth Guardians maintain. It takes only a few seconds."

"You're kidding, right? Teleportation isn't real."

"It is. I've been in the portal before. It's a little disorienting, but I can assure you it works just fine. Maybe I'll ask Virginia to chauffeur us somewhere for our honeymoon." Not that he needed to go anywhere at all, because all he wanted to do was make love to Anita all day and all night.

"I haven't even thought about a honeymoon yet."

"I'm not gonna rush you on that." He brushed his lips over hers in a featherlight kiss. "But what I do want right now is to blood-bond with you. I can't wait another moment."

She smiled sinfully. "In that case, we shouldn't waste time with chit-chat."

"I like the way you think. I knew there was a reason why I love you."

"Oh, I'm sure you don't love me only for my brains."

Cooper palmed her ass and yanked her against him. "I think you're on the right track, Deputy."

"Actually, it's detective now."

"Mmm-hmm."

Cooper pulled on the seam of Anita's sweater and drew it over her head, freeing her. Beneath it, she wore a T-shirt, but from the way her breasts bounced freely, he knew she wasn't wearing a bra.

"I like it that you don't wear a bra," he murmured as he snatched the T-shirt and took it off her to reveal the olive skin beneath.

"You do, huh? How about you show a little skin too?" Her lips puckered, tempting him.

"That can be arranged." Unceremoniously, he rid himself of his shirt and tossed it on a chair. But he didn't stop there, and continued undressing. He loved the way Anita watched him as he removed layer after layer until he stood in front of her without a stitch on him.

He caught her gazing at his cock, which was hard and heavy. Desire shone from her blue irises, and she licked her lips.

"Now you," he demanded, pointing to her pants and shoes. "Or do you need help?"

She smirked. "And have you shred the few clothes I brought to San Francisco with me?"

She motioned to his hands, and when he followed her look, he realized that his fingers had turned into sharp claws. He hadn't even noticed that his vampire side was already emerging, eager to bond with the woman he loved.

"I'm sorry," he said as he watched her take off her shoes.

"Don't be," she said, her voice huskier than he'd ever heard it. "I like it. That wildness… it's a turn-on." She shimmied out of her jeans.

He ran his eyes over her nearly nude body, and his throat went dry when she finally stepped out of her panties. He put his arm around her waist and pulled her to him.

With his other hand on her nape, he brought his face to hers. "I haven't thanked you properly yet for saving my life."

"I have the feeling you're gonna do that shortly."

He palmed her ass and pressed her to him, his hard-on digging into her stomach.

"Mmm-hmm." He captured her lips and kissed her possessively, before he released her mouth again. "But there's something you have to learn first."

"What's that?"

With his fingers under her chin, he tipped her face up so she had to look at him. "When I tell you to save yourself, you've gotta listen to me and not ignore my order. Do you know what could have happened?"

The thought sent an ice-cold shudder down his spine.

"It turned out fine." She slid her hand onto his nape and pulled him to her. "But if you think that I'll follow every order you give me, think again. I'm not a shrinking violet."

"Hmm," he grunted. "Stubborn as ever."

Anita laughed softly. "Would you really want it any other way?" She rubbed her groin against his cock, making his heart beat faster and a moan dislodge from his chest.

"Are you trying to pacify me with sex?"

"Is it working?"

He lifted her up into his arms and laid her down on the bed. "What do you think?"

Her eyes glinted with mischief. "As we both know, distracting you with sex works really well."

The memory of Anita giving him a blowjob in his car resurfaced. It was true, he had no defenses when it came to her. But it didn't bother him. He liked to feel vulnerable when he was with her. He liked to open his heart to her.

Cooper rolled over her, her thighs parting automatically to accommodate him. He shifted and adjusted his angle. For a second, he paused at the entrance to her body, while he locked eyes with her.

"I love you, Anita."

He plunged into her with one thrust, seating himself to the hilt, his balls slapping against her flesh.

"I love you, Cooper," Anita murmured on a moan, before he sank his lips on hers and kissed her.

They moved in synch with each other, slamming together again and again. Perspiration on their bodies made every movement smooth and sensual. Her plentiful juices created a welcoming sheath for him, and their moans and sighs provided the background music for their lovemaking. The knowledge that after tonight, Anita would be the only woman he would make love to and drink from for the rest of his life, made his heart pound even more excitedly.

He couldn't wait much longer to make her his. Restraint was overrated. He needed her now.

Cooper ripped his lips from hers and slowed his thrusts, but remained inside her, while he allowed his fingers to turn into claws once more. With one sharp barb he cut into the skin of his shoulder. Blood seeped from the small wound.

He looked into Anita's eyes. "You have to drink from me now. And I'll drink from you."

"Yes." Her breath ghosted over his skin as he lowered his shoulder toward her mouth.

When he felt her lips connect with his skin, he gasped at the tantalizing sensation. Anita latched onto him and drew his blood into her. A tingling went through his entire body, and made his cock jerk inside her. He dropped his face to her neck, his fangs fully extended now. He licked over her skin, then drove his fangs into her flesh. A moment later, her rich blood coated his tongue, and ran down the back of his throat. Everything inside him was in flames.

He'd heard many of his fellow vampires and vampire hybrids talk about the blood-bonding ceremony, but nothing could have prepared him for this intense experience. Every sensation, every feeling was deeper, more real. The love he felt in his heart suddenly flooded every cell of his body, and then reached even further. He felt another body just as intensely. He felt Anita, felt her love for him, sensed her happiness and her physical pleasure. Just like she could feel his love and pleasure now. They were one, their bond strong and unbreakable, their love eternal.

I love you, Baby. You're mine now. He let the thought drift to her.

Cooper? It was Anita's voice in his head, even though she was still drinking from him, just like his fangs were still in her neck.

Oh, Cooper, I didn't know that it would be like this.

Are you all right, Baby?

Better than all right. I'm finally home. I've been looking for you all my life. You're mine.

And you're mine. Forever and always.

I love you.

I love you more.

And he would prove it to her every single day and every single night, worshipping her body, showering her with love, and protecting her from all evil no matter the cost. 'Cause he'd been looking for her his whole life too.

Reading Order Scanguards Vampires & Stealth Guardians

Scanguards Vampires

Prequel Novella: Mortal Wish
Book 1: Samson's Lovely Mortal
Book 2: Amaury's Hellion
Book 3: Gabriel's Mate
Book 4: Yvette's Haven
Book 5: Zane's Redemption
Book 6: Quinn's Undying Rose
Book 7: Oliver's Hunger
Book 8: Thomas's Choice
Novella 8 ½: Silent Bite
Book 9: Cain's Identity

20 years pass

Book 10: Luther's Return
Book 11: Blake's Pursuit
Novella 11 ½: Fateful Reunion

Book 12: John's Yearning

Stealth Guardians

Same time period

Book 1: Lover Uncloaked

Next

Book 2: Master Unchained
Book 3: Warrior Unraveled

Next

Book 4: Guardian Undone
Book 5: Immortal Unveiled
Book 6: Protector Unmatched
Book 7: Demon Unleashed

8 years pass

Scanguards Hybrids

The Scanguards Hybrids will also be numbered within the Scanguards Vampires series (SV 13 = SH 1) to preserve continuity.

Book 1 (SV 13): Ryder's Storm
Book 2 (SV 14): Damian's Conquest
Book 3 (SV 15): Grayson's Challenge
Book 4 (SV 16): Isabelle's Forbidden Love
Book 5 (SV 17): Cooper's Passion
Book 6 (SV 18): Vanessa's Bravery
Book 7 (SV 19): Patrick's Seduction (2025)

ABOUT THE AUTHOR

Tina Folsom was born in Germany and has been living in English speaking countries since 1991. Tina has always been a bit of a globe trotter. She lived in Munich, Lausanne, London, New York City, Los Angeles, San Francisco, and Sacramento. She has now made a beach town in Southern California her permanent home with her American husband and her dog.

She's written over 50 romance novels in English most of which are translated into German, French, Italian, and Spanish.

https://tinawritesromance.com
tina@tinawritesromance.com

facebook.com/TinaFolsomFans
instagram.com/authortinafolsom

www.ingramcontent.com/pod-product-compliance
Lightning Source LLC
Chambersburg PA
CBHW022122310726
48972CB00007B/2153